JANE

The Cousins Of Pemberley: Book 4

LINDA O'BYRNE

ALSO BY LINDA O'BYRNE

The Cousins Of Pemberley series in order:

Cassandra

Catherine

Miriam

Boxset Edition containing books 1-3

*This book is in memory of my parents, Ernie and Kathleen Blake
from whom I inherited a love of reading and a vivid imagination!
I hope they would have been proud of the Pemberley
series, especially this one that is set in the Dorset countryside they
loved.*

Pemberley

Above Stairs:
Elizabeth and Fitzwilliam Darcy: children, Anne, Jane, Bennetta, Fitzwilliam and Henry.

Below Stairs:
Miss Reynolds - housekeeper, Mr Charlton - tutor, James - footman, Archie - head groom, Tabitha - maid.

Clifton Park:
Jane and Charles Bingley: children, Beth, George, Sophia and Alethea.
A frequent visitor: Mrs Caroline Tremaine, Mr Bingley's sister.

Wyvern Lodge:
Dr Richard Courtney and Cassandra - daughter of Lydia Allerton, née Bennet - and their baby, Victoria.
Susannah, Richard and Robert's elder sister.

Courtney Castle, Northumberland:
Sir Robert Courtney and Catherine - daughter of Mr Collins and the former Charlotte Lucas. Also Matilda, Sir Robert's daughter by his first marriage.

Cape Town, South Africa:
Mary Ogden, née Bennet.

On the High Seas:
Captain Nicholas Sullivan, his wife Miriam, Mary Bennet's daughter by her first marriage.

Longbourn, Hertfordshire:
Mrs Bennet, Mr Collins, his wife, the former Kitty Bennet and their daughter, Harriet.

Deerwood Park, Dorset:

Colonel Fitzwilliam - Mr Darcy's cousin.
Celeste Fiorette - a distant cousin
Mrs Oxley - housekeeper, Dixon - valet, Bates - gardener.

Robyns, Dorset:
Archer Maitland, his grandmother, Lady Goddard and
his friend, Dr Andrew Moore.
Miss Purkiss, companion to Lady Goddard.

THE SERIES SO FAR

❦

Book 1:
Cassandra

Cassandra Wickham, daughter of a flirt and a scoundrel, an innocent abroad in a world where money can buy you anything, even a bride.

When danger threatens and the man she thought she could rely on fails her, there is only one place she can turn to
for help -

Pemberley.

❦

Surely the Darcys will protect her, no matter what happened in the past to divide the two families?

Book 2

Catherine

Catherine Collins, a very ordinary young woman - plain, quiet, often over-looked but possessing a reputation for having great common-sense.
Or so her distant cousin Elizabeth Darcy believes and so recommends her as governess for little Matilda Courtney.

Catherine travels to Northumberland, full of good intentions to do her best and be a credit to the family.

But appearances and reputations can be deceptive - Robert and Martin Courtney will soon learn exactly what type of girl Elizabeth has sent them.

❀

Book 3:
Miriam.

Mary Bennet - overlooked, laughed at, despised - married a missionary and vanished into a life of service out in Africa. But now Miriam, her daughter, is coming to England, disliking everything she has been told about her family.

Her aunts and cousins are expecting someone quiet, dull and bookish, just like her mother, not the quick-tempered, impulsive girl who arrives.

How can this adventurous girl with her desire for freedom possibly fit into their well ordered world? And what havoc will she cause as she tries?

CHAPTER 1

DERBYSHIRE, ENGLAND, AUGUST, 1834

I t is a truth, universally acknowledged, that daughters give their mothers far more concern throughout their lives than do their sons. The mistress of Pemberley, Elizabeth Darcy, believed in that saying with all her heart when facing her usually sweet-natured and biddable daughter, Jane.

The halls and rooms of the great house were dim, the curtains and blinds drawn against the warmth of the late summer sun.

Out in the rose gardens, visitors were sitting under parasols, sipping cool lemonade, talking to her other daughters, Anne and Bennetta.

She needed to attend to them immediately but Jane had been so elusive of late that coming across her on the stairs had provided an unexpected opportunity to confront her.

She tried again with barely concealed impatience. "Jane, dear child, you are being stubborn. Anne insists she had no intention of hurting you; refusing to speak to her, running off to Colonel Fitzwilliam in Dorset, neither of these will solve the problem."

"Mama, I just need to get away. I feel so hurt, so betrayed. Anne might not have meant to ruin my life, but that is what she has done! How can I possibly face her every morning across the breakfast table, knowing that Digby proposed marriage to her?

When I thought...I believed..."

Digby! Digby Frobisher! Elizabeth rued the day she had ever heard the name, bitterly regretting inviting him into their social circle. The handsome, fair haired young man had managed to wreck their peaceful lives in just a few months.

She tried again: she was concerned - Jane was normally pale, a frail, slighter version of her more robust twin.

Their faces were identical in form, but Jane's hair when unbound was a shower of gilt, Anne's a dark gold. Jane's eyes were the blue of a robin's egg whilst

Anne's gaze was harder, a sparkling cold sapphire.

But now Jane was not just pale: she was white and the great dark circles under her eyes spoke of sleepless nights.

"Jane, you never gave any indication that you had formed deep feelings for Digby.

I had no idea. Surely Digby himself did not know. Anne has told me that she only guessed andwas quite sure he was not the right man for you. She wanted to show you how fickle he was, that he was quite happy to transfer his attentions to her if she showed him they might be reciprocated."

"I am not the sort of girl, Mama, who goes around telling men how she feels about them! I am convinced Digby knew. He has broken my heart and Anne, however kindly meant her actions were, has aided him."

Elizabeth stared at her helplessly. How like her dear namesake, Jane Bingley, she was.

Memories of how Charles Bingley had been persuaded that Jane did not love him because she did not show her feelings, came flooding back. Had this been a similar situation?

Had Digby really thought that Anne's flirtation meant she cared for him, whilst Jane's behaviour painted a picture of indifference?

"I am sure your heart is not broken - perhaps just badly dented! Well, Jane, I cannot stop you travelling down to Dorset to stay with your godfather. Perhaps a few weeks in his sensible, quiet company is just what you need."

"Thank you, Mama."

"Now, go and wash your face and come down to admire baby Victoria. Cassandra is so pleased with her little girl, although I don't think your Aunt Lydia is as enamoured as the rest of the family."

Becoming a grandmother is a momentous event in a lady's life. Sadly, Mrs

Lydia Allerton, did not agree. Leaving her husband at home - Colonel Allerton maintained that the Derbyshire air did not suit him, although Lydia knew it was her brother-in-law's disdain he disliked - she had reluctantly travelled from Newcastle to inspect Miss Victoria Courtney.

Now, sitting under a pink sunshade umbrella in the Pemberley rose garden, she tried to look enthusiastic as she gazed down at the bundle in her arms. But the screwed up red face under the white lace bonnet did not enchant her and only added to her sense of outrage at this further marker of the passage of time.

"You had better take her, Cassandra," she said to her daughter, holding out the infant. "I think she should go back inside before she starts crying."

"Why, Grandmama Lydia, anyone would think you weren't mightily impressed by your granddaughter."

Elizabeth Darcy didn't know whether to laugh or cry. She found the thought of her little sister's new title amusing in the extreme, but on the other hand, it made her realise just how quickly the years were passing. Indeed, her oldest children would be twenty this coming Christmas.

"Lord, Lizzy, I'm sure she's a very fine baby," Lydia said with a sigh of relief as her daughter carried her precious child away. "But the fuss they make of her has to be seen to be believed. Wyvern Lodge is in a constant turmoil with people rushing around as soon as the child makes a sound. I've told Cassie to let her scream upstairs out of earshot, but she refuses to heed me."

She reached for a glass of iced lemonade and laid back in her chair in satisfaction. It was a hot day; sitting in the shade, in the rose garden of Pemberley, all was quiet elegance, the air heavy with perfume. The only sounds were some sparrows squabbling in a lavender bush and the trickle of a little fountain nearby.

It wouldn't have suited her to live in such peace all the time - no, she preferred a noisier, busier life - but for an hour it was pleasant. She shut her eyes and very shortly a small snore rose into the perfumed air.

Elizabeth glanced across at the woman sitting quietly under the second umbrella. Miss Susannah Courtney, aunt to baby Vicky, had said very little since she arrived with the Courtney party on this visit to Pemberley.

In her late thirties, Susannah was a neat, brown-haired person with a gentle expression and soft voice. Although in no way subservient, she tended to keep herself in the background at family gatherings and Elizabeth had noticed with exasperation that Lydia treated her almost as if she were a servant instead of a close relation by marriage. She also noticed that Susannah ignored this, never disturbing the peace with arguments or disagreements.

"Susannah, this might be a good moment for me to speak to you. There has been no opportunity so far today. New infants do tend to take up everyone's time and attention!"

"Certainly. Is there something I can do for you?"

Elizabeth hesitated and glanced across the rose garden to where Anne and Bennetta, were talking to Cassandra. Of her other daughter, Jane, there was still no sign. She sighed: the girl was probably packing, eager to leave Derbyshire at the earliest moment, happy to distance herself from her family.

Elizabeth was at a loss how to heal the wounds that recent events had inflicted. Jane had always been the quiet one of the family, but now it was as if she was on one side of a tightly shut window and everyone else in the world was on the other.

She turned back to Susannah. "I have a great favour to ask of you. Jane intends to travel to Dorset tomorrow, to stay with her godfather, Colonel Fitzwilliam. She has already written to him to expect her. She is determined to go and I cannot persuade her otherwise. Sometimes, even though she is the quietest of my children, there is a very stubborn streak in her character. Mr Darcy says she inherits it from me, but I cannot see the resemblance myself."

Susannah frowned. "I am aware that she is fond of Mr Darcy's cousin. She often talks of him."

"She always runs to Colonel Fitzwilliam as soon as she encounters any difficulty in her life. I have begged her to stay home and sort out the problem, but she refuses. To Dorset she will go. Apparently there has been - well, I cannot call it an argument because no one has raised their voices, but a very unhappy falling out between her and her sister."

Susannah did not need to ask which sister. Anne, Jane's twin, with her blonde beauty and supercilious expression, had never been one of her favourite acquaintances. Ever since the Darcys and Courtneys had been linked by marriage, Anne had always made Susannah acutely aware that as a woman long past marriageable age, she was just a spinster sister, an unpaid housekeeper for her younger brother and as such of no consequence. While her circumstances were entirely true, it was, nevertheless impolite in the extreme to make such a distinction.

"How can I help?" She was fond of Jane and had always disliked the way she was constantly put in the background by her domineering twin, always deferring to her wishes and had often hoped that one day she would stand up for herself.

"Will you... is it possible for you to accompany Jane? I worry about her so much. I do not like the thought of her travelling on her own when she is in such a distressed state of mind. I fear I would not rest easily at night, although she has been to Dorset by herself before, of course. She was there just after Christmas. I would send Bennetta with her, but the last thing Jane needs now is the company of a beautiful, self-confident young girl."

Susannah felt her lips twitching and fought to keep a straight face. "Well, you can certainly not call me beautiful or young, and although I think I have my fair share of confidence, I shall do my best to hide it in front of Jane!"

"Oh I am so sorry... I..."

"Please! I quite understand. My feelings are not hurt in the slightest. I would love to visit Dorset. It is not a county I have ever explored. I always travel north, of course, when I visit the family at Courtney Castle."

"Could Richard spare you?"

Susannah smiled, a little wryly and glanced at Lydia's sleeping figure. "I know I am of use to Cassandra, especially now she has Vicky to care for, but at the same time I am sure she and Richard will be delighted to have the house to themselves for a while. And there is still a week left of your sister's visit. I must admit I shall be grateful not to be at home during that time. We do not have a comfortable relationship; I think it comes from when I innocently asked her how she wished to be addressed as a grandmother!"

Elizabeth tried not to smile but failed. "The thought of Lydia being a grandmother fills me both with amusement and also horror at how old I must be if my little sister has now reached that stage in life, although to be fair, she did have Cassandra when she was very young."

"Yes, I fear she did not take the news of Victoria's arrival well. But enough of this. The trip to Dorset - I shall be delighted to accompany Jane. We have always been good friends. Am I right in thinking this will not be a long visit to see Colonel Fitzwilliam?"

"A few weeks, no more. Hopefully, when she returns, Jane will have forgotten her disappointments and this disagreement with her sister, and life can return to its even keel again."

Susannah considered that it would be a good thing if Jane returned determined to be a person in her own right and not just "Anne's twin" but thought it unwise to say those words to her hostess. She changed the subject. "The house seems very quiet with Henry and Fitzwilliam missing."

Elizabeth's usually brilliant dark eyes became shadowed. "It has been a very odd few months. The whole household was put in turmoil by my niece Miriam's arrival from Africa and even more so by her sudden departure to marry the sea captain! We still await letters from her and Mary telling of the wedding which was supposed to have taken place in Cape Town. Then Fitz left to spend August with a school friend and as you know, Mr Darcy has taken Henry to Portsmouth where he is to join a ship of the line as a midshipman."

"I was sad not to meet Miriam when she was here, but I could not leave Cassandra when she was so near her time."

"Oh, I quite understand. I feel as if some exotic bird has flown through the halls of Pemberley, disturbing everything. I would never have believed that Mary, so quiet, so solemn, could have such a daughter. But then our children never turn out as we expect them to.

"And I have had to say goodbye to my dear Henry - to me he seems very young to start such a hard and dangerous life, but I am assured that it is the right thing to do, for him to have his own career in the navy, away from Pemberley which of course, Fitz will one day inherit. As you may imagine, Henry cannot wait to hear cannon fire and be involved in some dreadful battle. The fact that I lie awake at night, picturing all sorts of injuries and worse does not seem to be important to anyone!"

She bit back the words, "Especially Mr Darcy," because that would have been disloyal to her husband, whom she loved dearly. But on this subject they did not agree and although they had not exactly quarrelled about Henry's naval career, she felt that her opinion did not matter. At least they agreed on how undesirable Digby Frobisher was as a husband for either of the twins. Mr Darcy - who would have been quite happy to have kept all his daughters at home, unmarried, for the rest of their lives - had been unusually vocal about Digby's behaviour.

"So you will accompany Jane? I will arrange for the carriage to stop at Wyvern Lodge tomorrow morning, if that is convenient for you."

"Certainly. I have only met Colonel Fitzwilliam the once, that was at Cassandra's wedding, but he seemed an extremely agreeable gentleman. He did me the honour of asking me to dance and we sat next to each other at breakfast. I was very impressed by his knowledge of the world and his genteel manners. It will be a pleasure to make his acquaintance again."

"I fear I cannot tell you more of the disagreement between Jane and Anne because that would mean breaking a confidence. But, of course, if Jane tells you herself, then please feel free to give her any advice you can. Mine, I am afraid, is of little use. Apparently 'I do not understand about love!'"

She stood up and adjusted her parasol. "Now, I will awaken my lazy sister and announce that tea is ready in the drawing-room. You must have some refreshment before you leave. The girls' elderly nurse, Nanny Chilcot, whom, as you know, has rooms in the east wing now she has retired, has, I believe, been called into action to care for Victoria so we can all eat in peace. Indeed, I will be surprised if we manage to extract the infant from her arms when your carriage is called!"

She turned to her duties as mistress of Pemberley and tried to push her worries about Jane to the back of her mind.

So many years had passed since the twins had been born and Elizabeth was certain that most people would have long forgotten that she had almost lost the younger twin. Anne was a healthy infant but Jane had been tiny, fragile and her parents were told by the doctors that she might not survive. For weeks they had hardly strayed from the nursery, desperate for the child to thrive.

Thankfully, as the months passed, Jane had grown stronger, although she never had her sister's robust constitution; always the first to be ill, to catch a cold, to tire when walking or riding. Elizabeth knew she had treated her differently from the other children; shielding her from anything unpleasant, not allowing her to ever take unnecessary risks, always concerned that she was not over-tiring herself.

Bennetta should, of course, have taken her place as the child most in need of care, but then Bennetta, whose arrival in the world had almost ended her mother's place in it, had never and would never rouse the same tender emotions in Elizabeth. She loved her wild child dearly, but apart from two years previously when she had fallen from her horse and lost her memory for several days after hitting her head, she had never had a day's worry about Bennetta's health.

Now she was beginning to realise that this constant protection of Jane had, perhaps, been inadvisable. Throughout her nearly twenty years, Jane had never had to make her own decisions or been allowed to suffer any discomfort. She had never learnt to deal with any hardship. Was that why this silly affair with Digby Frobisher had affected her so badly?

Elizabeth sighed, woke her sleeping sister and gathered her guests together for tea. Daughters were a great trial and she wondered if her mother had lain awake worrying about her five girls. Then she smiled and thought, 'Mama worried about getting us married. Our characters were our own affair.'

Upstairs in the cool of the library, the girl who was causing her mother so much concern was gazing out of a window at the splendour of the great parkland below her. This room had a northerly aspect and so was cool even on the hottest of summer days.

Nobody had needed to sculpt or force the surroundings of Pemberley into beauty, no Capability Brown had been hired in the past to provide a magnificent landscape - nature had managed that all on her own. Admittedly, in one or two places, a tree had been felled to produce a distant view of woods and high hills but great oaks and Spanish chestnuts cast their shade on the lawns.

The flower gardens on the southerly side had been extended by the Darcys in the years since their marriage, and fell away in tiers of white, red, pink and yellow, roses and lilies. Little paths wound through the flowers and in places small fountains burbled bright cascades of water into pools.

Jane, who was usually only too happy to sit and read, occasionally glancing up to enjoy the scene before her, now sat on the deep window sill, half hidden behind the heavy brocade curtains. She knew she could not stay there much longer. It would be extremely discourteous to Cassandra not to go downstairs and admire the baby.

But Anne would be there and the thought of facing her twin at the moment filled her with dread. How could she have been so callous, so unkind? Did Jane mean so little to her that she could hurt her in this fashion?

"I truly believe she does not see me as a person at all," she murmured to herself. "All our lives, I have just been a pale copy of her, to be ignored, not someone with real feelings and emotions."

Then somewhere deep inside her head a voice muttered, "But you liked being overlooked, allowed to go your own way, enjoyed being 'just Jane' so that no one queried you or argued. You never had to defend your thoughts because you never told anyone what they were. It isn't all Anne's fault!"

But she was too unhappy to listen for long or give the voice any attention:

she stepped down from the window sill and straightening the pale blue silk that billowed over her petticoats, she tightened the darker blue sash and brushed tears from her cheeks.

'No one here understands,' she thought. 'Mama loves Papa, of course, but I am sure she has never felt this way, never had someone tell her how ardently they admire and love her and then... Well, I am going to stay with dear Colonel Fitzwilliam. I'll be safe there at Deerwood Park. Free from Anne's barbed comments, Bennetta's knowing looks and Mama's questions.'

"Jane! Jane! Oh, here you are. I guessed you would be in the library."

In a riot of dark curls, her younger sister, Bennetta, rushed through the door in a swirl of lemon spotted muslin, the huge sleeves which her father disliked so much, tied above and below her elbows with dark green ribbon. Jane could not remember a time when Bennetta did not rush: she seemed to run through the whole day, whirling from room to room, from plan to plan. Was she ever unhappy? Jane thought not and envied her most deeply. Surely Bennetta would never know the pain of betrayal by people she loved.

"Mama has sent me to find you. Aunt Lydia and Cassandra will be leaving soon. You must come and say your goodbyes and admire Miss Vicky. Lord, Jane, what is wrong with you? Even Anne has held the baby, although I think from the look on her face, Miss Vicky might have disgraced herself at that very moment! And I have run out of complimentary things to say about someone so small and pink. Now, do come. And try to be cheerful. You are making such a fuss over a silly man! There are so many men in the world to meet and attract. Crying over just one seems ridiculous to me."

Jane was silent as she followed her sister downstairs to make polite conversation with the departing guests. There was no escape from comments and speculation whilst she remained in Pemberley. She could not wait to escape and be in the sympathetic company of someone who would always put her first, only have *her* well-being at heart.

She said her goodbyes and was surprised but delighted when Susannah whispered that she was to accompany her on the morrow and was so looking forward to visiting Colonel Fitzwilliam's country home.

Two days later, a carriage travelled slowly up a steep hill in the county of Dorset: Jane and her companion were traveling in luxury and comfort. It was another hot day but with September almost on them, the heatwave that had covered the country was finally on the wane; indeed, from the state of the muddy road it looked as if there had been heavy showers in that part of Dorset that morning, although now the sky was clear.

They had passed fields that were being harvested, the workers bent double in long rows, billhooks flashing as they cut down the lines of wheat. In other meadows, groups of women were binding the cut wheat into bundles, children running around, laughing and playing. On the higher hill slopes, flocks of sheep grazed.

At a reasonable pace, because the ladies did not wish to be thrown around inside, the carriage travelled on, through neat villages of thatched cottages, fording shallow streams and stopping occasionally for the team to be rested.

The remains of a picnic box packed with inviting bites to tempt even the most ladylike of appetites now lay on the carriage floor, almost empty. They had made good time on the journey from Derbyshire, stopping one night at Longbourn, in Hertfordshire, to visit Jane's grandmother and Aunt Kitty, then skirting around London instead of driving through the noise and bustle of the great city.

Jane had been glad that their visit to Mr and Mrs Collins had only been for one night. She had to admit she was not fond of her Aunt Kitty or her husband. The former was a large lady, very fond of her food, with a bad complexion, complaining voice and manner. Mr Collins also had a great deal to say but Jane thought him pompous and his ingratiating manner annoyed her.

Although she tried to find a dutiful affection for her grandmother, she found the very elderly Mrs Bennet silly and annoying and marvelled, not for the first time, that this was her dear mama's mother.

There was only one subject of conversation, the marriage of Catherine - Mr Collins' daughter by his first marriage - to Sir Robert Courtney. At least Jane had the satisfaction of seeing Susannah treated with more respect and appreciation than shown by her Aunt Lydia . As Robert's elder sister, she was received with all polite attentions and given precedence at the dinner table, even though she was unmarried.

Apart from endlessly talking of "Lady Courtney", the Collins' household revolved around the child Harriet; an unattractive little girl, as tall as she was wide, with a stubborn disposition, not helped by being spoilt to extremes by her parents and grandmother.

Glad to be away from Longbourn, Jane gazed out of the window and saw not the beauty of the countryside but her own pale reflection under her pale green hat; she looked white and drawn, her eyes shadowed in dark circles. There was a little dirt on the inside of the window and, with a gloved finger, she drew a round face with a smile curving across it, then rubbed it out hastily. She couldn't recall the last time she had smiled.

Susannah sighed and tried to think of something to say that would brighten the day. It distressed her to see Jane in this pitiable state. She was such a gentle soul; the thought that someone could have hurt her to this extent was painful.

The carriage jolted violently as they crested the hill and made their way cautiously down the track on the other side Archie, recently promoted to head coachman at Pemberley, applied the brake, cursing as Tabitha Ford, the young maid sitting next to him, squealed and grasped his arm, although the postillion had dismounted and was holding the horses' heads to stop them going too fast and slipping on the rough surface.

Susannah wished she knew more about why Jane was so keen to leave home. Not a word had been said about her reasons for the trip and Susannah could only hazard a guess that a young man must be at the centre of the disagreement. She could think of nothing else that would cause such an upset between sisters.

"Jane, my dear, you seem so sad. I do not wish to force a confidence from you, but if there is any way in which I can be of assistance, please tell me. I find your current condition so distressing."

"Oh I am sorry. I had no intention of making everyone in my life feel as miserable as I do. I just feel... I find it hard to put into words..." She stopped. How could she possibly tell this calm, good-natured woman how unhappy she had become.

"Tell me immediately if I am wrong, but I sense this is something to do with a young gentleman, a certain Mr Digby Frobisher. I shall not pretend ignorance; oh, don't look so surprised, no one has been talking about you to me, but Bennetta tells all the gossip to Cassandra and I cannot help but overhear."

Digby! Jane shut her eyes, trying to banish the picture in her mind of his fair hair, good-looking face and a manner and words that had once seemed to promise her all the affection in the world.

Just then the carriage reached the bottom of the hill and came to a halt. Archie dismounted and came round to the window. "Miss Jane, we have about ten more miles to go before we reach Deerwood Park. I need to rest the horses for a while, so if you and Miss Courtney wish to alight for a breath of air, please do so."

"Thank you, Archie."

They stepped down with his help and wandered across the road to where a stile led onto a footpath that vanished away into a thick wood. Jane sat on the step, trying to discipline her billowing skirts and gazed at the trees, their branches swaying in the breeze, but she was not seeing the splendour of the day, just a crowded drawing-room in Mayfair.

"I first met Digby at Catherine's wedding to Sir Robert last year. We had a wonderful long and heartfelt conversation about the plays of Shakespeare. We danced and he made sure I had a glass of champagne. Then I met him in London, before Christmas. Time has gone by so fast. We had... I believed we had a... a connection."

She felt hot colour flood up into her cheeks as she remembered. "We spoke of books, we had both seen an exhibition of Ancient Greek artefacts at the British Museum that were of interest. We discussed important things, like the growing problem of unemployed men gathering in London because there is no work to be had in the countryside. Although he seems like a man about town, Digby has a very serious side to his nature and I felt honoured that he had let me see that aspect of his character."

"I envy you. To find a man whom you can admire and respect is a blessing."

Jane sighed. "There was no time for us to become closer. I had already promised to visit Dorset to stay with Colonel Fitzwilliam after Christmas, but in the weeks that followed I received letters from Digby. Oh, Susannah, they were such lovely letters! Warm and kind but very proper. No sense of over familiarity, just consideration and intelligence. It led me to believe... "

"That he cared for you?"

"Yes," came the whispered reply. "And then because we had not celebrated our birthday which falls just before Christmas, Anne wanted to hold a ball at Pemberley. Our cousin Miriam had arrived from Africa, if you remember, and it was to be a grand occasion for her, too, and everything seemed exciting. To my astonishment, Digby drove over from Cheshire that evening with his family. I was not expecting to see him, but oh, I was so pleased. And Anne ruined the evening!"

"Not deliberately, surely?"

"She asked him to dance, she flirted, she encouraged him to stay by her side all evening. As you know, the great artist, Edmund Avery, had painted a portrait of us Darcy children and it was to be unveiled that evening. I so wanted Digby to be by my side when that occurred, but Anne had other plans."

Susannah looked grave. "But surely, if he was your particular friend...?"

"Oh, she thought it a fine joke. A tease. Afterwards, she said she had no idea I was fond of him in any great way and was sorry for her behaviour. And so I forgave her."

With a rustle of pale green silk, she stood up abruptly and, careless of her thin leather shoes, walked a little way along the muddy road in the deep shade cast by the trees.

"A day or so later I had a letter full of apologies from Digby, hoping that our friendship had not been spoiled in any way by what he called his 'attempts to prove himself affable to my twin sister and so win her approval of any future connection between us'. He...he professed to ardently admire and love me!"

"Goodness, that is practically a proposal!"

Jane laughed but it was not a happy sound and she walked further along the road, as if she could not bear to stand still for too long.

"I am glad to hear you say that because I thought so, too. After that we met twice in London - the first time was at a large gathering held for Bennetta's coming out in July. I was so happy. We danced, we sat on the terrace, oh Susannah, I could not possibly have imagined his feelings for me. I am not the sort of girl who thinks every man she meets will fall in love with her.

"Then just two days later, Digby came to call at Matlock House, to thank my parents for the pleasant evening and we walked together in the garden - although I admit I sensed a certain restraint in his manner towards me. However, I imagined that was because his family had of late suffered from a disaster. Everyone was talking about it at every social occasion."

"The Frobishers live in Cheshire, I believe. Yes, there were rumours about them. Did not Mr Frobisher Snr lose a vast fortune out in the West Indies?"

Jane nodded. "Indeed, in Antigua, but Digby said very little about it although it was clear he was concerned for his father. However, rightly or wrongly, I believed that they were still a wealthy family and would easily weather the financial storm."

"A gentleman's lack of a very great fortune would not have mattered to you if you truly loved him. He was not likely to be destitute and ask you to live in a hovel!"

The breeze swirled along the hedgerow, trembling the late blossoms of honeysuckle that trailed amongst the briars, sending their perfume spinning through the warm air.

Jane looked back in her mind at all that had transpired. "Of course not. He had already told me in general conversation that he had money of his own, left by a doting grandfather, but he made no offer although he was as warm and affectionate in his behaviour towards me as ever, only, as I said, a little more formal. I thought it just a matter of time, that when his family problems had been eased and he could concentrate on happier things, he would approach Papa for my hand."

"And had you told him of your feelings?"

"Not in so many words, no, but Susannah, he could not have been in any doubt that I cared for him."

The older woman looked doubtful; in the two years since she had first met Jane Darcy, she had never seen any indication of strong emotion cross her face and although she had never been in love herself, she knew that gentlemen sometimes needed confirmation that their advances would not be rejected.

"Quickly, my dear, tell me the end of this story. We must return to the carriage. I can see Archie signalling that he is ready to set off once more."

Jane raised her chin and stared bravely at her companion. "Oh the end is very easy to report. Last week, Digby came to stay at Pemberley. I am sure you can imagine how pleased I was to see him, although I was puzzled, I didn't understand who had invited him. It turned out to be Anne. The day after he arrived, he went to Papa and asked for Anne's hand in marriage!"

Susannah stood still in the middle of the road. She had no words to express her horror.

"You may well look surprised. Perhaps you can imagine my shock, my despair."

"I don't understand; are you saying Anne is in love with Digby Frobisher?"

Jane shook her head impatiently. "No, of course not. Digby is far too insignificant a person in society for Miss Darcy of Pemberley to marry. She refused his offer and he left without even seeing me. She says she led him on for my sake; to show me that he was nothing but a fortune hunter, that appearances can be deceptive. That he would have settled for me, but when she pretended to like him, he saw a chance of a better catch."

"A clumsy way of helping. A word or two in confidence to you would perhaps have been more advisable. But you don't believe she acted in your interest?"

Jane bit her lip, her blue eyes misted with tears she refused to shed. "I don't know. I feel so betrayed. Even if she is telling the truth, why, as you rightly say, not speak to me about it? She is my twin. I had lately confided in her that I thought I loved Digby. She knew how much this would hurt me but went ahead anyway."

"What does your mama say?"

"Oh Mama is cross with her but believes that she acted from the best of intentions. But you have not yet heard the worst of what occurred. The next day I received yet another letter from Digby - oh, he writes so well - he should write romances, the type of book Bennetta reads!"

"But what could he possibly say in mitigation?"

"That he had always truly loved me - and that in a few month's time, perhaps we could resume our affectionate relationship. He seems to think that I will be quite happy to be second best, that this is a perfectly good reason for breaking my heart!"

"You surely did not reply?"

Jane shook her head. "Of course not. I burnt the letter and decided to come down to Dorset to stay with dear Colonel Fitzwilliam. I cannot face Anne at the moment and I am scared that Digby will arrive at Pemberley again with more lies and apologies. Susannah, I fear I love him so much that I will weaken and give in! I have been so used to being second best to Anne all my life, it almost seems like the natural thing to do. I think that upsets me most of all."

Susannah tried to inject some confidence into her voice. "Well, I don't think you would ever do that. I am convinced that you have plenty of courage to stand up for what is right, even if you have never had to use it before now. You know exactly what type of man Digby is and although you have been grievously hurt, it is over and done with.

"To be fair, we know that not everyone can marry for love. Gentlemen sometimes see a union as more of a business arrangement and as long as both parties are agreeable, such a marriage can work. But I can see that you do not think like that. Well, a holiday with Colonel Fitzwilliam will soon set you back on your feet. He is such a sensible man and I am sure that in his sympathetic company you will recover quickly. There are so many good men out there in the world. Certainly, if you are so inclined, you will find someone to love and admire very soon who will never see you as second best."

To her surprise, Jane turned from the top step where she was climbing back into the carriage, her eyes flashing.

"That's what Bennetta says. Lots more men to attract! No! I shall never marry. How can I ever trust a man again? How could I believe any words of love he spoke to me? I would always remember Digby and doubts would rise up in my mind. No, I am finished with men completely. Apart from those in my close family, I trust none of them!"

And as Susannah gazed at the icy expression in her eyes, she realised that her friend had retreated behind a wall built of grief and despair and wondered if she would ever emerge from there again.

CHAPTER 2

J ane stepped up into the carriage, leaving Susannah to follow, but before they could continue their conversation, a clatter of hooves on the roadway sounded and two horses came cantering around the bend, far too fast for the muddy surface. At the sight of the carriage, the first one reared, neighing wildly and only superb skills kept his rider seated as he fought for control.

Bedlam ensued as the carriage horses tried to bolt, but luckily the postillion was still holding their heads and Archie rushed to help him bring them under control. The carriage rocked violently and Jane and Susannah bit back screams as they were jolted from their seats onto the floor.

The second rider was not as lucky or as skilled as the first. His mount came to an abrupt halt and deposited the man neatly over its head into a ditch under the hedgerow where he struggled to get up, splashing and gasping in the muddy water.

"Good grief, man! What are you thinking of, blocking the road in such a fashion?"

The first rider leapt from his horse and approached Archie. A big man, broad shouldered under his black riding coat, with dark ruffled hair and, under heavy black brows, deep brown eyes that were at that moment full of anger.

As he reached the coach, he saw the Darcy crest on the door and hesitated, some of the arrogance fading from his voice. "My apologies. Is everyone safe? No one hurt or injured?"

Jane struggled up from the floor, pushed down the window and stared out, angry and shaken, her green hat askew, the feather on top bent sideways. The man gave a start, then smiled in a fashion that lit up his taciturn features.

"Miss Darcy! Anne! By all that's wonderful - Anne, what are you doing down here in darkest Dorset? Anne - but no..."

His voice trailed away as he gazed into blue eyes that were softer than the sharp sapphire that had intrigued him so much recently in London. The lady's hat had been knocked sidewards by the crash and the plainly dressed fair hair was not the complicated design of braids and curls that he had noticed with such pleasure on another occasion. "Not Anne."

"I am afraid you have the advantage over me, Sir," Jane said coldly, trying to push her hat straight. "You obviously have mistaken me for my sister. I am Miss Jane Darcy. And I must protest that galloping at speed round a blind corner on a public road is not the most sensible thing to do!"

The man bowed. "Anne's twin sister - she has spoken of you. I apologise for the mistake, Miss Darcy, but you are so alike I think I must be forgiven. I also ask your forgiveness for nearly contributing to an accident, although it was criminal of your man to stop the carriage just here on a sharp bend."

Jane bit back her indignant comments; if this was indeed a friend of Anne's then it would not be polite to engage in an argument, but she still thought the men had been careless. There could have been villager walking along the road, even a child. Suddenly she remembered her manners. "And this lady, rubbing her elbow from its hard contact with the floor, is Miss Courtney."

"Madam! My heartfelt apologies once more. Allow me to introduce myself, if I may. Archer Maitland at your service, and the fellow dripping weed and water in the ditch is my good friend, Dr Andrew Moore. Andrew, Miss Jane Darcy and Miss Courtney."

The other man stumbled out onto the road, laughing through the mud on his face, even as he rescued a large piece of weed that was tangled into his wet brown hair.

"I told you my riding skills are negligible, Archer, but you would insist I accompany you. But I am in one piece, which is a miracle. The water and mud - a great deal of mud - cushioned my fall. Ladies - " he turned and bowed to

Jane and Susannah. "If I had a hat - mine seems to have vanished under the ditch water - I would doff it to you. Please take it for granted."

For the first time in weeks, Jane felt her lips trying to smile; the gentleman was a comic figure. "Sir, you are extremely wet. Please do not let us detain you from home and a warm bath, although as a doctor, you are probably quite aware of that need."

"Alas, I am not a doctor of medicine, Miss Darcy."

"Oh, Andrew has all sorts of degrees and titles from schools and universities. You've never known such a fellow for reading and learning."

"Well, I was certainly skilled enough to tell you that we were riding too fast, Archer! And that my skill on horseback is far less than yours. A fact that the beast in question was quite well aware of, in my opinion, hence him depositing me in the ditch."

"You are not hurt, Sir?" Susannah had joined Jane at the window.

"Goodness no! My pride is a little dented and I fear these breeches will not survive to see the light of another day, but otherwise all is well."

"Are you on your way to Colonel Fitzwilliam's residence?" Mr Maitland asked abruptly. "I know there is a family connection and this road only leads to the village of Compton Forge and Deerwood Park itself."

Jane nodded, irritated by his forthright manner that was almost bordering on arrogance; here was the type of man who asked questions and expected immediate answers. He reminded her of her sister! Well, if the two of them were friends, they must suit each other very well and she wondered why Anne had never mentioned him. Bitterly she thought her sister had probably been too busy with Digby Frobisher!

But such thoughts would have to wait; coolly she replied, "Yes, Sir. We are visiting with Colonel Fitzwilliam and must hurry now to continue our journey. We wish you a good-day and hope you have a safe ride home."

Mr Maitland raised his eyebrows at a tone in her voice that was bordering on dismissal and swung back onto his horse. "Of course, Miss Darcy. We would not wish to detain you any longer than necessary. I am sure we will meet again, very soon, under happier and drier circumstances."

With cries from the driver and a crack of his whip, the carriage at last jolted into movement, leaving the two men to stare after it. Finally, as the sound of the horses died away, Andrew Moore, brushed more weed and mud from his breeches and said, frowning, "My friend, surely it would have been polite to have told Miss Darcy that we are promised to dine with the Colonel this very evening?"

Archer Maitland patted his horse's neck. It wasn't often that his behaviour could be called ungentlemanly, but he realised his friend's words were justified.

"Oh, admittedly it would have been the correct course of action, but her uncalled for chilly demeanour made me disinclined to follow the normal dictates of politeness. And the middle of a public road is not the place for long explanations, especially with a girl whose icy stare dries the words in your mouth. Now, do catch your horse, who seems to have tangled his bridle in that bush, and let's make haste home across the fields. You, my friend, need a hot bath before you are fit to mix in company."

Archer hardly listened to the rest of his friend's comments as they headed for Robyns, the country estate his grandmother had purchased on the death of her husband, Admiral Goddard, where she ruled the staff with a rod of iron. He knew he had been less than friendly to the poor girl. His only excuse was that he was bone tired; his life as a lawyer in London had been extremely exhausting over the past few months and he had been looking forward to a few restful weeks in the country to prepare himself for the many law court battles that lay ahead.

Now as he rode, he recalled a conversation he had had with Miss Anne Darcy whom he had indeed met in London at the home of a certain society hostess, Mrs Caroline Tremaine.

He had admired her brilliant blue eyes, even if her forthright ideas and opinions did not always chime with his own. Anne Darcy was the sort of girl whom he could see as his wife - brilliant, charming, the perfect partner for an up and coming member of the legal profession, one who was destined for politics and ultimately, high office.

He smiled as he recalled his formidable grandmama's words of approval when she met Miss Darcy at a soirée. She had privately told her grandson to ask for the girl's hand in marriage immediately, that he would be a fool to miss such a golden opportunity. Being related to the Darcys of Pemberley would open doors to him socially that were at present firmly closed.

Now, as he put his horse to a fence and cleared it with feet to spare, he remembered an evening when Anne Darcy had admitted to being a twin, the elder twin, as she insisted. On being asked to described her sister's character, she had informed him that Jane tended to shun society, had always been delicate, protected and cosseted by over indulgent parents. It was Anne's opinion that her sister, much as she loved her, needed to learn to stand up for herself and not to rely on friends and family constantly to smooth her path through life.

Anne had made it clear that it irritated her when people always rushed to make Jane's life easy. "You can have no idea, Mr Maitland, how wearying it is to be told constantly by your parents to take care of your sister. The number of times that we have not gone out in the evening as the late hour would make Jane tired, the walks and carriage rides we have cancelled because they were scared it would be too much for her. And at every turn, I have been required to look after her - as if I had no other role to play in life."

She had tossed her head, the little gems on her headdress glittering in the candlelight. "Do not mistake me, Sir. I am fond of my sister and have no wish myself to be looked after, as if I am some wilting flower. But just sometimes I wish that Mama and Papa would give me the same care and attention as they do Jane, whether I need it or not."

Then she had laughed and her fan had opened to its widest to hide her expression, which, just for a moment, had bordered on wistful.

Archer had sympathised; he, too, had no time for the cosseted sort of girl who got her own way by fainting or bursting into tears at the slightest setback. Anne had painted her twin as just such a person.

That conversation had ended with an odd remark which at the time had struck him as a little unkind and left him feeling that his goddess was perhaps not as perfect as he had imagined.

"Well, at least it won't matter if Jane never marries, and la, I cannot see that she ever will because what man would want a frail wife who needs constant attention? But she will surely inherit her godfather's estate in Dorset and so will be quite self-sufficient and no burden on me or my brothers in the future."

Archer didn't know why Jane Darcy's off-hand attitude during their sudden meeting on the road irritated him so much. He had no time for girls who expected their slightest whims to be obeyed, who hid their real feelings and used tears and emotion to bend life to their expectation.

He could well imagine that she was a young lady who was completely unaware of all the upheaval that was abroad in the country at the moment, as working men began to clamour for more pay and better conditions. Archer would have bet several guineas that Jane Darcy paid less attention to politics than the trimming on her latest bonnet.

He was aware that was why he admired Anne Darcy: she was a young lady who always seemed in control of her own destiny, who spoke her mind and had decided views on most matters. She was elegant, beautiful and very well connected.

He knew his grandmother, Lady Goddard, would be only too pleased if he announced his intention to marry the Darcys' eldest daughter. Even though she had purchased Robyns, she still retained her London address in Mayfair and spent many weeks of the season there. Every time Archer met her, she expounded on the virtues of a wife who would bring lustre to his career in law and in the future world of politics.

He was not naive - he knew that to succeed amongst powerful men you needed money. His parents had left him very little on their deaths, but he knew his grandmother would happily give him the funds needed, as long as she approved of his future wife.

Anne Darcy would be a sparkling hostess at his dinner table and make him the envy of all his friends and acquaintance. With all that in mind, Archer Maitland was not quite sure why he had hesitated to ask for her hand. But recently, with his grandmother's words of advice ringing in his ears, he had decided that the next time they met, he would propose that she became his wife.

He had no doubt at all that she would accept. He sensed that she did not love him but, as Mrs Maitland, would have an extremely interesting and powerful part to play in his future career. And he was definitely not going to make the same mistake his mother had made and marry someone who was unsuitable out of love.

At last he turned in his saddle to shout across to his friend. "I wonder if Miss Jane Darcy knows that Colonel Fitzwilliam has another visitor at the moment?"

"Oh, you mean the ravishing Celeste, she of the flashing dark eyes? Isn't she some sort of a distant cousin to the Colonel and the Darcys?"

Archer nodded. "I think it will be most interesting to see the two young ladies at the same table. Smouldering hot night and chilly winter day, both vying for their cousin's attention." And he laughed and urged his horse into a canter, leaving his friend staring after him, his pleasant, mud spattered face creased with concern.

Dr Andrew Moore knew he was not the most astute of men. An eminent archaeologist, he was never happier than when kneeling in a trench in some foreign land, gently scraping away the soil in order to discover clues to the life and times of the people who had lived there centuries ago. Engrossed in his books and papers from various learned societies, he often seemed bewildered when faced with modern day life.

He had known Archer Maitland since they were at school together where Andrew had been mercilessly bullied, first for being so clever and second for coming from a very humble family background, until Archer had intervened, teaching the bullies a lesson they would not forget in a hurry. Since those days the two boys had become firm friends.

Andrew had been amazed when Archer offered him friendship. He was completely unaware that Archer, under his forthright manner and blunt behaviour, had a passion for justice and fair play. It was why he had chosen to study law and it was accepted by all their acquaintances that he would rise to the top of his profession very quickly and eventually enter parliament.

As he grew older, Andrew had realised that Archer's family life was not as happy as his own. He learnt that Archer's grandparents, Admiral and Lady Goddard, had disowned their daughter, Violet, when she married Mr Maitland. A lowly lawyer in a small country town with no way of progressing in his profession, was not the husband they had wished for their only child. Mr Maitland had died when Archer was fourteen and he and his mother lived in very reduced circumstances in a small town near Winchester in the county of Hampshire.

Somewhat reluctantly, his grandparents had paid for their grandson's education at a good school and when he reached the age of eighteen, gave him a sum each year to sustain himself. Archer was fond of them and visited regularly, always hoping that in some way he could bring about a conciliation between them and his mother. But neither side was prepared to make the first move at improving relations and, when Archer turned twenty, his mother followed his father, almost thankfully, into the graveyard.

Now, years later, Andrew could see that the pride which had made the Goddards and their daughter so stubborn was just as prevalent in Archer's character. The little boy who had refused to accept a holiday with richer school-friends because he felt he could not invite them back to his own modest home had turned into a man who kept all his emotions locked away, determined not to show any weakness to the world at large.

Archer had grown closer to Lady Goddard when the Admiral died and Andrew, too, often found himself in her company, although he did not care for the way she expected to control every facet of his friend's life.

He had been delighted to receive Archer's recent invitation to accompany him on a short visit to his grandmother's new home in Dorset. It had come at a most opportune time. Andrew was hoping to travel out to Greece where new, exciting excavations were beginning on the site of the Acropolis in Athens. His parents had moved to Wales with his younger brothers and sisters and he had already given up his London lodgings when the trip was delayed, so it seemed fortuitous that Archer should offer this invitation to stay at Robyns until his new travel arrangements were verified.

Now he urged his horse into a trot, shivering as the breeze chilled his wet shirt, looking forward to a bath and clean clothes. He hoped Archer wouldn't play too many games with Colonel Fitzwilliam's distant relations. He never meant to be unkind, but then, thought Andrew, as he clung to the horse's mane and urged it into a canter, neither did a leopard with its prey.

The late afternoon was slowly turning into evening: the wind had dropped and somewhere a blackbird was singing his last song of the day. The sun was setting in a glory of peach and apricot as Colonel Fitzwilliam opened the massive oak door that led into his rambling old house, stood on the stone steps and gazed anxiously down the length of the long driveway to where it finally curved out of view and vanished under an avenue of lime trees towards the lodge gates.

His visitors were late and he only hoped they had not run into trouble on the rough Dorset lanes. In this hidden valley tucked away under the range of hills that protected it from the sea, progress was slow in coming and once you left the main road, the potholes and uneven surface were a liability when travelling.

Jane's godfather was not an elderly man - but a career in the army had caused his health to suffer: he limped badly and found riding a trial. Although not quite an invalid, he led a quiet life, busy with his collections of silver, books and manuscripts, running his estate with care and kindness, seeing few people except close friends and relations.

He was well cared for by a loyal staff, headed by his housekeeper, Mrs Oxley, and only ventured away from Dorset to stay with the Darcys once a year and to his house in London every six months. His once dark hair was shot through with silver but he was still a handsome man with a pleasing appearance.

Colonel Fitzwilliam had fallen in love over twenty years ago with Miss Elizabeth Bennet, but he had never shared his feelings with that lady - indeed, he had soon realised that compared to the all-consuming, white hot passion his cousin Darcy felt for her, his affections were mild. But mild or not, he had never loved anyone else and had long settled for comfortable bachelorhood.

He had always taken his duties as godfather to Jane Darcy very seriously. He loved the gentle, quiet girl who had not been expected to live more than a few days when born. He was keen, as were her parents, to protect her from all harm. Sometimes in the dead of night, when he could not sleep from the pain of the injuries he had received abroad, he wondered if this was the type of daughter he might have had with Elizabeth. But as dawn rose, he pushed those thoughts to the back of his mind.

Anne Darcy, even as a child, had annoyed him by her supercilious manners and arrogant behaviour. Bennetta and the boys treated him politely but obviously felt he was just another elderly relative who had to be respected but who knew nothing about their world.

Jane was different: since childhood she had sought out his company and it had been obvious over the years on the Darcys' visits to Deerwood Park that she was the one who looked forward to seeing him the most. On her he lavished all his affection and he was seriously worried by a recent letter from Elizabeth, telling of arguments and divisions in the family.

The sound of wheels on gravel and the jingle of harness sent a wave of relief through him. The Darcy coach was rounding the bend. Just then a young lady came out of the house and slipped her arm through his.

"Oh 'ave they arrived? They are so late! I dislike lateness, it is very bad mannered, but then I expect being so rich, Jane Darcy feels she can do as she wishes, although I think she should perhaps show you more consideration. You should be resting your poor leg. But perhaps I am unkind. They may have been delayed on the road. Forgive me, dear Colonel, I was concerned that you had been worried and that dinner will be late when you have other guests arriving and your poor cook will be distraught! Me, I am so delighted to make Jane's acquaintance. It is good of you to give shelter to all your cousins."

Colonel Fitzwilliam gazed down at the beautiful face turned up to him, the sparkling black eyes and affectionate expression. He smiled; the arrival of this distant relation had both surprised and delighted him. The Italian girl had only been at Deerwood Park for three weeks but in that time she had impressed him with her love of life and been pleased with the little attentions she showed him.

"And I am certain she will be over-joyed to meet you, too, Celeste. Don't look distressed. I know only too well that it is concern for me that makes you speak harshly. I am sure you will be good friends. Look, here she is now."

Celeste gripped his arm tighter and turned her gaze to where a slight figure in pale green silk with a hat to match - a colour that did nothing for her - was alighting from the carriage. So this was Jane Darcy. Well, she was pretty, in a fair-haired, insipid, English sort of way, and well dressed - although not in the very latest fashion, her sleeves should have contained far more material and surely she was only wearing three petticoats when four was the fashion.

Celeste stroked the skirt of her crimson silk; the Colonel had been very generous lately and she had bought several new outfits from a shop in Dorchester.

Jane was smiling as she walked up the steps to the front door, but Celeste could see that she was very pale and there was an air of sadness and restraint about her person. A rival? Oh yes, the Colonel would feel very protective of this girl. But Celeste could see nothing in this person that could cause her to believe she could stand in the way of her plans.

Jane was delighted to have arrived at the house she considered her haven, her safe harbour from the world. From her very first visit as a small child, Jane had always loved Deerwood Park: her parents had often brought their whole family to stay with Colonel Fitzwilliam when they were small.

A few minutes earlier she had felt a swell of anticipation as the carriage clattered through the village of Compton Forge with its tiny Norman church and cluster of cottages around the village green. She had lowered the window, oblivious to the dust thrown up by the horses and pointed out all the familiar sights.

"Look, Susannah, there is the duck pond from which Henry had to be rescued when he had just learned to walk, and there is the village shop which sells everything you could possibly want and where Mrs Ramsden used to give out biscuits, but only to children who had been good. She still serves behind the counter. There is the Green Man, a very old inn, built in good Queen Bess's time, so they say. It is an odd name, is it not? I have no idea where it comes from.

"And, see that big tree we are just passing - one of the village children dared Bennetta to climb it and she did, right to the very top, and she was confined to her room with just bread and water for two days as punishment! And there is the field where Anne's pony used to graze. He is long gone, of course, but even when she was small she was a fine rider."

Susannah smiled and nodded with interest but she was well aware that there was no mention in Jane's memories of any escapade she might have been involved in as a child. It was as if she had always been kept safe, locked away in a gilded cage, always the observer, outside the family inner circle, watching but not taking part.

Two farm labourers, on their way home from the fields, looked up at the carriage passed and doffed their hats, recognising the Darcy crest emblazoned on the doors. A group of women gossiping on their doorsteps, turned and bobbed deferential curtsies.

Now the carriage had left the village behind and was sweeping down a long road, through gates already opened in anticipation by the lodge keeper, into the main drive. It swept under a tunnel of green where the branches met and entwined overhead, turned an abrupt corner and there, under the shelter of a hillside, the mansion house of Deerwood Park lay snugly before her.

Over two hundred years old, it had been built towards the end of Queen Elizabeth's reign and the creeper covered red bricks, small mullioned windows and tall carved chimney pots stood untouched, the same as the day they had been built.

Jane had once heard her sister remark that it was a crime that Colonel Fitzwilliam did not tear down the old monstrosity and build a lovely new house, full of high-ceilinged rooms with large windows.

It had been one of the few times when she had argued heatedly with Anne. She loved Deerwood Park with all her heart. Pemberley was wonderful, of course, and her home, but it did not appeal to her romantic nature as did this old, rambling building with its steep stairs, twisting passageways and cavities locked away behind panelling and false shelves, that were memories of the dreadful times when Catholic priests had been hidden away from their persecutors.

She stepped down from the carriage, not waiting for Archie's help, and smiled in pleasure at the sight of her godfather standing at the top of the steps. Her smile only faltered a little when she noticed the small, dark haired girl clinging to his arm.

"Jane, my dear child. You have arrived safely! I have been worried. There is such unrest everywhere and travelling has become distinctly difficult of late."

The Colonel eased his arm from the girl's grasp and took both of Jane's hands in his. He smiled past her and bowed his head in acknowledgment. "And Miss Courtney! How delighted I am to see you here at Deerwood. Come in, come in. I have ordered refreshments for you."

"Colonel Fitzwilliam, it is so good to see you again. And..." Jane hesitated and dropped a small curtsey to the girl.

"My dear, this is a distant cousin of mine and an even more distant one of yours - Signorina Celeste Fiorette."

Jane held out her hand in astonishment; she had never heard of this relation but as the slim white fingers grasped hers with a grip that was too tight, almost painful, she found herself gazing into beautiful dark eyes that were as cold as a winter's night sky and at complete odds to the smile on the foreign girl's lips.

CHAPTER 3

"But my dear Jane, are you saying you had no knowledge of this young lady before today?" Susannah was sitting on her friend's bed, watching as she made her final preparations before going downstairs for a late dinner.

Jane had changed into a pale lemon dress which, although fashionable with its tight waist and full skirt, drained all the delicate colour from a face that was already far too pale. Their maid, Tabitha, had put up her hair in a tight, braided coronet and Susannah wished that for once she would display it in the cloud of fair waves that changed her from pretty to beautiful.

It had taken her a very short time to wash and change from her own travelling outfit into a plain brown silk that she knew to be old-fashioned but was cool on this very hot evening. She longed to explore the house which seemed so old and exciting, but that adventure would have to wait until the morning. They could not be late to dinner on their first evening.

Susannah could already see the fascination a building such as Deerwood Park might have for a person with romantic inclinations such as Jane. Her own bedroom was small and oddly shaped with no two walls the same length. But it was comfortable, tucked away at the end of a twisting passage, with a tiny diamond-paned window that overlooked an apple orchard where the trees were bowed to the ground with fruit.

The wooden floor sloped steeply and she had smiled to discover that her bed was propped up by wooden blocks on one side to stop the occupant from sliding out onto the floor in the middle of the night!

In all the confusion of arriving, she had not had a moment to speak privately to her friend. There had been an awkward moment when it was revealed by the housekeeper that Jane would not have the spacious bedroom she usually frequented on her visits to Deerwood Park. Celeste was using that and although the Italian girl charmingly, with many apologies, said she would move immediately if given a chance to pack all her belongings but it might take a while because she had so much scattered everywhere, Jane had obviously politely insisted that any room would suit her just as well.

Tabitha had been sent downstairs to have her own supper in the kitchen and the two were now alone. Jane fussed with a blonde tress that refused to stay pinned into place.

"No, never. Well, I vaguely knew there had been a great scandal in the Fitzwilliam family, but I was never that much interested in old history. Papa's mother - whom Anne is named after of course - Lady Catherine de Bourgh and the Colonel's own father, had a much younger sister, Rose. Of course we were never told the details, but Bennetta discovered recently - from gossiping with the servants, I fear - that Rose, who was wild and wilful, ran away from home when she was just fifteen and eloped to Italy with one of the grooms!

"It caused the most dreadful situation. She was disowned by the family and never mentioned again. It was as if she had never existed. I believe, although I have never seen it for myself, that my great-grandfather, Earl Fitzwilliam, even crossed her name out of the family Bible!"

"And this Celeste is her granddaughter?"

"So it would seem. I think Papa will be amazed to hear that she exists. I am only surprised that she came here to the Colonel and did not present herself to the Earl himself. Although he does not have good health, so perhaps she thought it kinder to be introduced by a family member."

"The Colonel seems delighted to have her here. And she seems to be very much at home at Deerwood Park."

Jane stood up, smiling. "I am delighted that there is another cousin to include in our family circle. No doubt we will get to hear all about her life in Italy, which will be interesting. I wonder how long she intends to stay in England? And it is good for the Colonel to have company. I would wish to be here far more often than is possible because I think he gets lonely on his own. Now, we must go down to dinner - I am not particularly hungry, but I am sure you must be."

She led the way down the twisting oak staircase and across the panelled hall to the dining-room. A footman leapt forward to open the door but as she stepped through into the candle-lit room, Jane stopped so suddenly that Susannah almost bumped into her.

"Jane, my dear. Come in, sit down and let me make more introductions."

The Colonel smiled warmly at her. "This gentleman is Mr Archer Maitland. The grandson of an old acquaintance of mine, Lady Goddard, who purchased the Robyns estate, just a few miles distant on the far side of Deerwood hill. Archer is staying in Dorset for a short while, an escape from his busy life in the law courts of London. And here is his friend, the celebrated archaeologist, Dr Andrew Moore. Gentlemen, my god-daughter, Miss Jane Darcy and another friend, Miss Courtney."

Archer Maitland strode forward and taking Jane's hand, bowed over it, his dark eyes gleaming in the candlelight that flickered and flared as a gentle breeze slipped through the half open windows. He was smiling, enjoying her surprise.

"Miss Darcy, we meet again! I fear you are astonished to see us here and will probably be annoyed that we did not mention that we were to be fellow guests when we met earlier."

Jane gently pulled her hand away, realising she was irritated more than astonished. Why had the wretched man not mentioned that they were close neighbours? "Indeed, Sir, I am confused that you did not speak of it."

"But not appalled, I hope?" Andrew Moore, who was standing by the window, crossed the room to take Susannah's hand in turn and bowed over it, his good-humoured face creased with an anxious frown.

Jane summoned her wits, which had been lost for a few minutes and turned away from Archer towards his friend. "Oh no, Sir, just surprised. And it is a pleasure to see you warm and dry once more. And certainly with far less mud about your person."

"Indeed, we have heard all about Dr Moore's escapades this afternoon," the Colonel said. "I am only thankful that no one suffered any lasting injury. Now, please be seated everyone. The soup will surely be getting cold with every minute that passes."

Jane smiled and started towards the seat on the Colonel's right hand which was her normal place when she visited, then realised that Celeste was already sitting there.

The Italian girl gazed up at her, her dark eyes full of contrition. "La, I am afraid I have taken your place, Jane. First your bedroom and now your seat at the table. You will think me very remiss but we do not stand on these outdated manners at home in Sicily and I believe the Colonel, too, is beginning to think that sometimes life can be far too ordered for comfort."

Celeste flicked open her fan and turned to the Colonel, her eyes full of affectionate merriment above the lace folds. "But of course Jane, I will move immediately if you wish to take precedence. I believe you are, in fact, nearly a year older than me. I have only just turned nineteen and the Colonel told me that your twentieth birthday is in December."

"I insist that Miss Jane sits here next to me." Archer held out the chair before the footman could do so and Jane had no choice but to nod her thanks and sit, trying to cover her confusion as best she could, only too well aware that Celeste, in glittering gold silk, made her own pale lemon evening dress seem washed out and boring.

She sighed; this was exactly how Anne made her feel. Her mama had never dressed the twins in identical clothes, wanting them to have their own personalities, but Anne had always chosen brighter colours, more dramatic styles, lower necklines.

'Really, Jane,' she thought crossly. 'Does it matter how you look? Dear Colonel Fitzwilliam won't care and I have not the slightest desire to attract either of these two gentlemen. My feelings for Digby are still as strong as ever, no matter how badly he has treated me. Indeed, it seems that Mr Maitland has already met Anne, so he will be only too aware of her attraction.'

"I am sure your sister insists on all ceremony around the Pemberley dining-table," Archer said, leaning back to allow his soup plate to be filled by a footman from a great blue and white tureen. "We have met when she has been staying in London with Mrs Caroline Tremaine; I found her to be a young lady with very strong views on such things."

"Indeed, Anne is perhaps more particular than I am, Sir, especially on formal occasions. But our family meals are very relaxed. My younger sister and brothers make it so. They are not great believers in staid behaviour!"

"I am afraid I have missed out on that side of family life. I am an only child, although Andrew there has four younger siblings."

"I am sympatico with you, Mr Maitland. I, too, am an only child. It can be very lonely when you are growing up. I long to meet all the Darcy family," Celeste put in brightly. "The dear Colonel speaks so warmly of your parents, I am sure I will be immensely fond of them. And what of your family, Miss Courtney?" she continued, leaning forward a little to direct her words to Susannah who was sitting across from Jane at the end of the table, next to Andrew Moore. "You must surely miss them, living as Jane's companion. Are they farmers? In trade, perhaps?"

"Oh, but Miss Courtney..." the Colonel began but Susannah interrupted him smoothly, without hardly looking up from her plate.

"I do not live at Pemberley, Signorina Celeste. I live nearby with my brother and sister-in-law."

"Susannah's brother is a doctor," Jane said. "She is a good friend, not just a companion, although, of course, she is my closest companion on this holiday."

She was about to add that Susannah was also sister to Sir Robert Courtney of Courtney Castle in Northumberland, then realised that her friend was pressing down on her foot under the table and swallowed her words. For whatever reason, the connection was obviously not to be mentioned at the moment.

It was of course, in her opinion, the height of bad manners to inquire in such an offhand fashion about someone to whom you had just been introduced, but, Jane thought doubtfully, no one else seemed to think anything out of place had occurred. Perhaps she was too old-fashioned, as Anne often said. It was 1834, not 1734! She knew she had a tendency to live in the past and abhor modern manners.

And Celeste was a foreigner; Jane was sure their ways of living were very different in Sicily. The girl obviously meant no harm and was now chattering away to the Colonel, insisting that he tried this or that delicacy from the platter of cold meats and pastries which formed one of the courses.

Jane tried to concentrate on what Mr Maitland was saying but found her attention drifting. She sighed: this evening was turning out so differently from what she had imagined on the journey to Dorset.

Her unhappiness over Digby had been soothed by the thought that she and Susannah would sit with her godfather, exchanging news of Pemberley and catching up on all the local gossip from Compton Forge. But she had hardly spoken two words to the Colonel since her arrival; Celeste had monopolised his attention the whole time. Instead, she must spend her meal being polite to Mr Maitland and Dr Moore.

She found the younger man, far more approachable than his dark haired friend. He had interesting comments to make about historical sites in Greece and Italy and Jane found him an easy dinner partner.

To her distress, she realised she was neglecting the gentleman on her other side, but could sense that he did not find her company congenial. He appeared tired and his apparent disapproval of her made her uneasy. Aware that she had once more failed to be of interest, she retreated even further behind cold words and short replies to any question he asked.

"We can learn a lot from our ancient ancestors," Dr Moore said as the footmen brought in the final course. "But I wonder if the Greeks knew how to make a dessert such as this - with gooseberries, cream and iced liqueur. I must compliment your cook, Colonel Fitzwilliam. Keeping such a dish cold in this weather is an achievement."

"The Colonel has an ice-house in the grounds," Jane said. "It is built deep underground, close to the lake. When that freezes in the winter, great blocks of ice are stored in straw and wood and because the room is so cold it takes a long time to melt away. My papa was so impressed that he had one constructed at Pemberley."

"Is the ice-house somewhere you visit often, Miss Jane?" Archer Maitland asked. His tone was polite, but his friend looked up sharply and immediately changed the subject from ice-houses to what he hoped to find out in Greece on his next archaeological dig.

"I am sure it will be even hotter in Greece," Archer said with a smile. He pretended to shiver. "It is distinctly chilly in here tonight, I fancy."

"Perhaps you are sitting in a draught, Sir?" Jane said, stunned into reacting at this not very well concealed barb. "You must be careful, Mr Maitland, although I believe cool air is always advised for those who have a tendency to be hot-headed."

To her surprise, the stern, hawk like features broke into a grin that was almost boyish and she caught a glimpse of someone very different as his dark eyes gleamed. "You are quite right, Miss Jane. I shall heed your wise words."

"Poor Mr Maitland!" Celeste's husky voice purred down the table. "Being criticised for being hot blooded! Why, Jane, I fear you would not care for many of the young gentlemen you would meet in my country. We prize those whose passions are easily aroused. Indeed, I believe gentlemen in any part of the world would prefer their companions to show their emotions rather than hide them away."

And she laughed and tapped the Colonel on his arm with her fan, gazing at him with her brilliant dark eyes.

There was an uneasy silence until Susannah neatly changed the subject with an interested question to the Colonel about the age of the house.

Jane sipped her wine in silence but her thoughts were tumultuous. Was Celeste right? Would she have kept Digby's admiration if she had shown him just how deep her own feelings for him were? Could he possibly have decided that her quiet, cool exterior covered an inner person who was just as cold and retiring, someone who really didn't care for him? It was a frightening thought.

When dinner was finished, with a hot cheese relish for the gentlemen and iced rosewater for the ladies, the party moved into the drawing-room where the windows were still open a little to let in the cooler night air.

Jane had always loved this room - the low ceiling, criss-crossed with ancient beams, the oak panelling, each panel embossed in the centre with a wooden rose. The heavy chairs were covered in patterned damask and thick rugs lay scattered across the old floorboards, cut from oaks that Jane believed had been saplings at the time of the battle of Agincourt.

"You were very reserved at dinner, Miss Darcy." Carrying his coffee cup, Archer Maitland crossed to her side and seated himself next to her. "I hope you were not too fatigued by your journey and the heat to enjoy your meal? Or perhaps it was the company that tired you."

"The company, Sir?"

"I am sure it was a great surprise to find a cousin you knew nothing about in residence here at Deerwood, and then Andrew and I have also helped spoil the quiet evening I imagine you thought you were about to enjoy. I remember Anne telling me that you prefer a life of peace and solitude, that you spend more time in the Pemberley library than dancing or visiting."

Jane felt her cheeks redden and flicked open her fan. There was nothing in Mr Maitland's words that she could dispute, but it was the tone in which he spoke them that irritated her.

"It is true that I enjoy reading, but I do not consider that a fault. I am afraid my sister is somewhat extravagant with her opinions. I have no wish for continual solitude; I enjoy the company of many people."

"But I have never seen you in London society? Miss Anne Darcy is often to be found gracing the assembly rooms and balls when she stays with Mrs Tremaine. Are you never tempted to do the same? Or perhaps you do not care to dance?"

To her horror, Jane realised that tears were welling up in her eyes. She blinked rapidly, mortified to think that Mr Maitland might think he was the reason for them. It had been a sudden memory - Digby dancing with Anne at the Pemberley ball. Until that time she had truly believed that he liked and admired her more than her twin and the pain she had felt during that evening was still raw, when even Bennetta had danced with him twice and he had ignored her completely.

"Archer, you have monopolised Miss Jane for too long." Dr Moore was standing in front of her, an expression of concern on his kind face. He had been watching from across the room, and seen the fleeting change of expression cross her features.

Archer Maitland stood up immediately, vacating his chair for his friend. "A thousand apologies. I think I will give orders for our carriage to be brought round. It will not do to outstay our welcome. Hopefully the weather will be cooler tomorrow. Perhaps if you and Miss Courtney will have recovered your energy, you will accompany Andrew on a walk through the woods and show him some of the more intriguing sights of the area."

"I am sure we would be pleased to have his company."

"And you, Sir? Will you be joining us?" Susannah asked.

Archer shook his head. "Sadly, I must accompany my grandmother on visits tomorrow. But I would suggest, Miss Jane, that you show Andrew the waterfall and the strange circle of standing stones that are to be found nearby. Indeed, their age and purpose is lost in time and such ancient things are of great interest to him.

With that, he bowed to Jane and the rest of the company and left the room, leaving her feeling thankful that he had gone and annoyed that she had not had the chance to tell him that she loved to dance and was considered better at the art than either of her sisters!

She turned her attention to Dr Moore, her ruffled feelings soothed by his gentle words. Here was a gentleman whose manner and demeanour were very much to her liking. No barbed comments but kind conversation that needed no effort to understand. They discussed a time and place to meet the following day and she felt soothed by the pleasure he showed at these arrangements.

Eventually a footman appeared to inform Dr Moore that the carriage was waiting and with many promises for the following day, he left.

"Such a clever gentleman," Celeste said brightly when the door closed behind him. "And I do believe you have made a conquest, dear cousin."

Jane laughed at the absurdity of the remark. She was not the type of girl who attracted men on their first meeting.

"He is a pleasant man," she replied. "Indeed, I think he is the type of gentleman who would always be polite and considerate to any young woman he met. I do not think I would ever imagine myself to be in a special position where that is concerned or set out to be the target for his attentions."

"I fear I have annoyed you! Made an embarrassment! But you must forgive me. I was only thinking what a happy thing it is for a man to be attracted to you. What a delight it would be for all your family and connections to see you settled in life. I am so sorry. I should not have spoken. Perhaps I used the wrong words. I try very hard to speak English well, but I know I am not always correct. Oh please do not look at me like that! As if you are so angry with me."

Celeste's lip trembled and her eyes filled with tears, as if she was upset that her remarks had caused Jane distress.

"My dear, do not worry yourself so." Colonel Fitzwilliam was all concern, placing a kindly hand on the young girl's shoulder. "Jane knows that you meant no harm, don't you, Jane?" And he flicked a warning glance at his god-daughter.

"Of course." Jane was bewildered. The Italian girl's sudden flood of emotion seemed so exaggerated and unnecessary. She was not aware that she had given her any angry glance at all and it was upsetting that the Colonel should think that she had.

"Well, I for one am very tired. It has been a long day." Eager to calm the situation, Susannah stood up and moved to the door. "Jane, it is getting late - let us retire. Colonel Fitzwilliam, I bid you goodnight and thank you again for your hospitality in this lovely house. I look forward to exploring it tomorrow. I am sure it has all sorts of secrets to reveal."

The Colonel took her hand and bowed over it. "The pleasure is all mine, Miss Courtney. I will be delighted to show you all that Deerwood Park has to offer."

Jane followed Susannah from the room and, taking a candle from a foot-man, followed her up the winding oak staircase.

"Sleep well, dear Jane," the older woman said as they reached the passageway leading to her own room. "We will no doubt talk in the morning when we have had a chance to think over the day's events."

She smiled and Jane watched as the gleam from her candle vanished into the dark, then turned to find Tabitha waiting in her bedroom to unpin and brush her hair and help her undress.

The bed was not the one she was used to and when the maid had gone, pulling back the heavy curtains so the moonlight glittered in across the floor, she blew out her candle, sure she would not sleep a wink.

The journey, her distress over Digby, her pleasure at seeing the Colonel once more, Andrew Moore's kind eyes, Celeste's odd behaviour, all raced through her mind. But, as she fell at last into slumber, her main thought was annoyance that she had failed to tell Archer Maitland that she liked dancing!

CHAPTER 4

J ane awoke the next morning, restless and flustered by weird dreams. She had been standing in a church, attending Anne at her wedding to Digby Frobisher. Astonishingly, the vicar had been Archer Maitland who had turned to her, asking why she didn't object when she was so obviously against the match?

She had struggled to speak through her tears, wishing to say that all she wanted was for everyone to be happy, but the words would not come and Mr Maitland was laughing at her, and the church bells were ringing louder and louder - until with a start she woke to a calm morning with the soft sunlight filtering in through the windows and the bells became the brass rings on the rails as Tabitha drew back the curtains.

Thankfully the temperature seemed far more amenable; the intense heat had lifted and the very first light mists of autumn were drifting over the woodlands that she could see from her windows. The bright green of the leaves was slowly fading and the first yellows and bronzes were appearing as the end of the year edged nearer.

It was a fine day for walking and she was keen to show Susannah and Dr Moore all the glories of Deerwood Park, the waterfall and the odd stones that she was sure would intrigue him. She was pleased that Mr Maitland wouldn't be accompanying them; she found it hard to picture him wandering through a woodland scene, admiring the foliage. It was her opinion that he was more likely to admonish the leaves for turning yellow!

"Are you comfortable in your room, Tabitha?" she asked her maid as she was helping her dress. "I know this is your first time here at Deerwood. Grace Frost always maided me until she left Pemberley to take up a position in London."

The young girl nodded as she ran a comb through the fair tangles that cascaded around Jane's shoulders. She was well aware of why Grace had left Derbyshire but that was not a conversation she could have with Miss Darcy. She was quite sure her lady had no idea of the scandal that had surrounded Grace's sudden departure with the artist Edmund Avery, just as she was sure that Jane didn't realise all the servants knew about Mr Frobisher proposing to the wrong sister and being turned down and Miss Jane being that upset about everything.

"I'm sharing with the Italian lady's maid, Miss. But it's a big room up on the top floor, so we've plenty of space."

"Oh, I didn't think, of course Signorina Celeste has brought her own maid with her from Sicily."

"Why yes, Miss Jane. Her name's Luisa but she doesn't speak much English and that she does speak, I can hardly understand." She sniffed, disdainfully. "Must admit they have odd customs in foreign parts. Us Pemberley maids know better than to speak before we are spoken to. Why Luisa chatters on to her mistress just as if they were sisters! It would never do at home."

Jane fell silent, pondering on how brave Celeste must be to leave her own home and country and travel to England, not knowing what sort of welcome she would receive from her distant relations. No wonder she took refuge in speaking to her maid in their own tongue: the need not to think and translate every word must be so welcome.

She tried to picture herself travelling alone to a foreign country with just a maid for company and failed. Why, she could not remember a single time in her whole life when she had ever done anything on her own, unguarded, unchaperoned. Even on this trip to Dorset it had been arranged that Susannah accompany her as well as Tabitha. She hadn't been consulted and although she was delighted to have Susannah's company, she couldn't help feeling aggravated that no one had asked her if this was what she wished.

She sighed; why only last year their cousin Catherine had ventured up to

Northumberland on her own to work at Courtney Castle. Miriam, their cousin from Africa, had travelled across oceans and endured all sorts of perils! Why, even Grace, the maid who had tended her for several years had gone away on her own to work in London. So why did her mama and papa think she needed constant protection? Was she really so feeble and helpless?

When Tabitha had finished pinning up her hair and helped her to wash and dress, she hurried downstairs, worried that she might be late because she knew her friend was an early riser. As she had expected, Colonel Fitzwilliam and Susannah were already at breakfast. They were laughing as she entered, obviously enjoying each other's company.

"I must apologise, Godfather, Susannah - I am tardy this morning."

"My dear girl, think nothing of it. You were obviously tired from all the travelling and, if I had given it more consideration, I should not have invited guests to dine on your first evening here." The Colonel beckoned to a footman who came forward with a choice of hot chocolate or cider. "Miss Courtney has been entertaining me most diligently in your absence."

"And is Celeste also tired this morning?" Jane asked, aware of an empty seat at the table.

The Colonel laughed. "Oh our little cousin never rises much before eleven. She is a fragile creature, you know. I am always most cautious to see that she does not overstrain herself in any way."

Susannah raised an eyebrow at Jane and then applied herself to her bread and honey. She thought she had never seen anyone less fragile looking than the buxom Celeste, but it was not her place to say so!

"So she will not be joining us on our walk this morning?"

"No, Jane. Indeed not. And I shall stay behind to keep her company. We have plans to catalogue some of my silver collection. Celeste loves to look at it and appreciates the finer pieces."

"She has good taste, then." Jane smiled across the table at her godfather. "You must inspect the Colonel's wonderful silver, Susannah. You will surely find it of great interest. Have you shown Dr Moore yet, Godfather?"

The Colonel nodded. "Indeed I have. He was very impressed. He says he has never seen such a fine collection outside of a museum."

"And did Mr Maitland also appreciate them? I somehow fear that anything old would be considered unfashionable by that gentleman."

"Jane, you are too harsh! Archer Maitland does not perhaps share his friend's enthusiasm for the ancient, but he can still recognise how important it is to have these links with the past."

"Well, I shall look forward to inspecting the pieces myself during this holiday," Susannah said peacefully. "But this morning I believe has been set aside for us to explore. Jane, I am keen to see the waterfall and the walk through the woods to the village you have spoken of so warmly."

Stout shoes, bonnets and parasols were the order of the day and Susannah insisted they took a light shawl each because it would be far cooler in the deep shade of the woods. She had no worries on her own account, but with Jane still in such an emotional state of mind, she was concerned in case she took a chill while her mood was so low. She knew from Mrs Darcy that Jane's health was always a concern and that she should be on her guard at all times in case she over tired herself.

Jane felt her spirits lifting as they left the gardens of Deerwood Park by a small wicker gate and followed the path that lead deep into the woods. It was a perfect day for walking and she was delighted to show Susannah the beauty of Colonel Fitzwilliam's estate.

"The woods continue all the way to the edge of the village," she said, slipping off her bonnet and letting it hang from its ribbons down her back. Its closeness to her face was making her feel hotter than was comfortable. "We can purchase a glass of milk from one of the villagers before we head back."

"It is certainly a beautiful place, Jane. I can see why you love it so much."

"I always feel safe here."

"Safe? But surely you are quite safe at Pemberley? You couldn't be more protected than in your own home."

Jane bent to pluck a tall wild flower that was growing near the path. It was so hard to explain that although she loved Pemberley, its vast rooms and corridors, the picture galleries, ballrooms and high painted ceilings made her feel small and insignificant. At Deerwood Park, with the small rooms and winding passages, she felt safe and secure.

"Hallooo!"

They had reached a small stone bridge that curved up and over what should have been a busy stream, but with the drought was no more than a thin trickle. Coming towards them along the path that led back up the hillside was Dr Moore, raising his hat to them.

"Good morning, ladies! What a wonderful morning for an outing."

"Good morning, Dr Moore!" Jane was delighted to see him, feeling the warmth of his regard, liking the way his eyes crinkled when he smiled, as blue as the coat he was wearing.

"Have you walked right over the hill, Sir?" Susannah asked.

"Yes indeed, Robyns, the Goddard estate, lies on the far side of the Downs. It borders onto the sea cliffs and extends to the north up to the crest of the hill. It is a steep climb, but an easy walk down on this side. I shall put the challenge of getting home out of my mind until the time comes to leave!"

"Mr Maitland suggested I show you the odd circle of stones near the waterfall. They are extremely ancient, so I have been told."

"I would very much like to see them, but not if it is out of your way. I would not wish you to be tired on my account."

Jane insisted that it would be no trouble and the three of them crossed the bridge and began the climb up the path that followed the course of the stream.

"Mr Maitland is engaged on calls with his grandmother this morning, I believe?"

"Indeed, I left him pacing around the hall, irritated that his grandmother had yet to make an appearance. Lady Goddard is a law unto herself and even Archer has to bow to her will, although I fear one of these days he will rebel."

Jane found herself smiling as she pictured that tall, arrogant man having to sit and politely sip tea with the ladies of the district and be forced to listen to their chatter and gossip, then chided herself quickly for having such mean thoughts.

৩✺৩

ARCHER MAITLAND HAD HAD A VERY FRUSTRATING AND IRRITATING morning. He hadn't slept well for months; he had been extremely busy with his law practice in London which had been involved with the distressing case of the six Dorset men from the village of Tolpuddle, who had been deported to Australia for treason. He had hoped that a couple of weeks of placid boredom would help him recover his energies. But memories of the previous evening's events kept flashing though his mind as he wrestled with his bed sheets.

He finally gave up trying to sleep and at dawn strode out through the grounds to a lake that lay a quarter of a mile from the house. The water here was fed by an underground source and so the level of the water had not been lessened by the drought.

Archer stripped off, hoping that an icy cold plunge would drive away his bad mood, but when he returned to the house, he realised he was still thinking of ice-houses, cold gooseberry desserts and a pair of very chilly blue eyes.

Breakfast did nothing to help his temper and the final straw was the half hour he spent in the hall, with the horses and carriage outside, waiting for his grandmother to appear. The tradition of calling and leaving cards, of sometimes taking a cup of chocolate or tea he felt was a complete waste of his time.

Usually he gave in to his grandmother's insistence on his attendance, but for some reason this morning his patience snapped; he left word with a footman that, with apologies, he would not be accompanying Lady Goddard, tore off his choking cravat, changed from his visiting clothes to plain shirt, linen coat and breeches and set out to walk off his bad mood.

He deliberately did not aim his steps towards Deerwood Park; he would leave Andrew to the joys of those ladies' company. No, he just wanted to stretch his legs and enjoy the fresh air.

With the house behind him, he strode out across the rough turf towards the hills. The steep climb up the chalky track made him realise how lazy he had become in London and he was more than grateful to reach the top where a breeze from the sea felt good on his hot skin and he was able to look down the far slope. Not completely to his surprise, he realised that below him spread the woodlands of Deerwood Park.

Then, to his astonishment, a yard or two before the summit of the hill, he could see the figure of a girl, hatless, the wind making a halo of her fair hair, reaching up to find a handhold on the giant boulder that lay just beneath his feet. He was about to shout down at her, angry that anyone could be so foolish, when he saw that there was nothing except her own balance in stubby little boots, holding her on the rocky path and a hundred foot drop to the hard ground below.

THE ANCIENT STONE CIRCLE WAS ONE OF THE ODDEST THINGS IN THE district and Jane was eager to show it to Dr Moore. Where a waterfall cascading down the chalky hillside - although no more than a gleaming trickle of water at the moment - fell into a deep, green pool, a wide circle had been cut into the woods and there were the strange grey stones, some standing buried in the turf, others lying sideways where they had fallen over the centuries.

Susannah exclaimed in interest and Dr Moore gave every indication of pleasure. Jane sat on a fallen tree trunk and watched as they moved round the circle, examining each stone in turn. Dr Moore had produced a small notebook and was making sketches and measuring distances with a piece of string that Susannah held for him.

Jane could recall her papa and eldest brother doing the same thing one far distant time when they had spent a few weeks one summer at Deerwood Park, apparently fascinated - as certain men obviously were - by how equally the stones were laid out and full of explanations and wonder at their existence.

Staring up the rock face, she wondered if it was possible to find the source of the waterfall, where the water sprung out of the hillside. Normally it was far too wet with spray and moss to venture higher - although she knew her brothers and Bennetta had all made the climb at some time when they were young - but this year the drought had made every path firm underfoot.

Memories of a far away picnic crowded in on her - everyone happy and busy, exploring, climbing, Mama sketching, Anne taking off her shoes and stockings and paddling in the pool where the waterfall cascaded.

But why did she have no memories of what she had done? All she could recall was being seated in the shade with her sketch book, being told not to tire herself after the walk and certainly not to plunge her hot feet in the cold water in case she took a chill.

Bennetta and Henry had scampered away to clamber up the rocks, pretending not to hear their papa call out after them. She could have gone with them, but she hadn't, she had been obedient and quiet and - the word 'dull' blazed through her mind and she pushed it aside. It was only right that her mama had worried over her health; Jane had been told from a very early age that she was not strong and mustn't tire herself without good cause.

Now her companions were busy on the far side of the stone circle and she realised that, although she had always found them interesting, she did not have the same feeling for the old stones as they obviously did. She stood up and quietly clambered across the first few rocks that led upwards in easy steps.

"Be careful! Don't go too far, Jane dear!" That was Susannah: once more someone was making her hesitate, tempting her to sit down, to be quiet and obedient.

Was this what Digby Frobisher expected? Probably! That she would forgive and forget, marry him and settle down quietly in the country to lead a blameless and loveless life, knowing she was second best, as always, to her sister.

Spurred on by sudden anger at herself for being so feeble, Jane looped up her skirt and petticoats and tucked them into her belt as she scrambled higher and higher. She looked down once and felt the world swing round her as she realised just how precarious her footing was. If the rough stones should start to slip and slide, she would go down, head over heels, to the bottom of the path.

A quiver of fear coursed through her and she could hear in her head all the voices warning her of putting herself into danger, the voices that had been part of her life for ever. She hesitated and then pushed the voices aside. For once she was going to accomplish a goal she had set herself. A few feet more and she felt a thrill of victory! There was a dark opening between two rocks, where a trickle of water wandered out and disappeared over the edge. She had found the source of the waterfall.

She turned triumphantly to wave at her companions far below, but they were busy and did not look up. Just then a seagull floated above her head, calling with its harsh voice and she remembered just how close she must be to the sea. Why, if she continued up the hillside, surely she would be able to see all the way to the seashore itself. It must be a wonderful sight.

But a few scrambling steps later, the path suddenly vanished. A vast boulder had at some time slid across it, preventing her from going any further. She found herself blinking back tears, not of pain, but of sheer frustration, when suddenly a voice said, "You little fool! Take my hand. Quickly!"

She gazed up, but against the brilliance of the sun she could only see a dark outline of a man, but she had no difficulty in recognising the autocratic voice and the hand held out to her.

For a split second Jane hesitated; she was loathe to admit that she was in need of assistance and even more averse to that assistance being given by Mr Maitland. But her common-sense prevailed. She was well aware that she did not have the strength to push herself upwards but she was reluctant to give up her goal when she was so close to successfully completing the climb.

Stretching out a hand she found it clasped in his; with one firm pull she was on top of the boulder, gasping at the incredible view that lay before her - she could see miles out to sea, to the dark line of the horizon - almost unaware of the tightness of the grip on her arm as Archer held her steady against his side.

Thrilled to have overcome her fear, she said, "Thank you, Sir. I would have been unhappy to have had to climb down and not seen this panorama of sky, sea and land. You may release me, now. I am in no danger of falling."

Archer was so angry that he could hardly speak. Miss Jane Darcy had obviously no idea that she had put herself into a most grievous position. Even now she could be lying with broken limbs at the bottom of the cliff face.

At last he said, "And what would you have done if I had not been here, Miss Jane?"

She looked up at him, startled by the anger in his voice, aware that his grip had, if anything, tightened even more around her arm.

"Why, I would have clambered down to my companions, taking great care, I assure you."

Crossly, she pulled her arm free; she was certain she would have a bruise there soon. She could not understand why he was so angry. She had not inconvenienced him in any fashion.

"It was foolhardy in the extreme. You could have killed yourself!"

Jane twisted away: insufferable man, lecturing her as if she were a small child.

Archer gasped as the long, fair hair was caught by the wind and wrapped itself over his face. For a moment he was blinded until he pushed the tendrils away. He had never seen hair as pale a gold as this. From what he could remember, Anne Darcy's was darker and he had never seen it loose, it had always been high on her head in a complicated arrangement, not loose and wild.

Jane, unaware that her rescuer was comparing her to her twin, spun round to him once more and said, "I have no idea why you are so angry, Sir. Perhaps we should go down and join the others. Indeed, here is someone come to find me."

A scrabbling of feet on the rocks, and Dr Moore clambered up the final steep slope towards them. "Miss Jane! Archer! I thought I heard voices. We were growing concerned, Miss Jane. We had no idea whom you were talking to up here. I am surprised to see you, my friend. I thought you were engaged with family duties this morning."

Jane felt a wave of relief. Dr Moore's friendly face and cheerful voice that held no hint of censure were a balm to her aggravated emotions.

Andrew gazed out at the view and then back down the path, suddenly away of how sheer it was. "Good Lord, that's a steep climb. You should not have attempted it on your own. You could have fallen and hurt yourself."

Archer struggled to control his temper. "That is exactly what I have been telling her! But perhaps you will have more success than I in conveying to Miss Darcy the imprudence of her behaviour."

"Ha! I think the better course of action is for us all to return to firmer ground. Colonel Fitzwilliam and Signorina Celeste have walked down to join our company and I fear he is a little distressed by your actions, Miss Jane."

Jane immediately felt a wave of contrition; she would never willingly upset her godfather and had to admit perhaps her desire to overcome her fears had rather outweighed her judgement on this occasion. But she was determined she would not give Archer Maitland the satisfaction of telling him that!

"There is a better path, just a little way along the top of the hillside. Come!" Without saying another word, Archer turned and walked away, leaving the others to follow.

Jane pulled on her bonnet once more, tied it securely under her chin and tucked her hair under it in some semblance of order. Andrew waited patiently, then tucked Jane's hand through his arm and helped her over the rougher parts of the track as they descended to where the others of their company were waiting.

CHAPTER 5

The walk through the woods into the village was undertaken in rather a subdued fashion: conversation amongst the party was muted. Archer Maitland had joined them and was leading the way with Celeste on his arm, while the Colonel and Susannah followed. Jane and Dr Moore brought up the rear and although he chatted cheerfully about all around, she found it difficult to respond in a like manner.

She had apologised profusely to the Colonel for alarming him by her behaviour, although she did not fully understand why he seemed to be upset. Surely she had never been in any real danger and she was certain that if it had been her young sister, Bennetta, who had ventured up the cliff, he would not have been so worried.

But there was no denying that her godfather looked quite white and drawn with worry and only Jane's insistence that she was perfectly well stopped him from cancelling the outing and returning at haste to the house.

As they reached the village, Archer and Andrew vanished into the Green Man Inn to discover if cold lemonade could be purchased and the Colonel, at the begging of Celeste who was anxious for new ribbons, accompanied her into the tiny shop to inspect the wares on display.

On the far side of the pond, a large willow tree cascaded its branches down into the water where a family of ducks were squabbling. In the shade of the branches stood a wooden bench and Jane pushed her way under and sat down, thankfully, because she realised she was far more tired than she cared to admit. She pulled off her bonnet again, not caring that her hair was flying free and gazed around in happy recognition. She had often sat in this half-hidden spot over the years, knowing she was safe...

Safe! There was that wretched word again. What was the matter with her? Every time she cast her mind back to the past, that was the word that came to mind. Why, she could not think of a single occasion in her whole life when she had not been safe, taken care of and protected from harm. So why did she cling to safety in such an odd way?

Suddenly the branches were parted and Susannah joined her, her smile warm and obviously not critical.

"Do come and join me in the shade, dear friend. I fear I am in disgrace," Jane said. "The Colonel can hardly speak to me, Mr Maitland does nothing but scowl and except for Dr Moore, this would be a very sorry outing. Are you angry with me too, Susannah?"

The older woman retied the ribbons on her straw hat and smiled at her friend, admiring the way the sunlight flickered through the willow leaves and shone on her fair hair. The unusual amount of exercise had brought a fine colour to her cheeks and she seemed to have lost some of that look of despair that had worried her friends and family so much.

"Not at all, Jane dear. I admit I was slightly concerned when I looked up and saw how high you had climbed, but within seconds Mr Maitland was at your side and I knew all was well."

Jane felt her temper rising. "There was no need for a fuss. Mr Maitland acts as if he had rescued me from some terrible fate. He really is an objectionable man. I have yet to have any conversation with him that does not include barbed comments and condemnation of my actions."

"On the other hand, Dr Moore is very amiable."

Jane nodded, knowing her cheeks were colouring. She had to admit it was pleasant to have a gentleman pay her such kind and considerate attention. Not that she was attracted to him, of course. She had vowed to have nothing to do with men for ever more and was determined not to be one of those young ladies who changed their affections in the same way they changed their bonnets!

Susannah changed the subject. "Do not think too badly of the Colonel. I was talking to him when we both noticed to where you had adventured. He was only as alarmed as I was myself."

"Then why is he now so upset?"

Her friend hesitated, then said, "Well, I am sure it was not her intention, but Signorina Celeste got very agitated, on your behalf. She kept insisting that you would fall, that you would dash your head on the rocks below and inflict some great injury on yourself. Her cries of alarm made the Colonel feel that you were in mortal peril and he became most concerned for your safety."

"Oh dear. What a tangle. Why did Celeste have to interfere?"

"She has a very excitable nature, no doubt, and I am sure she was worried. It is just a pity she reacted so violently and upset the Colonel."

Jane glanced at her friend and started to speak, then fell silent. There had been an odd tone in Susannah's voice, as if she was highly critical of the Italian girl but could not say so out loud.

"Why, here they are! Sitting comfortably in the shade, whilst we faint from hunger!" Celeste parted the branches with a cry of success.

Jane and Susannah left their seat to find the rest of the party standing waiting for them.

"I apologise if we have kept you from your luncheons," Jane said. "Was there no lemonade to be had at the Green Man?"

Dr Moore shook his head. "Well, there was, but although my doctorate is not in medicine, I suggested to Archer that it did not look at all wholesome. Indeed, the place was filthy and I could not recommend that we purchased anything to eat or drink there."

"But it always used to be a lovely, clean establishment! Papa and Mama often purchased little items for our picnics when we were young." Jane was distressed to hear the inn being so disparaged.

"I fear the decline of villages such as Compton Forge is the result of so called progress," Archer Maitland said. "The area no longer has such a large population as it did ten years ago. There is very little work for men nowadays. The small holdings and little farms have all but disappeared, swallowed up by the larger farmers, and so more and more families have left the area to seek employment elsewhere. They frequently go to London which is causing a great deal of overcrowding and poverty in the city. And the workers who remain are often not paid a good wage."

The Colonel nodded. "It has caused a great deal of distress and unrest, I must admit. That shocking affair in the village of Tolpuddle in February was, I fear, just the beginning of what might become a very ugly few years. And Tolpuddle is not so many miles away as the crow flies."

Archer nodded. "It was a bad affair and equally badly handled by the authorities. I have been busy at work, trying to help the families of those men who were deported to Australia. There is a great petition, being signed by thousands of people, to bring the men back. I am hoping that we might have some success, perhaps not this year but maybe next."

"Yes, I am aware that you have similar views to mine. Well, I employ the same number of staff as I have always done and pay them what I think is fair for their labour, but I know several of my neighbours have dismissed people such as under shepherds, labourers, herders and the like. It is very sad, but as Archer says, it is progress."

Jane stared about her; now she was looking with clarity, and not through the glow of happy memories, she could see that the village was a shadow of its former self. Several of the cottages stood empty, their thatched roofs had weeds growing through them. There were broken windows in places and even the dwellings that were inhabited looked mean and run down. The Green Man did indeed look dilapidated and dirty; the sign swinging over the door just a blur of old paint on warped wood.

She realised, too, that where before there had always been groups of young children out playing, who would happily run up, expecting pennies to be thrown, only two very grubby infants dressed in torn shifts were standing, gazing listlessly at the Deerwood party.

Of course she was well aware that earlier that year there had been disorder and outcry when six farmers from Tolpuddle had been arrested for swearing an illegal oath when they joined a society to protest against their poor pay. Even far away in Derbyshire, news had arrived of the great gatherings in London to protest the men being transported to Australia and campaign for their pardon and return.

She could plainly recall her papa throwing his newspaper down on the breakfast table in anger, stating that the people in authority were out of their minds and if employers only paid their workers a decent wage - for how could a family with small children exist on six shillings a week? - then the country could settle down once more.

"But surely something should be done, especially for their families!" Susannah sounded distressed and angry.

"La, please let us talk of something more pleasant," Celeste broke in with a laugh. "Me, I am hungry and eager for my luncheon. Come, Jane, walk with me. We will leave the men and Miss Courtney to their serious discussions."

"We must return to Deerwood Park by the quickest route, along the track." The Colonel turned to Archer and Andrew. "Will you gentlemen give us the pleasure of your company for lunch, or are you promised elsewhere?"

"No, we are entirely at your disposal, Sir," Andrew replied with a bow. "Although I am reluctant to impose on your hospitality for a second day running."

"Indeed, I have not spoken to my grandmother but I am sure she will be delighted if you will all come and dine with us on Friday." Archer Maitland spoke almost without thinking, aware of the surprised glance his friend threw in his direction. Lady Goddard was not a person who took kindly to surprises, especially ones that involved an extra four people for dinner at short notice.

"Oh how delightful. I am so anxious to see Robyns," Celeste said. "The dear Colonel has told me that it is one of the most delightful houses in the whole county."

Archer did not agree but bowed in acknowledgement of the compliment to his grandmother and the party turned to wend its way back along the road towards Deerwood Park.

Jane would have been more than happy to have spoken more with him about the plight of the poor people in the district, but Celeste left the Colonel and slipped her arm through hers, lowering her parasol behind their heads to shut out anyone else from their conversation.

"Jane - oh, you do not mind me calling you Jane, do you, cousin. I am afraid I just took it for granted that you would not be missish about such things."

"Not at all, Celeste. And may I say how much I admire your command of English which seems to grow more and more each time we speak. I'm afraid my ability with a foreign language is limited to a few words of French." She smiled, remembering. "We had a governess, a Miss Jemima Smith, whose job it was to teach us, but I'm afraid my two sisters and myself were not good pupils for the poor woman. I fear we made her life very hard!"

The Italian girl laughed. "Thank you, Jane. Like you, I had a governess, but as there was only me to teach, perhaps I learnt quickly."

"Are your parents - I do not wish to distress you - are they still alive?"

There was a deep sigh. "Sadly, no. They have both passed away. My mother died when I was born and I was raised by my father until he too died. That is why, because I was all alone in Sicily, I decided to try and make contact with my family over here in England."

"I am sure everyone will be delighted to make your acquaintance. I will write to my mama and insist you are invited to stay at Pemberley. But are you planning on living in England permanently?"

Celeste giggled and bent her head closer to Jane's. "Well, dear cousin, the Colonel has told me that I am welcome to stay as long as I please. That is so gallant of him, is it not?"

"Indeed. But then he is one of the most caring gentlemen I have ever known. I am extremely fond of him."

There was a deep sigh from the other girl. "Yes, I had thought that, too. Which is why I was surprised when you behaved as you did earlier. You upset him so much by putting yourself in danger!"

"There was no need for such alarm. Colonel Fitzwilliam is well used to my brothers and sisters exploring Deerwood Park. They have often been in far more hazardous situations than merely climbing a rocky slope."

"But Jane, you do not understand, I think. This was you. You have grown very close to him, I can see that. Perhaps too close. He worries about you so much. Why, never a day has gone past since I arrived that he has not shown concern as to your future well-being. When your carriage was late arriving he was quite certain you had been attacked by highwaymen! Why, even before you arrived, he seemed quite weighed down with anxiety from a letter he received from your dear mama. Do you think that is quite fair?"

"Fair?" She was confused and upset that her mama must have written to the Colonel, giving details of her doomed love affair with Digby Frobisher.

"Oh forgive me, I am speaking, how you say, out of turn."

Jane glanced behind them but the rest of the party had stopped to try and identify a bird that was singing high up in a tree. There was no chance of them being overheard.

"No, pray go on, Cousin. The last thing I would ever wish is to be a... a burden to my god-father."

"Ah! I was right to so believe. Indeed, when the Colonel told me how he found it hard to sleep from worrying - " she paused and bit her lip. "But that was a confidence, of course. Forgive me, I should not have said so much."

Jane shivered, even though the day was still warm. She was horrified at the other girl's words; that her actions, her habit of running away to the shelter of Deerwood Park when life became too difficult, had caused the Colonel's health to suffer. He had retired from the army having received a bad wound abroad. She felt ashamed; she should have realised that he was not as strong as her own papa, that he needed a quiet, peaceful existence.

"Thank you for being open and honest with me," she murmured at last. "I have been very selfish but it is a state of affairs that is easily corrected. I will make sure to do nothing to upset the Colonel for the remainder of my stay. And, indeed, I will arrange to leave earlier than planned."

"No, no, no. Oh dear no." Celeste sounded quite alarmed. "That would upset him even more." There was a long pause; Jane was finding it difficult to find the right words to mend the situation, then Celeste's fingers on her arm tightened.

"Jane - may I tell you a great secret, in complete confidence, of course."

There was nothing to do but to nod and give assurances.

"The dear Colonel has made it clear to me... that is, we have discovered that we have mutual feelings of regard for each other! No, no, please, I can imagine what you will say... that I am too young to enter into such a union, that we have only known each other for such a short time, that we are cousins. All is true. That is why it is such a secret. That is why, because of my feelings for him, I took it upon myself to point out that your behaviour was of concern to his health. And now - " thick dark lashes fluttered in embarrassment - "now I fling myself on your mercy. Please do not mention this to anyone, especially your family. I know the Colonel wants to tell the world himself, but only when we are ready."

If Jane had been speechless before, now she was in such a state of amazement and bewilderment that she hardly knew how to keep walking along the woodland track. She felt as if the very ground was shaking beneath her feet. The Colonel and Celeste! To be married!

She was well aware that women often entered into partnerships with much older men. If you were not lucky enough to come from an extremely wealthy family, then marriage was a necessity. And if a gentleman of mature years asked for your hand, then you would be a fool to turn him down. To have a home, children, a place in society, all of those were a fair return for marrying someone perhaps twenty or thirty years older than yourself.

To become the wife of her cousin would, obviously, be an extremely good match for the Italian girl, but even in the short hours Jane had known Celeste, she was certain she was someone who would enjoy a much more exciting life than that to be had as chatelaine of Deerwood Park.

"You have no reply to give me?"

"Yes, of course. If that is what you both decide, then I wish you joy and, of course, I will respect your wishes and tell no one of your plans."

"But Jane, you look shocked. Surely you can see that poor Colonel Fitzwilliam has been lonely for so long and you would not begrudge him a few years of happiness? I, for my part, am delighted to grant him that. And Jane, I beg of you, please do not mention this to the Colonel. I am breaking my word in telling you but I thought it was for the best, for his health's sake."

"Ladies! You have been exchanging confidences for too long. Pray let us join in your conversation. We have been discussing the state of unrest in the country and I am sure you have views on the matter."

Before Jane could form a sensible reply, Andrew and Archer had caught up to them.

Celeste smiled sweetly. "Just girlish chatter, Dr Moore. Indeed, Mr Maitland, Jane was just saying that we are very late for luncheon and that she wishes boring politics will not spoil our pleasant outing."

"The Darcy girls have not been brought up to get involved in politics." The Colonel, with Susannah on his arm, reached the group and Jane was relieved to see that the worried frown had vanished and he looked calm and happy. "Although the way young Bennetta argues a point of view would be challenging to anybody. Jane and Anne, however, prefer pleasanter ways of spending their time."

Jane started to deny that she was a person who had no opinions, to say that indeed she was deeply concerned about the strife in the country, the plight of the poor, then caught sight of Archer Maitland's face. She was sure she could see a look of contempt and fell silent. Let him believe what he liked; that she was just a frivolous, empty-headed female. There was no way she was going to justify herself in front of him!

CHAPTER 6

A leisurely luncheon at Deerwood Park was served in a small dining-room whose windows opened out onto the gardens and orchards. From her seat, Jane could look out and see men up ladders, beginning to harvest the apple crop. From the heavily bent boughs, she was sure it would be a good one, which meant there would be plenty of cider and apple pies and puddings in the weeks and months to come.

She found it difficult to take part in the easy conversation that flowed around the table and knew she was causing her godfather to cast her anxious glances once more. But her mind was in a whirl of confusion and when the coffee was served, she took her cup and moved to where a window seat gave her a sunny spot in which to sit and think.

Celeste and the Colonel! It was hard to credit what she had been told but the more she watched and noticed how much care he took about where the Italian girl was seated, if her glass was full, the way he chose certain choice pieces of meat and fruit for her from the serving dishes, she began to see his regard in a new light.

What she had, up until then, considered the actions of a concerned cousin, could indeed be deciphered in a very different fashion. And now she was worried because if this was the case, then Celeste could not possibly stay here at Deerwood Park, living alone with the Colonel without a proper chaperone.

The arrival of a very young cousin from abroad on a visit would have raised no eyebrows - it would be considered in exactly the same fashion as Jane herself coming to stay. But if a hint of romantic involvement was aired abroad.... Rumours would soon spread; the servants would gossip and both their reputations would suffer. There was no denying that they had been under the same roof for several weeks already, but she could do nothing about that. The future was, however, in her hands.

On the walk home, Jane had almost decided that whatever Celeste said, she would pack and inform Susannah that they would be returning to Pemberley in the next few days. But now she realised that if they left, then any ongoing scandal would be partly her fault.

She had no protective feelings towards Celeste, indeed she was sure the girl was quite thick skinned enough to survive any amount of gossip, but the Colonel was a sensitive man and any hint that his actions were morally wrong, would distress him. If his neighbours began to talk behind his back, he would be mortified.

Jane knew she could not allow that if she could prevent it somehow. She intended to write to her mother that very evening, asking for her advice. True, Celeste had said her relationship with the Colonel was a secret, but perhaps she could suggest that they were both invited to Pemberley. That would be the best thing to achieve. Indeed, her papa should know of Celeste's existence sooner, rather than later, as should the elderly Earl Fitzwilliam, the head of the ancient family to which her grandmama had belonged. Jane frowned: it was odd that the Colonel had not yet told his closest family that a new cousin had arrived to join them.

On the other side of the room, Archer Maitland stood, coffee cup in hand, half listening to Andrew and Celeste talking about some ancient ruins in Sicily, aware that Miss Courtney and the Colonel were still discussing the troubled political situation in quiet voices.

He glanced across the room to where Jane Darcy sat by the open window, the afternoon sunlight sparking glints from her fair hair. She looked a long way away, lost in her thoughts. She was frowning slightly, as if what she was thinking was not very agreeable.

For some bizarre reason, he wished that she looked happier. He had never seen her twin look anything but content and assured on the occasions they had met and it seemed unfair that this girl should appear to have all the worries of the world on her shoulders. And, he thought irritably, what could she possibly have to be anxious about? She was young, wealthy, the cherished, protected daughter of loving parents. Over-loving, if Miss Anne was to be believed.

Was that why she was frowning, perhaps? Did she feel she was not getting the required amount of attention from her godfather now that Celeste Fiorette was here at Deerwood? The Colonel's attentions towards his Italian cousin were warm and constant. That frown could be one of jealousy.

He swallowed down a mouthful of coffee that was far too hot and winced as it burnt his mouth. What was wrong with him, wasting his time on wondering what was going on inside that pretty head? Probably no more than trying to decide which dress to wear for dinner that evening.

Before he could consider his actions, he strode across the room. "Once more I find you are quiet at meal time, Miss Jane. I fear the Colonel's cook will begin to wonder that the flavours in her dishes fall sadly below your expectation."

Jane smiled: "Why Mrs Blunt has known me for a good many years, Sir. She is well aware of all my likes and dislikes and even if there was a dish I found fault with, I would only discuss it with her and not in front of guests."

Archer grinned suddenly and Jane realised it made him look years younger than the twenty five or six years she was sure he had celebrated.

"That remark brings back memories of my grandfather - he was a retired Admiral of the Fleet, a gentleman with a terrible temper that grew worse as he grew older - caused by gout, I do believe. I recall, as a child, seeing him pick up a whole dish of potatoes that he had decided were not properly cooked and hurl them onto the floor!"

"Goodness! What did your parents say?"

Archer's face changed and the frown returned. "Sadly they were divided from my grandparents on their marriage. I am afraid that they did not approve of my mother's choice of husband. It was a very sad state of affairs. They were all as stubborn as each other and no matter how much I pleaded for a reconciliation, they refused.

"My father died when I was fourteen; my mother and I remained living in the town of Alresford, near Winchester, where he had his law practice until her death. I found it hard to grieve for her. She loved my father so much; she just wanted to be with him."

He paused for a second, his eyes darker still with pain. "I went to live with my grandparents in London until my grandfather's death. That was when my grandmother decided she needed a country home as well as her London abode and purchased Robyns. And of course, by that time, I had moved out into my own lodgings."

Impulsively, Jane reached out and touched his arm. She could tell by his voice and the look in his eyes that the loss of his father had hurt him deeply. She could not imagine being without her own dear papa. Although he was a man with a reserved nature, not given to shows of outward affection, she knew herself to be loved dearly and the void in her life if he was to die would be unbearable.

Admiral Goddard sounded terrifying! How different had been dear Mr Bennet, her own grandfather. His visits to Pemberley when she was a child had always given her much pleasure. They had shared a great love of books and had often sat together in the library talking and discussing what they had read. And even though the money was not important to her, the bequest to all his female grandchildren in his will, "in order that they did not have to marry the first fool who asked them," had always made her laugh when she thought of it.

For a brief moment Archer covered her fingers with his own, then took a deep breath and reverted to his usual, slightly arrogant attitude. "You will meet my grandmama when you come to Robyns for dinner, Miss Jane. She will be intrigued - she has already had the pleasure of your sister's company in London."

"I fear she may well be disappointed if she expects another Anne at her dinner table. We are not alike, except in general appearance."

"I found Miss Anne to be a very accomplished and delightful companion."

Jane nodded, feeling as she so often did, that sensation of being second best to her glittering twin. "She is all of those things and more." A flicker of mischief crossed her face. "And an excellent dancer, of course. I am sure your grandmother noticed that particular accomplishment."

"I fear that we will not have enough couples at dinner to make up even one small set for dancing, so Grandmama will not be able to judge your abilities."

Jane stood up, smoothing down her skirts. "Then I fear, Mr Maitland, you will never know how I compare to Anne! And now, with your pardon, I think I will walk in the orchard and watch the men harvesting the apples. I love this time of year."

Archer bowed and stood sipping his coffee, watching from the window as the girl appeared, making her way along the grassy track between the heavily laden trees. He saw her stop and talk to the head gardener, noticing that the man carefully steered her away from any danger of being hit by falling fruit and guided her to a bench where she could watch the harvest in safety.

He could tell by the man's demeanour that Jane was popular with the servants and realised, with something of a shock, that Anne would never have dreamt of getting involved in such a countrified occupation.

"Are you comparing the young lady to her sister?" Andrew had joined him at the window, intrigued by his friend's expression.

"Oh, there is no comparison to be made. It is difficult to believe they are twins, even though on first sight they are alike to look at."

"You once told me that you were tempted to ask for Miss Anne Darcy's hand in marriage? Are you still of like mind?"

Archer shrugged irritably and swallowed the last drop of coffee. "Anne is a beautiful, accomplished woman. She would be a great asset to me in my career - as my grandmother is always happy to tell me."

"So you do mean to ask for her! And do you believe her feelings for you are such that she would accept?"

Archer stirred his spoon round his coffee cup, not noticing it was empty. "I think Anne would like the type of life I could offer her."

"And love? Does that enter into your calculations at all, my hard-hearted friend? I myself will only marry for love."

There was a long pause; Archer seemed distracted by the sight of a young gardener offering Miss Jane a particularly pretty pink and cream apple and her smiling acceptance of the fruit.

"Oh love! I have no time for such fancies and nor does Anne. It would be a good, suitable, advantageous marriage for both of us. And that is what marriage should be. I will not make the same mistake as my poor mother and ally myself to an unsuitable partner because of love. My father was a good man, but not the right husband for her."

A touch on his sleeve - he glanced down to find Celeste smiling up at him. "Oh Mr Maitland, I am sorry, I did not mean to overhear your words, but it is exciting that you might be marrying my cousin, Anne Darcy!"

"There is nothing yet settled," Archer replied hastily.

"Oh, I quite understand." Celeste tapped her fan mischievously on his hand. "Have no fear, your secret is quite safe with me, Sir. My lips are sealed."

And she drew a finger across her mouth in a dramatic fashion. "But we are all friends and family here. We wish the best for all of us, I am sure."

Andrew smiled. He found the Italian girl entertaining company, although she seemed to know very little, indeed nothing at all, about the wonderful Roman and Greek ruins on her island home of Sicily. But then young ladies didn't need to fill their heads with historical knowledge, although it was odd that she had never even visited certain towns famous their ruins.

"Well, I have no secrets to share with you, Signorina Celeste. My life is an open book. And, I daresay, a very boring one." He laughed. "Now, if you will excuse me, I think I will join Miss Jane in the garden. It is too lovely an afternoon to stay indoors."

Celeste fell silent, watching through the window as Andrew appeared, sitting next to Jane, helping himself to an apple from the basket in her lap. She was aware of a twinge of jealousy. What was it about this pale, fair-haired creature that men found so appealing? Irritation wriggled through her: Celeste was never happy unless all men in her vicinity were only showing interest in her.

She was aware of Archer Maitland by her side, his silence intriguing her. "Your friend, he has a tendresse for Miss Jane, I think," she ventured at last.

"What? Excuse me, Signorina, my thoughts were many miles away. Andrew and Jane Darcy? Why - no! I mean, well, there is no reason why not, of course, because you will never meet a more good-hearted, kindly fellow than Andrew, but he is in no position to take a wife. He leaves for Greece very soon, for one of his interminable historical digs."

"Greece is not that far away, not if you care for someone. And I am sure a wife could be very useful in such a situation. But then, even if he does, I fear his feelings will not be reciprocated."

Archer felt a wave of indignation; he was very protective of his friend whom he thought to be a good man, far better than he himself. "I think Miss Jane Darcy would be proud to have gained the affections of such a man."

"Oh la, of course, Mr Maitland! Of course. Forgive me, I meant no disrespect towards Dr Moore. A true gentleman, I do declare. It is just that - but no - I must not repeat servants' gossip. That is not the English way, although it is useful to have knowledge of all the facts when making up your mind about a person."

"Gossip?" Archer sounded disgusted.

"Oh, do not blame my poor maid, Luisa, for repeating what she has been told, Sir. Her English is not as good as mine and perhaps she misunderstands. The Darcy maid, Tabitha, told her that her mistress has come into the country to mend her broken heart. She is desperately in love with a Mr Digby Frobisher and Tabitha was sure that an announcement was about to be made when some argument occurred. He apparently asked for her sister's hand, was refused and left Pemberley very abruptly.

"Poor Jane. She looks so wan and unhappy and now we must understand why. To be heartbroken is a dreadful thing, to be made so by your sister is even worse. But I am sure that it was all some sort of confusion and that the young man will soon appear on the scene to make Jane happy once more. True love will never be overcome."

Archer did not reply. Digby Frobisher! He remembered a young puppy flirting with Anne Darcy at a soirée one evening in London. A shallow, worthless sort of youth, as far as he could recall, no occupation except to spend his parents' money and enjoy himself. Lord knows why he thought Anne would have accepted his proposal.

Well, Jane and Frobisher! It made it very apparent to him just what her character must be like if she had fallen in love with such a man. They were, in his opinion, very suited to each other and he wished them a happy reunion and much joy!

CHAPTER 7

J ane found it difficult during the following days to sort out her feelings for
all that had happened since her arrival at Deerwood Park. Her unhappiness over her sister's betrayal and Digby's dreadful behaviour was still
there, of course, because she refused to acknowledge that from a distance
it now looked less important than she had first imagined. It was Celeste's reve-
lations which caused her to lay awake at night, not memories of Digby's fair
hair and warm smile.

She longed to confide in Susannah about the Colonel's affections for his
distant cousin, but knew she could not break a confidence once given. She had
to admit that to her eyes, the Colonel seemed extremely happy; he was busy
designing a herb garden that he planned to grow outside the kitchen area.

At breakfast every morning, Celeste was full of good intentions and ideas,
but measuring out pathways and helping the gardeners transplant sturdy
bushes of mint, rosemary and comfrey soon paled and Susannah, who had
established a flourishing herb garden of her own in Derbyshire, had been
called into action to give advice to the Colonel whilst the Italian girl spent her
days sorting out her wardrobe and embellishing her hats with new nets and
ribbons.

To Jane's surprise, her godfather did not seem to mind being left to his own
devices by Celeste and she could only suppose that theirs was a relationship

which survived being apart quite happily, unlike her own parents who always seemed slightly unhappy when their partner was not at their side.

She had asked the Colonel if he had any objection to her telling her parents about their cousin's sudden arrival and had been cheered when he said he thought that was a good idea.

"Indeed I have been meaning to write myself. It is very remiss of me, but Celeste was most anxious that she get used to our English ways before meeting up with other members of the family, especially my cousin, the Earl. She wanted to improve her English, and you must admit that every day she gets better and better. And I do declare I believe she is a little scared of visiting Pemberley.

"Of course, Jane, for a girl from a small Sicilian town, a vast estate and great house would be very daunting. We, of course, are quite used to the size and splendour, but Celeste is nervous. Why, she even found Deerwood quite intimidating when she first arrived in England."

Jane, who could see no sign at all of trepidation in the girl's demeanour, found she had no sensible reply to this but was glad when her letter home was sent, telling of Celeste's history and arrival, suggesting that she be invited to visit the Darcys as soon as possible. She felt she had done all she could to safeguard the young woman's reputation and save her godfather from gossip.

Andrew Moore had ridden over from Robyns twice since their eventful day out but there had been no sign of Mr Maitland whom she was told was busy with his grandmother's business affairs.

Jane enjoyed Andrew's company but there were times when she wished he would speak of events that were happening in the world today and not constantly wish to lecture her about ancient civilisations!

This morning she had sat, trying not to fidget whilst he expounded on the wonders of Ancient Greece and had been naughtily very relieved when Celeste insisted that the young doctor escorted her to inspect the late fruit that was being brought to perfection in the glass houses.

"I think you have made a conquest, Jane," Susannah said as they waved goodbye to the young man from the driveway of Deerwood as he rode off after luncheon, waving his hat in the air with one hand and clutching desperately at his saddle with the other because his riding skills had not yet increased. "And forgive me for speaking out of turn, but I think you might be just the slightest bit interested in the gentleman!"

Jane laughed and linked arms with her as they walked round the house towards the kitchen gardens where the Colonel, his waistcoat discarded, was supervising the laying of little gravel paths between the hedges of new lavender plants, with Bates, the gloomy faced head-gardener.

Celeste was sitting under an archway of late flowering honeysuckle, eating a peach which Andrew had picked for her earlier, juice running down her chin, laughing at some remark the Colonel had just made.

Susannah turned to Jane to comment and realised there had been a big improvement in her demeanour over the past few days. If the pale faced, unhappy girl who had left Derbyshire hadn't completely vanished, then she was well on the way. There was more colour in Jane's cheeks and even her hairstyle was less severe than usual.

Susannah felt a sense of relief; obviously the memory of Digby was slowly being eroded by the attentions of the young archaeologist! Elizabeth Darcy would be delighted and she decided to write to Pemberley that very evening with the news.

"Oh Susannah, just because two people are comfortable in each other's company, does not mean they have romantic feelings for each other."

"Although feeling comfortable with someone is surely a great asset in a relationship." The older woman looked suddenly thoughtful as she gazed across the garden. "Having a liking for the same things, knowing your minds match on many matters, all that is important, I believe. I have seen what a happy state of affairs that can create with my own brothers and their wives."

"You are quite correct but I am quite certain there is more to love than both having a fondness for gooseberry cream, which is one of the few areas where Dr Moore and I are in complete agreement!"

"And do you have anything as exciting as gooseberry cream in common with Mr Maitland?"

"Archer Maitland? Goodness me, no. We argue every time we meet. Well, he argues and I refrain from being rude because he is my godfather's friend and I have no wish for any bad feeling at Deerwood! But you must admit he is an objectionable fellow."

Susannah shook her head. "I disagree. I find him knowledgeable and forthright, that is all. True, he does have a very straightforward manner of speaking, but I find that refreshing these days when so many gentlemen can spend several minutes and all their breath in just asking for another cup of tea."

"I am intrigued to meet his grandmother tomorrow night. Lady Goddard sounds a formidable old lady."

"Indeed she does. Dr Moore told me she frightens him into dropping things - plates, knives, forks, books! He was laughing when he spoke, but I feel there is probably more than a grain of truth in his remarks."

She shivered suddenly as a few leaves came tumbling down in gust of wind. "Autumn, I fear is finally with us. Mrs Oxley will no doubt be ordering the fires to be lit soon. I expect poor Celeste will notice the change in temperature more than us, especially coming from all that Italian sunshine."

Jane sighed: a memory had suddenly surfaced of talking to Digby about their shared hope to travel to Europe and discovering that he agreed with her on so many interesting places they wished to visit.

A little dart of disquiet broke into her reverie: had Digby been too eager to agree with her? Perhaps he had told Anne that he was in accord with her as well? It was so difficult to know what to think. She had believed with her heart and soul that he cared for her, but she had been wrong. That gave her cause to think that she had no judgement where men were concerned. Had all his fine words been a sham and make believe, just so he could marry into the Darcy family?

The whole idea was hurtful and left her feeling angry, not only at men who did not show their true characters, but with herself for being so feeble as to believe every word he had said. Well, she would not do that again: she would believe no man's sugar-coated words!

She watched as Susannah moved to Celeste's side and heard her suggesting that she would do well to put on her shawl as these English winds were sharper than the Italian ones she was used to and could be harmful.

Dear Susannah, always worrying about other people. Jane smiled to herself, thoughts of Digby vanishing. She wondered what her friend would say if she whispered the secret that had been entrusted to her? She would be surprised, perhaps even shocked. Indeed it was difficult to list just what similar likes and dislikes Celeste and the Colonel had in common, but obviously they were not letting such small problems stand in their way of happiness.

Jane fell silent as they all began to return to the house, only to relinquish her friend when the Colonel called across for Susannah's advice on the advisability of installing a little fountain in the centre of the herb bed.

As Susannah hastened to partake what little knowledge she had, Celeste linked her arm through Jane's as they walked on.

"It amuses me, dear Jane, that so many English gentlemen seem to enjoy playing around in mud. The Colonel is bespattered and Dr Moore cannot wait until he is out in Greece, getting his hands dirty, digging away for his old antiquities. Tell me, does your papa pass his time gardening?"

Jane smiled and shook her head. "I believe he and mama enjoy planning where new flower beds and statues shall be placed, but he leaves the actual work to people trained in that profession."

Celeste laughed. "The Colonel has Bates to help him, but he still insists on getting his hands dirty. I suppose Dr Moore has no choice but to dig and at least his results are of great interest to many people. He tells me that he will give a talk to the Royal Society when he returns from Athens. This is very important. He will be mixing with the highest people in the land. That is much better than growing the largest cabbage in all England!"

Jane glanced at her cousin's beautiful face. She looked thoughtful, as if pondering a difficult problem.

"When you are living here as the Colonel's wife, I am sure you can persuade him to involve himself in other, less muddy, hobbies."

"What? Oh yes, yes, indeed I shall. And, of course, it will be very cold in Greece during the winter."

Puzzled at this odd remark, Jane just nodded politely and led the way indoors to order tea to be served at once, trusting that that would bring the gallant gardeners indoors.

Overnight the wind increased and rain clouds began to gather from the west. The sunny days were obviously over and Jane was glad she had thought to ask Tabitha to pack warmer dresses and coats.

No visitors arrived at Deerwood that day - they were all to meet up at Robyns for dinner that evening. There was a mood of quiet anticipation throughout the house; Celeste, in particular, was very excited at the thought of the outing, insisting that Jane inspect her wardrobe and advise on which of her many dresses she should wear.

"The dear Colonel has allowed me to have, how you say, credit at a shop in Dorchester," she said, proudly displaying a silk and satin dress in emerald green, with huge, diaphanous sleeves in paler green gauze, embellished with many frills and flounces. Jane thought it far too grand for a simple country dinner, but the girl was so pleased with it that she didn't have the heart to pour cold water on her choice.

"I long to see Robyns and meet Lady Goddard. The Colonel does not go out into company nearly enough for a man of his consequence. This will hopefully be the first of many such dinners. Lady Goddard's friends in the neighbourhood will hear of our attending and ask us in return. And I am determined to persuade the Colonel to give a great dinner, with dancing. It would be very agreeable to hold such an affair before Dr Moore leaves for Greece."

She laughed. "He is such a charming young man but assures me he cannot dance. That he has, how he puts it, two left feet! But surely that cannot be the case. We shall see. I shall speak to the Colonel and insist on a dance here at Deerwood."

Jane would have liked to have given a word of warning, that she must not arouse the suspicion of the local population by acting as the chatelaine before a formal announcement of her betrothal was made. But Celeste was like a child in her excitement and could not be calmed.

Eventually she escaped back to her own room where Tabitha was waiting to style her hair.

"Which dress will you be wearing this evening, Miss Jane?" the young girl asked as she brushed and braided and twisted the long fair hair up into an intricate pattern, leaving just one tendril to curl down around each ear.

"I thought the pale pink." Jane glanced up into the mirror and realised the maid was frowning. "No? You do not approve?"

Tabitha blushed. "Oh Miss Jane, it isn't for me to approve or disapprove. The pink's pretty right enough, but oh Miss, I do love to see you in the cream silk."

Jane hesitated; she wasn't even aware that she had brought the cream dress with its wide sleeves and heavily embroidered bodice to Deerwood. She thought she had bundled it up and thrown it to the back of her wardrobe because she had been wearing it in London when dancing with Digby. She could only imagine that Tabitha had found it, and thought it had been discarded for washing.

She had to admit, once the dress was on, that it suited her better than the pale pink, not that she was bothered about how she looked. She was quite certain that old Lady Goddard would disapprove of her on principle, because she wasn't Anne. And as for the two gentlemen - she pushed her thoughts away.

What did it matter if Archer Maitland approved of her dress? Surely her thoughts and ideas were more important than what she was wearing?

"Miss Jane - " Tabitha was holding out her dark brown velvet shawl, obviously hesitating to speak but anxious to do so.

"Yes, Tabitha."

"Miss Jane, I've heard from some of the other servants that there is a sort of village celebration tonight at the Green Man Inn, because the harvest is all collected and good. It happens every year, they do say. I know it isn't my day off, but..."

"But I am going out and all you have to do is sit in your room, sewing on all my missing buttons and ribbons!" Jane smiled. "It sounds a jolly affair. Why, there might be dancing, you'd enjoy that, Tabitha."

"Oh, I couldn't dance with farm boys, Miss Jane. That would never do. But I've never seen a harvest celebration and...."

"Of course you can go. But please be back at the house by ten o'clock and make sure you do not walk alone though the woods. Stay with the other servants."

Tabitha curtsied. "Thank you, Miss Jane. I'll do just what you say." She crossed her fingers behind her back as she spoke, because everyone knew that meant you weren't really telling a lie. She wasn't sure if the other Deerwood maids were going to the village - and she certainly wasn't going to ask that irritating Luisa to go with her - but she was so bored here in the country and any sort of celebration must surely be exciting.

By six o'clock, with the wind gusting around the house, rattling the old window panes, Jane, Susannah and Celeste were sitting waiting in the drawing-room. The housekeeper had, indeed, had the fire lit and the flames gave a welcome heat to the chilly room. A footman had reported that the carriage was outside but the Colonel had not yet appeared.

"What can be keeping the dear man," Celeste said, jumping up and pacing across the room in a rustle and flash of emerald green from beneath her evening cloak.

"Cousin, sit and rest. You will overtire yourself."

Just then the door opened and the Colonel appeared, but he looked pale, was still wearing his day attire and was leaning heavily on the arm of his valet, Dixon. The three women started forward in alarm.

"My dears, pray do not fret yourselves, but I fear I will not be able to accompany you tonight. My leg - the one that carries the wound I received - I am afraid I wrenched it whilst gardening." He smiled across at Susannah. "You did warn me to be careful, Miss Courtney, but I was so determined to place the fountain in the right place myself!"

"But Colonel, surely if you sit very still and do not walk about, a meal will be of no hardship? Will Lady Goddard not think it rude if we do not go." Celeste looked appalled, her plans for the evening in ruins.

"I am sure Lady Goddard will understand perfectly. She would not want you to sit at her table in pain." Jane threw a cross glance at her cousin. Surely she should be thinking of the pain her loved one was suffering, not what a neighbour would say?

"Celeste, my dear, wipe away that frown. Indeed, you must all go. It would distress me to think I had deprived you of such an outing. You will enjoy seeing Robyns and I know Lady Goddard is most anxious to meet you all, especially you, my dear."

"How kind of you, Colonel!" Celeste was suddenly all smiles again, the scowl that had for the moment wiped away all her prettiness, now banished by his words. "And you can have a quiet evening here in peace. Come Jane, Miss Courtney, we must not keep the carriage waiting. It is bad for the horses, so I have been told."

Susannah stepped forward and took off her cloak. "I shall stay here with the Colonel," she said firmly. "Lady Goddard knows nothing about me and I am sure will not miss my presence in the slightest." She motioned Dixon to help his master to a comfortable chair by the fire. "There are many interesting books here on the shelves. I will read out loud for a while and then we can order a light supper before retiring."

Jane hesitated. She wanted to go to dinner at Robyns as much as Celeste, but surely it was her duty to stay with her godfather. "But Susannah..."

"Run along, Jane. Celeste is quite right. You must not keep horses waiting. All three of my brothers have given me that piece of information many times over the years!" And she settled herself into the chair on the other side of the fire, picked up a large, leather-bound tome and gave them a kind smile of dismissal.

CHAPTER 8

T here was still a little light left in the gloom as they journeyed to Robyns and Jane could see just how quickly the summer green had left the trees in the past few days. Yellow, brown and bronze were now the colours of the countryside. The wheat fields had all been harvested and stood empty with their pale stubble awaiting the horses and ploughs to prepare them for sowing the new crop.

They were traveling in the Fitzwilliam carriage, a large comfortable conveyance which soon covered the miles of narrow roadways that led inland and then southwards again towards the sea which was hidden behind the low sweep of hills.

Jane gazed out in interest as, in the dusk of the evening, with the wind blowing clouds in rags across the sky, the pale stone house with its flat face and many tall windows came into view and the carriage swung up the driveway to the front door.

Robyns looked stark, severe and unwelcoming to her eyes, and she wondered if Archer Maitland approved of the design. It was modern in style but had none of the grace and grandeur of Pemberley which had been built a good sixty years before. Jane knew, without doubt, that Anne would find this house pleasing and just to her taste but she could not bring herself to admire it.

There was, however, very little time to make a proper judgement as the front door swung open as they descended from the carriage and a footman ushered them into a wide hall where a maid was waiting to take their cloaks.

Jane just had time to take in marble floor, admire an impressive chandelier and glance at the large oil paintings of elderly ladies, all of whom seemed to possess dark eyes and long, thin noses and portly, red-faced gentlemen, several in naval uniform.

Then they were ushered by the footman into a drawing-room where the present day owner of the thin, arrogant nose was seated in a tall chair, presiding over all she surveyed.

Jane curtsied, aware of Celeste trembling at her side, then stood, raising her gaze in acknowledgement of the older woman's quick nod of greeting. She was not the slightest bit afraid of meeting this Lady Goddard. Being a shy, retiring person had not stopped her from knowing that she was a Darcy of Pemberley and a social match for anyone.

Lady Goddard was very elderly, tall, thin with a mass of grey hair dressed in a severe fashion, pulled back tightly from a face that showed very little expression. Jane had a fleeting thought - this was a woman who had never cried, never laughed, never found any happiness in life.

Sitting next to her on the sofa was a lady of middle years, but with a face lined with worry and a lifetime of hardship. She was busy sorting a giant tangle of embroidery silks, the colours splashing down her black skirt in crimsons, emeralds and bright yellows.

Archer, who had been leaning against the mantlepiece, came forward, smiling, and Jane realised that his dark eyes and dark brows had obviously been inherited from his grandmother, but luckily he had missed out on the long nose.

"Miss Jane Darcy, and Signorina Fiorette - how good to see you both. We were growing concerned as the minutes passed and you did not arrive. May I be allowed to introduce you to my grandmother, Lady Goddard. Grandmama, Miss Jane Darcy - who is, as you can see, the twin of Miss Anne Darcy whom you have already met in London, and Signorina Celeste Fiorette, a distant cousin of the Fitzwilliams."

"Lady Goddard. It is a pleasure to meet you."

"And this is my grandmother's companion, Miss Purkiss, who seems to have been given a most impossible task to finish by dinner time."

"Miss Darcy, I am delighted to make your acquaintance. So glad you have arrived safely, these narrow lanes, so difficult for horses... Please excuse me for not rising...these silks...such a muddle...but Mr Maitland, Sir, you are quite wrong. I shall easily sort these threads and if I do not finish, then I am sure I can eat later when I have done so."

"Stop chuntering, Purkiss! Of course you will eat with us. The silks can wait. Indeed, they seem to be in more of a tangle than when you started!"

Lady Goddard raised her lorgnette and gazed at Jane. "Yes, I can see the likeness to your sister. Archer told me you were twins but that it was not difficult to see the differences. Miss Anne has more vibrancy in her manner and dress, but I am sure you are only too aware of that yourself. Welcome to Robyns. And Signorina Fiorette?" She raised her lorgnette again and gazed at the girl. "I do not know anyone of Italian descent."

Jane flinched inwardly at the scarcely hidden barb but luckily Celeste's English, although extremely good, was not yet up to hearing sarcasm and she said enthusiastically, "It is so good of you to invite us here, Lady Goddard. The Colonel sends his utmost regrets but in incapacitated this evening and so has had to withdraw from the party."

"That is uncommon sad." Dr Moore strode forward, looking concerned. "Nothing too major, I hope. He seemed well this morning when I called."

"Indeed not, Sir," Jane replied. "Just a flare up of an old war wound but the change of circumstances caused us to be a little late. I do hope we have not delayed dinner too badly."

"In my day, young ladies would not have been told about war wounds," Lady Goddard said, holding out her hand for Archer to help her from her chair. "It smacks of indelicacy."

"I cannot see that a wound gained in the defence of your King and Country is anything to be ashamed of, Ma'am." Jane hadn't meant to speak out so indignantly, but she hated the thought of her dear godfather's pain being dismissed so easily.

Lady Goddard stared at her and Archer grinned to himself. His grandmother looked as if a mouse had turned in mid escape and snarled at it's pursuer.

"Well, let us hope for a quick recovery," he said smoothly. "Now, I can see our housekeeper speaking in the hallway to a footman so I imagine that dinner is served. May I take your arm, Miss Jane, and escort you to the table?" He took her arm, she could feel the warmth of his fingers on her skin and was horrified to find she was shaking.

Jane was aware of Lady Goddard's look of displeasure as she sailed past them and walked to her seat at the top of the table in the long, beautiful but severely decorated dining-room. Candles had been lit but the room was still quite dark, the drapes tightly pulled against the evening sky.

"You really must not annoy my grandmama, Miss Jane," Archer murmured as they followed Lady Goddard. "It is very bad for her digestion and we all suffer here at Robyns if that delicate system is disturbed!"

Jane bit her lip; had she been annoying? She knew her mama would be very displeased if she had. "I can assure you I have no intention of upsetting anyone, Mr Maitland."

Archer sighed theatrically. "And there lies your whole problem. Look at Celeste there, irritating Grandmama by flirting with Andrew, whom she looks upon as her special pet, because he is such a pleasant fellow, a far nicer person than I am, as I am sure you would agree. But I can already see that Grandmama admires her spirit."

Jane glanced up and found his face was solemn and stern, but the look in his eyes told of humour and mischief. What a contradiction Archer Maitland presented.

She refused to take the bait and resolutely turned her attention back to the dinner table. She had a strong suspicion that he was teasing her and she didn't like the feelings it gave her. None of the young men she had encountered in life so far had teased her. Digby - oh Digby! - had always treated her with great politeness and consideration, as if she were a piece of precious porcelain that could break at a touch.

She could see that indeed Celeste was flirting with Andrew and was very tempted to tell Archer that his friend was in no danger, that Celeste and the Colonel had formed an attachment, but of course she could not break her word.

Course followed course, large portions admittedly but all of it bland, with no seasoning. Colourless and, in Jane's opinion, unappetizing. Across the table, in the flickering candle-light, she could clearly see Celeste's expression of distaste and disappointment. She had obviously been expecting a fine meal, not this poor fare.

Then, even as Jane watched, her cousin pushed her portions uneaten around her plate and then, to her horror, slipped a large piece of chicken into her napkin. A squeak from Miss Purkiss told that she had spied what was happening but before Lady Goddard could notice, Andrew whipped it up and tucked it away in his coat pocket!

"Another jacket ruined," Archer murmured in Jane's ear. "Muddy ditches, greasy chicken, steep cliffs, really Miss Jane, since meeting you and Celeste, my friend and I seem destined for all sorts of disasters. Do you always have this effect on gentlemen? I wonder what is in store for me next? Your sister never mentioned that flaw in your character, never disclosed that you had revolutionary blood in your veins."

Jane felt a flare of unusual anger. This was unfair and unkind. She was well aware that her twin, however much she loved her, thought her a timid person with a nervous disposition. She was not the type of girl who caused problems.

"I am no revolutionary, Sir," she snapped. "I prefer a peaceful life. I am afraid I am not the courageous type." She looked up into his dark eyes and realised he was teasing again.

She took a deep breath; she was allowing him to annoy her, which was, of course, just what he wanted. "Perhaps one day you will meet Bennetta. If we have a firebrand in the family, it is my little sister. Nothing frightens her, I have never known her to be anything but brave."

Archer twirled the wine in his glass and lifted it in a mock toast. "I shall await that pleasure with interest, but in my opinion, courage is easy if you are brave but far more praiseworthy if you are not."

Lady Goddard looked up sharply, frowned at something she apparently didn't like in her grandson's tone, then tapped her fork against her plate. "Miss Jane Darcy, I had the pleasure of knowing your Great Aunt, Lady Catherine de Bourgh."

"How interesting, Ma'am. I am afraid we were not close. I only met her a few times before she died. I believe her daughter, Lady Anne, visited Pemberley before her marriage to Viscount Burgoyne but that was before I was born. I am afraid that following their sad demise, we no longer see their daughter, Lady Merryn. Her grandfather, Lord Bowyer, wishes her to live a quiet life at home in Devon. I believe my parents have offered hospitality to her on several occasions but it has always been declined.It is rumoured that she suffers from poor health."

"Yes, I know Lord Bowyer - a difficult man - not one who has much knowledge of young women! Catherine de Bourgh was a friend of my older sister, so there were quite a few years between us, but I admired her greatly and we became quite close as the years passed. Indeed, I still have the letter she wrote to me on your father's odd marriage to your mother. Which was, of course, a most remarkable and lamentable affair."

Jane realised her fists were clenched in her lap, her nails biting into her palms. Abominable old woman! How dare she be so rude about her darling mama. Before she could find the words to reply politely, Celeste broke into the conversation, her dark eyes gleaming with curiosity.

"Why was it lamentable? My distant cousins, the Darcys of Pemberley, are much admired by everyone, so I have heard. I am longing to meet them."

Jane took a deep breath, then realised that a large hand had taken one of her clenched fists under cover of the table-cloth and was holding it fast.

"Yes, Grandmama, please explain. I have not yet had the pleasure of meeting Mr and Mrs Darcy, but as you know, I am proud to claim acquaintance with Miss Anne Darcy and I am sure I will meet her parents in the future."

Lady Goddard heard the challenge in her grandson's voice and hesitated. She was anxious for him to marry Anne Darcy, even if her mother was a nobody, her grandmother a fool and one of her aunts had the most dubious of reputations. Why, it was even common knowledge now that a first cousin was illegitimate!

In any other family, these things would be enough to keep them from associating with respectable people, but there was one big difference. Mr Darcy was incredibly rich and had friends in high places. This Jane might say they no longer met with Lord Bowyer but the family connection was still there. His grand-daughter, Lady Merryn, who would surely marry into the aristocracy, was a cousin of Pemberley.

Lady Goddard was determined that Archer would enter Parliament and make himself a name in political circles. For all the disgrace of their marriage, the Darcys could be extremely important to him. She had already made it plain to him that she favoured Anne Darcy as his wife. Archer was not a fool - he quite understood that the money he would need to succeed in a new career would only be forthcoming if he agreed to her plan.

"My dear Lady Goddard - " Andrew broke into the tense silence, his voice plaintive and sad. "Are we to have that delicious pudding served to us soon? I can smell treacle tart and I know there are to be spiced plums with the cheese."

The old lady's stern features relaxed a little. She was fond of Andrew Moore and often allowed him liberties of behaviour which she would not have sanctioned from Archer. She did not know nor did she query why this was. His honest, open countenance and brown hair that would never stay neatly styled, the untidiness of his dress, the way his cravat was always coming loose, all these things should have irritated her. If someone had told her he bore a remarkable likeness to a certain young man she had liked far too well over fifty years before, who had died in some needless cavalry charge, she would not have believed them.

"I do declare, Andrew, that you eat more than three men put together," she said, trying not to smile and gestured to the footmen to bring in the desserts.

"You should have let me speak, Sir," Jane said softly as the various dishes were being laid before them. "I feel I have let down my parents by not defending them."

Archer sighed. "You must learn to choose your battles wisely. Your parents need no defence of their marriage from you. Grandmama is from a different age, her ideas are set and nothing you can say will alter them. She is a tyrant in many ways, she seems hard and uncaring and probably is! She refused to speak to her own daughter, my dear mother, for years and years and no matter what I said, I could not change her mind."

Jane was silent for a minute, cutting a slice of cheese into tiny squares. She tried to imagine how she would feel if her own mother refused to speak to her. It left her with a dreadful feeling inside, of sorrow and abandonment. But how could Archer Maitland be so at ease with his grandmother if she acted in such a way?

"But..."

"Ah, I know what you are going to say, Miss Jane, that surely my first duty was to my parent. But believe me, my mama was just as hard-headed and stubborn as my grandmother. She adored my father, was mortified by her parents' treatment of him and refused to make the first move of reconciliation and so it was stalemate. Obviously she had my deepest affection but I am also fond of my grandmother. I learnt to navigate between the two of them, like a small vessel in a storm trying to avoid two mighty rocks!"

Jane glanced up swiftly: his tone was light-hearted, almost flippant, but she could see the pain in his eyes that the situation caused him and she fell silent, knowing that any words from her would only be platitudes because she could not truly understand how two women could act in this way.

Suddenly Lady Goddard rang the handbell next to her wine glass and stood up. "Ladies, we will withdraw and let Dr Moore and my grandson enjoy their brandy. Please do not take more than one glass, Andrew, you know it does not agree with you. Purkiss - perhaps if you have had enough spiced plums, you will favour us with a few quiet tunes on the pianoforte. Signorina Celeste - take my arm and sit next to me. I wish to ask about Italy. It is many years since I travelled there."

Jane found herself accompanying Miss Purkiss as they left the dining-room. "Have you been with Lady Goddard a long time?"

"Oh, yes, a good many years, Miss Darcy. My mother died when I was a child. My father had the honour of serving under the Admiral, although only as a very lowly officer, and when he died in a sea battle, indeed, died saving the Admiral's life, I was left with no means of support, and sadly as I did not have the type of education that would have allowed me to take up a role as governess, the Admiral was kind enough to offer me a place in service to his family. So kind, so very kind."

Jane followed her into the drawing-room and stood next to the very ornate and beautiful pianoforte as Miss Purkiss hurried to sort her music. The companion played very well, and as the first tune began, she stood, listening in pleasure and wondering how difficult it must be, not only to be continually grateful, but to have to show this gratitude every day of your life?

She glanced across at Lady Goddard and Celeste - her cousin looked uncomfortable, fidgeting with her fan and the lace on her sleeve. Obviously the old lady's questions were proving burdensome. She only hoped they weren't about Roman architecture or statues because from conversations she had had with Celeste herself, the girl was sadly uneducated about the culture of her home country.

LOUNGING AT THE TABLE WITH BRANDY GLASS IN HAND, ARCHER AND Andrew were comfortably at their ease. Archer loosened his cravat and grinned at his friend.

"You and the beguiling Celeste are becoming good friends. I have a suspicion you are smitten by the young lady's charms."

Andrew sipped his brandy. "I admit I find her enchanting and extremely good company. I like her complete disregard for what is considered proper social behaviour."

"I admit I do not know any other Italian girls. Well, not of good birth, anyway! Perhaps they all behave as she does. Does she speak much of her upbringing and background?"

"I gather that her mother died at birth and she lived with her father's family until he, too, passed away."

Archer swirled the amber spirit round and round in his glass, enjoying the aroma. "I allow it must have taken a great deal of courage to travel to England in search of her distant relations, without even a proper chaperone."

His friend nodded thoughtfully, then frowned. "Sometimes, when we are speaking and not being overheard, I think she is going to tell me much more, then she hesitates and the subject is dropped."

"A secret?"

"Whatever it is, it would not stop my liking for her. Anyway enough of my affairs - what about your own? Is it to be the elegant Anne Darcy who will become the next Mrs Maitland or do you look elsewhere?"

Archer looked up sharply and shrugged. "I always swore I would never marry just for love. I will not end up like my poor father, living in poverty. You know my position. If I marry Anne then my grandmother will continue to fund my career. If I do not, then the money will cease."

"She only behaves that way because she cares for you."

"Yes, I am aware of that. That is why I hesitate to upset her."

Andrew finished his brandy with a gulp and stood up. "My friend, she has you trapped in a beautiful cage. Oh the bars might be made of velvet, but it is a cage, nonetheless. And I would not discard love so lightly. Marrying one sister when you care for another - that is a recipe for disaster. No, no, do not object to my words. I have eyes in my head! And now I suggest we join the ladies. Our futures lie in our own hands and we need to be brave enough to do the right thing."

CELESTE LOOKED UP EAGERLY WHEN THE DOOR OPENED AND THE TWO gentlemen appeared. Andrew moved to sit by her side, but Archer crossed to the pianoforte and as Miss Purkiss continued to play a little folk tune, he flicked through the sheet music.

"Ah, I thought I remembered seeing this here." He placed the piece on the music stand, and Miss Purkiss came to a discordant stop.

"But this is a waltz, Mr Maitland," she whispered. "Lady Goddard does not care for such music. She thinks it is indecent."

"But I am sure that just this once, she will relent. We do not have enough couples for ordinary dancing, but the joy of the waltz is that you only need one other person. Andrew was expressing a wish to dance with Signorina Celeste and I am sure you would not want them to be the centre of all attention on their own, Miss Jane? And, if my memory serves me correctly, you must show me that you are just as skilled at this pastime as your sister."

And before she could comment, his hand was on her waist and he was pulling her close to his body. With a little squeak of near despair, Miss Purkiss began to play the waltz music and Archer steered Jane out onto the highly polished floor and, with a wicked smile, swirled her round into the scandalous dance.

CHAPTER 9

For a few moments, Jane could not breathe – all she was aware of was the warmth of his fingers through the thin silk bodice of her dress, and when he pulled her even closer to guide her in a circle, she could feel the pressure of his legs against hers even through the layers of her skirts and petticoats!

When she managed to draw breath, she realised Andrew and Celeste were also dancing; she could hear them talking and laughing over the sound of the piano.

"Why, Miss Jane, I do believe your skill does outshine that of your sister." Archer's voice in her ear forced her to raise her gaze from his shoulder and look up into his face.

She found her throat was dry and swallowed hard to get out her words. "I doubt that, Sir and I fear by her expression that we have annoyed your grandmother."

Adroitly, Archer swung her round again to avoid the other couple. "Please don't worry. I will make my apologies to her when we stop and tell her you could not refuse without seeming churlish. After all, you are the guest and if your host wants you to dance, then you are surely forced to agree?"

Jane tried to keep a stern expression on her face, but suddenly she found herself trying not to smile. She had always loved dancing and had forgotten that she had vowed, after Digby, never to dance again except perhaps if she was forced to, with her papa or brothers. And she was so pleased that she was wearing this dress, one that suited her so well.

Archer tightened his grasp on her hand. "Why, Miss Jane, are you laughing? Don't tell me my skills are such that I am causing you amusement?"

"No, Sir, your skills are quite adequate for a waltz. I commend you. I fear poor Celeste is not faring as well. Dr Moore has trodden on her toes several times already."

Archer gazed down at his companion's fair head, at the ridiculous curl hanging down each cheek and for a second lost his step. Quickly recovering, he tried to examine his feelings. Dancing with Jane Darcy had been a sort of joke, an attempt to cut through the chilly veneer she showed towards him. For some reason he had found it annoying that she could be warm and companionable to Andrew, but not to him.

But now, holding her in his arms, he found he was wishing they could dance on forever - no, this was ridiculous! This was no Anne Darcy, this was not a girl of brilliance and wit who would be a help in his political career. She was quiet, nervous, used to being taken care of with no sensible or modern thoughts in her head. Why, he forced himself to remember, this was the girl who had fallen in love with that fatuous oaf Frobisher. Surely that showed him what type of person she was?

Jane felt as if she was floating round the room. How could it be possible for two almost strangers to be so in step with each other? Her whole body felt soft and relaxed and she found she was wishing they could dance on forever - no, this was sheer folly! She was forgetting all her solemn vows to have nothing to do with men ever again - especially men like Archer Maitland whom obviously preferred her sister and was probably at this very moment wishing it was Anne he held in his arms.

"You dance with your heart," Archer murmured. "Most young ladies dance with their heads. Your sister, for example."

Jane glanced up and felt a rush of colour to her face as she saw the intent way he was looking at her.

Suddenly the music came to an abrupt halt and Jane realised Lady Goddard had walked across to Miss Purkiss and stopped her playing. Archer stepped back, smiled, bowed and escorted Jane to a chair. Celeste joined her, looking flushed and happy; Jane only hoped she didn't look the same.

"I must apologise, Grandmama," Archer said smoothly. "I know you are not a devotee of the waltz, but I fear I must practice sometimes because I have to be proficient when I return to London. This dance is all the rage in the best circles and I know you would not want me to look like a country bumpkin in front of some of the highest in the land."

Jane could see the indecision on the old lady's face; she was obviously angry with the performance but reluctant to make her grandson seem a fool.

"I take your point, Archer, although I still think it is morally reprehensible to dance so close to young ladies you hardly know. Of course, if Miss Jane's sister had been here, it would have been an entirely different matter."

"Of course, but alas she is not." Archer's voice hardened and there was an uneasy silence until Andrew broke it in his usual fashion of trying to keep the peace.

"Tell me, Archer, what is the significance of the term 'Green Man Festival'? I overheard two fellows talking in the lane as I took my walk this evening."

"Oh Andrew, you needn't bother your head with village affairs," Lady Goddard said.

"It's a very old local custom, a dance of some sort held in Compton Forge every year at harvest time to celebrate an old deity, the Green Man," Archer explained. "Although who or what he was they cannot tell you. Just that if you do not do him homage, the next harvest will be blighted! The dancers gather in the village and progress up to the waterfall and the circle of standing stones you were looking at the other day. I believe there is then some sort of ceremony. Quite pagan, of course. The reasons are completely lost in time."

"How interesting. Would you not care to attend?"

Archer laughed. "No, my friend, I would not be welcome and nor would you. We are foreigners to the local Dorset men."

"Oh, it sounds charming. A village dance. I would love to see it!" Celeste's eyes shone with excitement.

"I'm afraid that is quite out of the question, Signorina. If men who are not natives of the area are frowned upon, I can assure you that no women are allowed anywhere near the inn whilst the dance and procession is in progress."

"Oh, of course, the Green Man Inn," Jane said, glad of having to think of something other than dancing with Archer. "I've often wondered where it got its strange name from. The sign outside is too old and faded to see clearly."

Her voice died away as a thought struck her. Her maid, Tabitha, had asked permission to attend a dance in the village that evening. But surely the other staff at Deerwood would know that women were not allowed and would prevent her from going?

"Are you certain we cannot attend?" Celeste pouted; she thought a dance in the dark of night sounded exciting.

"I can assure you that no young woman, no matter what her station in life, would go near the Green Man tonight," Archer said gravely. "These old country customs are steeped in tradition and the locals take them very seriously. It could be very dangerous to interfere in something that is centuries old."

"Quite right, too," Lady Goddard said dismissively. "It is certainly not wise or proper to enquire into the pursuits of the local populace. Luckily, all our servants have been with us for years and are Londoners by birth. They would not care to indulge in such fripperies. And now I will ring for coffee. I think we have had enough dancing this evening. Too much exercise is not beneficial for young ladies."

Jane sat for the rest of the evening in a state of high confusion. Tabitha was her responsibility; she had learnt that lesson from her mama over many years. The servants who took care of the Darcys were due their protection. She had given her maid permission to go to the village dance, admittedly in ignorance of any danger, but it would still be her fault if harm befell her.

Archer couldn't help but notice her abstracted air and was not alone. Celeste brought her coffee cup back to the table where she sat and whispered to him - "I think dear Jane is miles away in her thoughts. Perhaps it is memories of the young man she had such tender feelings for this summer that take up all her attention."

A few non-committal words were his reply and he swiftly turned his attention to his grandmother, who was obviously still annoyed by the dancing. The evening was coming to an end and finally the carriage was called for, cloaks were brought and Jane and Celeste were making their thank-yous and goodbyes.

Archer escorted them out into the dark night and checked that the postillion had two bright lanterns lit, one attached to a horse's bridle, the other on a pole he carried before to illuminate the track. Celeste was handed into the carriage and as Archer turned to assist Jane, he realised she was in urgent conversation with the driver.

"Nay, Miss Darcy, I daren't drive you there. Lord, what would the Colonel say if I did that?"

"But John, it won't take us more than five minutes and..."

"Is there a problem, Miss Jane?"

The girl spun round, fair hair cascading from inside the hood of her cloak. "Oh Mr Maitland - please, tell John here that he must drive me down to the village before we go home. My maid, Tabitha, has gone to the dance tonight at the Green Man."

"Good Lord why! Who allowed that?"

Jane flushed deeply at the accusation in his voice. "I take full responsibility, Sir. She asked leave to attend and I saw no reason at the time to stop her going. Of course, if I had known it was forbidden, then I would have told her so."

Privately Jane thought that Tabitha, who had originally joined the Darcy household in London before moving up to Pemberley, was a very sensible, forthright girl who would have laughed at the thought of a bunch of farmers, waggoners and shepherds being a danger. She was well aware that all the servants hired from big cities looked down their noses at their country cousins.

Archer bit back an angry response; this was not the time for recriminations. "John - I will accompany the ladies. Drive to the Green Man. I am sure all will be well, but I agree we must find the young woman as soon as possible. A lot of drink is taken on these occasions."

A look passed between the two men that conveyed all they suspected might happen to an innocent girl out alone on a night such as this. Archer gave a brief word to a footman to tell his grandmother and Dr Moore where he had gone and then his hand was under Jane's elbow and she felt herself almost thrown up into the carriage.

With the side lights flickering and the postillion running in front with a lantern, the horses moved off, far too slowly for Jane's liking, but she realised it would be unwise to travel faster. She was aware of Archer sitting opposite her, his face dark with anger. He did not speak, even when Jane broke the silence by giving a bewildered Celeste the reason for his presence.

"But Jane, I do not want to go to the village! I am tired, very tired. I shall fall ill if I do not get to my bed very soon. Surely the maid will be quite all right. Such girls are used to rough ways and manners. Luisa, my servant, is quite capable to looking after herself. I would not dream of running after her."

The streak of Pemberley stubbornness that Jane had inherited from her father reared its head again. "Tabitha is my responsibility. I gave her permission to leave Deerwood and go the dance. I know you are tired, Celeste, but here, wrap this rug around you and try and sleep. You can stay in the carriage where it is warm. Hopefully we will not be very long."

"But why do we not go home first and check to see if the silly girl is back?"

"I don't wish to alarm the Colonel or Susannah. They will have retired for the night. If we do not find Tabitha at the inn, then we will know she is hopefully back at Deerwood."

Celeste continued to grumble under her breath but eventually fell silent, the swaying of the carriage lulling her into sleep. Jane wished fervently that she could do the same, but knew that was impossible. But she also wished her cousin was awake and speaking to her. She was only too aware of Archer's dark, irritated expression every time he looked in her direction. She was tempted to speak but resisted: she was at fault but not through negligence: his anger was unjustified.

The subject of her scrutiny was fighting back the inclination to voice his feelings, which he knew would be unwise. He wasn't angry with Jane Darcy, far from it - he thought her concern for a servant was admirable - but he was angry at these old traditions that had been allowed to flourish unchecked - whatever their beginnings, centuries ago, surely they had little place in modern society, especially when their simplicity seemed to have changed into something far more sinister.

If crimes were committed and came to the ears of the local authorities, then it could have drastic consequences for all concerned. as Archer knew only too well after his recent involvement with the Tolpuddle case. He was tempted to explain to Jane how he felt but then a glance out of the window made him realise where they were.

"We are very close to Compton Forge. Listen, Miss Jane, you and Celeste must stay here in the carriage with John and I will go into the Green Man and investigate. They won't like me being there, I daresay, but I shall see immediately if your maid is present and bring her out to you."

Jane reached out to touch his sleeve. "Please, take John and the postillion with you. We shall be quite safe."

Archer shook his head, his expression grim. "It would be hopeless ordering either to enter the inn uninvited tonight. They are local men, quite aware of what transpires on a night such as this. No, I must investigate on my own."

The carriage drew up with a jingle of harness and stamping of hooves. To Jane's surprise, Archer smiled at her as he jumped down, then there was just the shape of him against the black of the inn and he was gone.

She could hear John and the postillion muttering together, their lanterns flickering, throwing vast shadows against the timbered walls of the Green Man Inn. Overhead the ancient sign swung, creaking in the wind, invisible in the dark but Jane could remember the faint outline of a green face that had been painted many, many years before, worn away by the passage of time.

There were a few faint lights at the windows, candles, she thought, and she could hear music in the distance - a drum, pipes and whistles - playing an odd tune that made her want to tap her feet and dance. So the party was still in progress but she was sure the sounds weren't coming from the Green Man. They were too far away.

She shivered, casting an envious glance at the sleeping Celeste, huddled inside the fur carriage rug. Archer had been gone for several minutes; how long could it take to check inside the inn for Tabitha? But she wasn't even sure if the maid was there. Suddenly she realised the music was getting louder; it seemed to be coming closer and she pushed open the carriage door to hear more clearly.

"I'm a-going to drive home, Miss Darcy," John shouted down from where he was now seated up on the box. He sounded worried. "We shouldn't be out here tonight. Not Green Man night, 'tisn't right."

"But we must wait for Mr Maitland..."

"I reckon he would want you two young ladies taken home, Miss." The coachman sounded more and more concerned and Jane heard the whip cracking and the cries to the horses as the postillion's lantern led the team round in a circle to head back the way they had come.

With the door open before her, she had acted even before the idea was fully formed in her mind. One foot on the step, a small jump and with the cream silk of her evening dress billowing around her, she was on the grassy verge of the lane and even as she turned and looked, the carriage was moving away, the lights growing dimmer, John and the postillion both unaware that one of their passengers was missing.

It seemed even darker with the lanterns gone; the wind gusted in strongly from the direction of the sea, blowing back the hood of her cloak, pulling long fair locks from their pins and sending them cascading down across her shoulders. Jane pushed them back, aware that she had never felt more scared or alone in her life. This was madness, she could only guess at how appalled her parents would be at this behaviour, but she also knew she couldn't just tamely go back to Deerwood Park, leaving Tabitha out here unprotected.

"Anne and Bennetta would think this fun, exciting, an adventure," she murmured to herself. "What is there to be afraid of, except my own silly imagination. I don't believe in ghosts and devils and such like. I will find Mr Maitland and all will be well."

Jane turned towards the inn, not stopping to wonder why she was so certain that Archer was the one person she wanted by her side. Just then she realised the candles in the windows had been extinguished and the sound of the music was now accompanied by the tramp of many feet. And a weird green light began to show up on the leaves of the trees and bushes further up the lane where the track curled around towards the hills.

She must move, hide somewhere out of sight, but before she could step to the side of the roadway, a group of cavorting figures leapt into view and were on and surrounding her, the music thrumming shrilly in her ears as they advanced.

Light from a green lantern shone in flashes across faces painted green, devils' faces, with glaring eyes and wild green hair and shaggy beards. Some had horns apparently growing out of their heads, some were wearing deer antlers and they surrounded her in a whirling, shouting mass, the pipes shrilling, drums beating, green hands reaching out to pluck at her cloak, her dress, her hair and they were drawing closer and closer, moaning and hissing, intent on all sorts of evil she could only imagine...

Archer Maitland, coming out of the inn, stood in horror for a second and then shot forward, pushing his way through the surging throng of dancers, desperate to reach Jane. What in hell's name was she doing here. He had to reach her... save her...

"Stop this nonsense! Stop it now!" This was not the voice of a terrified girl, this was Miss Jane Darcy of Pemberley. "Peter Dixon! I know it's you. I can recognise you under that silly mask. What would the Colonel say if he knew what his valet is doing tonight? And those are shoes with Deerwood crests on the buckles - why, Josiah - is that you under all that green paint? Shame on you, Sir. And you just promoted to footman. I have never been more astounded. And Bates! I have heard that cough whilst you are gardening often enough. No wonder you have a bad chest, Sir, if you are out cavorting in the damp of night. Now stop this music and go home, all of you."

Archer stopped in his tracks and stood, shaking with laughter as three of the group melted away, back into the dark and the music started up again as the rest headed off out of the village. He guessed they were going through the woods, up to the waterfall and the grey standing stones for the final rites of their festival. The eerie green light vanished into the trees, leaving just the starlight to illuminate the village.

Jane stood, trembling, the anger that had fuelled her, dying away, leaving her shaken and close to tears.

"Bravo, Miss Jane! Bravo!" Archer strode forward and grasped her hands in his. "I believe you have been deliberately misleading me. You said you were not brave. Well, that was certainly not the actions of a coward!"

Relieved beyond belief at seeing him and trying hard to keep her voice from quavering, she replied, "I have to admit I was scared at first, Sir, but when I realised at least three of them were men I have known for years, it came to me just how silly they looked. Prancing around in ridiculous costumes, all sense of dignity and decorum lost."

"Will you tell the Colonel what his valet, footman and gardener were doing this evening?"

Jane shook her head. "No, that would not be fair. I am sure they are off duty. I am unharmed and I take it that you have not found Tabitha at the inn, so hopefully she decided not to attend the dance after all." She shivered as the chill wind cut through her thin dress and evening cloak.

Archer noticed and immediately shrugged off his coat and draped it around her shoulders. "Come, we must walk back to Deerwood as fast as we can in order that you do not take a chill. I imagine we will meet the carriage coming back to find us when John realises that only one young lady is inside!"

"I suppose you think me very foolish for abandoning safety, but it was done with the best of intentions."

Archer's hand tightened on her arm as they hurried along the road. Yes, he had thought her foolish, but he had also thought it was the bravest thing he had seen for a long time. He was, however, less inclined to consider the feelings that had swept over him when he had first seen her there, surrounded by the angry mob. They were feelings he had no right to experience. He had only known her a few days and he was expected soon to ask for her sister's hand in marriage.

"Yes, very foolish," he said at last and they fell silent as the sounds of the approaching carriage came clearly through the night air.

CHAPTER 10

In the county of Derbyshire, in the great house of Pemberley, Elizabeth Darcy sat at her pretty writing desk in the small but elegant morning-room that had been her personal domain for over twenty years. Pen in hand, she was half way through a letter to her daughter and anxious for her husband's advice.

"So, my dear, we are agreed, we shall move to London for a few weeks and Jane must bring this Celeste up from Dorset immediately."

Mr Darcy was standing at the long window, gazing out over the beauty of Pemberley. His estate was glorious at every time of the year but with the woods a mass of amber, yellow and bronze, it was particularly vibrant and magnificent during the autumn months. Sadly it had been raining hard for two days and the beauty was a little diminished.

He turned back to his wife and seated himself on the other side of her desk. To his eye she looked hardly any different from the feisty Elizabeth Bennet he had fallen in love with many years ago. Motherhood and the duties of being mistress to his vast establishment had not diminished the sparkle in her eyes. He struggled to keep his thoughts in order and answer her question.

"Yes, I am at a loss as to why my cousin has kept the girl's existence a secret from the family. Her very being causes all sorts of complications with wills and inheritance matters. The Earl will not be pleased, but luckily his health is such that he sadly feels unable to meet her at present. I fear I grow concerned for his well-being and that son of his thinks of nothing but hunting and is as likely to break his neck as not!"

Elizabeth gently turned the conversation back to her own concerns. Her husband's mother, who had died long before she had met him, had come from an ancient family who prided themselves on their bloodline that stretched back into the mists of written records. A new member arriving suddenly from abroad had caused considerable consternation.

"Celeste Fiorette, a pretty name - and you had no idea she existed?"

Darcy shook his head, irritation written clear on his face. "No, Lizzy, none at all. We were told very little of that piece of family history when we were growing up. I knew, as youngsters do from servants' gossip, that there was a scandal concerning Rose, my mother's sister who was, of course, younger than her by some considerable years. My father told me, just before he died, that Rose had run away with an Italian groom and been disowned. It had been firmly believed by all, that she had died out in Italy. There has never been any mention of her marrying the groom or having a daughter, let alone a grand-daughter!"

He stood up and paced impatiently around the room. "I have written to the lawyers to ask them to make immediate enquiries. But, dear Lizzy, do you think there is any truth in Jane's poorly hidden hint in her letter that this Celeste and Fitzwilliam are to be married? Do you think you may have imagined the indication? It seems quite incredible: he is not a young, impulsive fellow anymore."

Elizabeth tried not to smile. Was it so surprising that a man of almost the same age as her own husband could fall in love?

Darcy turned and caught the mischievous expression in her eyes. For a second he was offended that she was laughing at him, then remembered the way they had spent a good part of the previous night together and found himself smiling back at his only love.

"We shall soon find out the truth of the matter in London. I daresay that once Celeste is established with our family at Matlock House, if the Colonel has strong feelings for her, then he will leave Deerwood and adjourn to his own house in town to be near her."

"Jane sounded in better spirits."

Elizabeth nodded her agreement. "Indeed, and I have received a short note from Susannah saying she is much improved in health and disposition which is very good news. I am praying that all the heartaches and unpleasantness of the past few months are now over. I have spoken again to Anne about her behaviour and although it was clumsily done, I do believe she only had her sister's best interests at heart. Anne is always so sure she is right in everything she does."

She fell silent for a moment, tempted to say that his eldest daughter had inherited so many of Mr Darcy's more unlovable character traits, then decided this was not the best moment.

"I only hope that Jane is not over exerting herself in any way. But I cannot think that there is much to do at Deerwood at this time of year except rest and restore her energy.

"Jane writes warmly of this Dr Moore and Anne tells me that she has met Mr Archer Maitland several times whilst staying in London with Caroline. I shall need to find out more about that relationship. Anne has already refused Digby Frobisher and several other young men to my knowledge. Perhaps this Archer Maitland is more to her taste."

Mr Darcy leant back in his chair and admired the new Turner painting he had just bought and hung on the wall of his wife's private drawing-room. He sighed heavily.

"Daughters are a great trial, my love. I have no great affection for your mother, as you well know, but of late, I have begun to have a little sympathy with her having five of you to deal with. Three are quite enough! The boys do not cause me nearly so many sleepless nights."

Elizabeth bit her lip. The health of her youngest, Henry, who was now a very new midshipman in the navy, caused her concern. She did not understand why her husband could accept so readily that Henry might come to harm at any time. It was the one thing that they disagreed upon and she could see no way to resolving the problem.

"Mama! Mama! Are you there?" The door was flung open and their youngest daughter stood, her long black curls sparkling with rain drops, her eyes shining, her cheeks rosy from running. "I met the post boy on my walk and ran straight back - here, letters from both my brothers for you and, much more exciting, a letter from our dear cousin Catherine with such good tidings. There is to be a new resident at Courtney Castle in the next few months!"

"Bennetta! Look at the state of you. Your petticoat is at least three inches deep in mud!"

The young girl gazed down at her ruined skirts and then looked up in bewilderment at the sound of her parents laughing together at a memory of one of their first meetings they would cherish for ever. Their laughter gave Bennetta a very odd feeling, one she had often had before and hated - that of being shut out, excluded from the bubble of happiness that surrounded them.

Oh, to be fair her mama often reached out and surrounded her with love and affection, but Bennetta knew deep down that her papa still struggled with the scars she had inflicted on him when her birth had put his wife in danger of dying. He loved her, she knew that, but there was always that reserve that hurt her so much that she continually pushed it away, busying herself with everything and anything to stop thinking about the feeling of loss it engendered in her.

So she did not ask what had caused their laughter and having learnt from them that they would all soon be travelling to London, she left them happily reading the latest news from Henry, who was at sea with the fleet and from Fitz who had just gone back to college.

Upstairs, she met Anne in the passage as she hurried to her room, guiltily aware that she was shedding mud at every step.

"It is official - we are to go to London to meet our new cousin, Celeste. Jane is to escort her up from Dorset. I long to hear all her stories of life in Italy. I wonder if we will be able to understand her? I have no Italian at all, except for a few words from various songs. And there is splendid news from Catherine - there will soon be a new addition to their family!"

Her elder sister shrugged; she still thought it most odd that their poor Collins relation was now Lady Courtney and she had absolutely no interest in this Celeste. "Then let us hope Catherine produces a boy, otherwise the poor thing will have to keep on having children year after year!"

"Really, Anne, you are so weird. Surely having children is all part of marriage. Well, I am happy for them, even if you are not." She poked out her tongue, forgetting that she had now reached the vast age of 18 and swept past her sister into her room.

Miss Darcy continued down the stairs, pushing all thoughts of Catherine and Celeste to one side; they were of no consequence to her. She was delighted to be going to London; she was sure to meet up with Archer once more and was quite convinced that this time he would propose marriage.

She paused on a landing where a vast gilt edged mirror hung. Her reflection, as always, pleased her. She knew she was beautiful, knew she was witty and elegant and would enjoy being the wife of a prominent lawyer and possible member of parliament in the not too distant future.

Anne did not love Archer and was certain that he did not love her. But they got on well together. His formidable grandmother was all in favour of the match and it would take her away from dull country life in Derbyshire, give her her own establishment and a chance to use her redoubtable talents to further her husband's career.

She stared around her at the grandeur that was Pemberley, the sweeping staircase, the glorious painted ceiling, the portraits of distinguished ancestors gazing down at her and fought back the black tide of resentment she always felt - that this would one day belong to her young brother who didn't care for it in the same passionate way she did. She was the eldest Darcy child, but she would never inherit Pemberley because she was a female. Life was very unfair.

Another thought brought more irritation - Jane! She would be coming to London with Celeste. There would be more tears, long silences and an air of suffering, just because her silly sister could not see that Digby was a young man who didn't care whom he married as long as they had money.

Anne had been told by her mother that she had handled the whole affair badly, but she did not have any doubts in her mind. In her own way she was fond of Jane and had just wanted to show her twin that Digby was a man lacking character. But Jane obviously had no difficulty in overlooking that. She grieved for her lost relationship and Anne had to admit that she did feel a few faint pangs of regret about that.

Patting a loose strand of hair into place, she continued down the stairway. Her mama wanted her to write to Jane, to say she was sorry to have encouraged Digby, but she could see no reason why she should apologise. Her twin would have spent several pleasant days being spoilt and pampered by Colonel Fitzwilliam, who never paid Anne anything more than the merest of compliments. She would no doubt have received all his sympathy and be far happier than before.

Her foot on the stair faltered. Goodness, from the tone of her thoughts it was almost as if she was jealous of Jane! How ridiculous was that? Jane could not look forward to a marriage to a handsome lawyer with an exciting career in politics ahead of him. Admittedly Anne would be marrying for convenience, not love, but what was wrong in that. You would be a very lucky young woman to marry for love, even in these modern days of 1834.

She sighed: she wanted Jane to be happy. Well, perhaps Digby could be invited to call on them in London. Surely Jane would accept him if he proposed again and then that would be to everyone's advantage.

🙰

A FEW DAYS LATER, JANE SAT IN THE DEERWOOD DRAWING-ROOM IN FRONT of a blazing fire. The weather was chilly and wet, the garden paths too muddy to tempt her out, the leaves torn from the branches in the woods, whirling in great swoops to batter against the mullioned windows. It was raining hard again this afternoon and she was glad to be indoors.

She had said nothing to Susannah or her godfather about the events at the Green Man. Several of the servants had been incapable of looking her straight in the eye the following morning, but seeing she was ignoring the situation, they had grown more cheerful, only working more assiduously to be of service to her.

Jane herself had found it difficult to keep a straight face when dealing with Dixon, the pompous valet, because she could still picture him covered in green paint with fake horns stuck to his forehead!

Tabitha had told her, almost casually, that the housekeeper had forbidden her to leave Deerwood on that evening. No reason had been given and the girl hadn't been too bothered because there had been a sing-song in the kitchen with tea and cake.

Jane had found it difficult to come to terms with her own behaviour. A few weeks ago she would not have dreamt of putting herself into danger: she would have alerted one of the senior servants and ordered them to fetch Tabitha back from the village. But she was no longer so timid; it was as if her whole life had been spent under a smothering blanket of care and concern. Now she had torn the coverings apart a little and ventured outside of the warm cocoon into the chillier but bracing world outside.

Her next decision would be whether to retreat once more and allow her friends and family to protect her, or fight for the right to follow her own path.

She would be twenty years old just before Christmas. A grown woman. And making amends with her sister was one of the things she must do. Regardless of Anne's intentions, the outcome had been to show her just how wrong and shallow her feelings had been for Digby. Why, it was even difficult now to remember exactly what he looked like!

The rain continued to batter against the windows and hiss down the chimney onto the flickering flames. The Colonel had retired to his study after breakfast as he did every morning - he was still suffering from the wound in his leg and the damp weather did nothing to improve his plight.

Celeste had drifted around the house in an irritable mood until Andrew Moore had arrived to leave his card and she had begged him to accompany her into Dorchester, to which request he had gladly agreed. Jane was glad they had taken the carriage; anyone out on horseback at the moment would be drenched in minutes.

The post had just been delivered and Jane was anxious to discover all the news from Pemberley. A plate of buttered muffins and a pot of hot chocolate lay on the table between her and Susannah who was bent over a small garment she was embroidering for her little niece. A fit of coughing struck her and Jane looked up in concern until it subsided.

"We have not had the pleasure of Mr Maitland's company these past days," Susannah said, putting away her handkerchief and bending her head once more to the delicate stitch work. "Although Dr Moore manages to visit us regularly."

Jane looked up from the letters that were strewn across her lap. "Mr Maitland is obviously far too busy to bother," she said tartly. "Dear Dr Moore comes to speak to the Colonel about the ancient silver and other little pieces of Roman pottery in which they both have an interest."

Susannah nodded and fought to stop another bout of coughing. "Yes, I quite understand that, but it is surprising how today that talk took about ten minutes and then he found it necessary to accompany Celeste into Dorchester in the carriage."

"Poor Celeste is not finding our autumn weather to her liking. And she does so love shopping." Jane bent her head to the packet of letters and murmured absentmindedly, "It is good of Dr Moore to take the time out of his day to amuse her, especially as the poor Colonel is still in pain. Her maid accompanies them so all is good and proper."

"Yes, but Jane dear - "

"Oh my goodness, Susannah - " the younger girl interrupted in consternation as she read one of her letters. "We are to leave Deerwood immediately and go to London! And we are to take Celeste with us."

She read her mama's words over again to make sure she had not misunderstood them...

"your papa and I were astonished to learn of Celeste Fiorette. Apparently it was not known to the family that Rose Fitzwilliam, who was very much younger than her sisters - your papa's mother and Lady Catherine - had a child in Italy after she ran away from home. The old Earl would not have her name mentioned. It was as if she ceased to exist. So my dear, you have presented us with a pretty problem because wills and inheritances are involved and your papa is busy corresponding with lawyers out in Italy. Thankfully, he speaks and writes the language extremely well.

"Now, you may say I am mistaken, but I got the strong sense from your letter that there is some understanding between Celeste and the Colonel. There is a very big difference in their ages, but I suppose it would be a great advantage to both of them if they were to marry even though they are cousins; he would no longer be alone and she would have protection in a foreign land. Forgive and ignore my remarks if you did not mean to give that impression. But if it is indeed true, it would be quite inappropriate for her to stay at Deerwood unchaperoned.

"I have today written to both of them - I have invited her to join us in London as soon as you can all travel. We have decided to spend some weeks at Matlock House. Mr Darcy has a great deal of business in town and Bennetta is determined to have a winter ball. She declares that she will never meet any suitable young men up here in Derbyshire. It is my opinion that your young sister will never find a man she thinks suitable!

"Susannah will obviously wish to continue home after a short stop in London. Indeed she may well care to travel on up to Northumberland as we have had the exciting news that dear Catherine is hoping to provide Sir Robert with an heir in a few months' time! Mr Darcy has asked me to say that he will happily provide a carriage for her journey north if that is her wish.

"And you yourself, my darling girl, are you fully recovered in spirits? Your letter sounded cheerful. Obviously meeting up with new people in different surroundings has helped you forget all the travails of this past summer. Your papa knows the name of Dr Moore - he is distinguished in archaeological circles. Anne says she is acquainted with Mr Maitland - in fact from the way she blushed when I spoke to her, I believe she has more than a passing liking for the gentleman. Has he given you any indication of his feelings for

her? Your papa says he is well known as an up and coming man and destined for politics. I'm sure such a life would suit Anne very well.

"So, can you please me, dear Jane, by writing to your sister and making amends in that direction? You know Anne; I am sure she wishes only the best for you but you will wait for ever for her to make the first move at reconciliation.

"We are all well. Letters have been received from Fitz and Henry, who boasts he has never even been sea-sick! Our only dark cloud is your dear Aunt Jane's health which still continues to cause me concern. But she is in good spirits and looks forward to hearing all your news from Deerwood."

Jane would have loved to have shown the letter to Susannah, but instead she read out the parts that affected her; obviously she could not divulge what Celeste had told her of her attachment to the Colonel. Indeed, she felt guilty that her worries had been so clear to her mother. She thought she had dropped but the slightest hint.

"That is so kind of your papa but I think I will spend a few quiet weeks at home. Travelling is so very tiring and I shall need to visit Northumberland once the new addition to the Courtney family has arrived. Here is a letter just arrived from Catherine that I have yet to read. I am sure it will give me more details of the happy event and how she is faring. "

Jane gave a worried glance at her companion. She did not like the flush on her cheeks or the continued cough.

"I shall miss your company in London, but I can well understand that you may long to get home, to your own bed. I will write to Mama today telling her of your wishes. I have a long list of clothes that she will need to bring down from Pemberley for me. If Papa's business affairs take longer than he expects, we could be in London for several weeks and the cold weather will soon be upon us. There is mention of a winter ball - Bennetta cannot bear to think of the ballroom at Matlock House not being used when she is living there."

Susannah bent over her work once more, wishing she did not feel so poorly, wondering if she dare ask how Jane was now feeling about Anne's behaviour earlier in the year. Nothing had been said and her companion had lost that air of desolation and grief which had so alarmed her family; hopefully her despair and feelings of betrayal were now all in the past.

She wondered if the attentions of Dr Moore had played their part? Compliments and warm words from an attractive man would always help to heal a broken heart, but she was very concerned that Jane did not read more into his behaviour than was wise. She had the strong feeling that Dr Moore's admiration was fixed in a different direction and worry flared through her mind at the thought that even more heartbreak might be in store for her young friend.

Jane stared into the fire, enjoying the warmth on her face, watching the flames licking around the logs. So Anne was attracted to Archer Maitland - she couldn't understand why that made her feel so irritable. He had made it clear that he admired her. Indeed, Jane had always felt that every time they met, Archer had been comparing her to her sister and not in a favourable fashion.

No, they were both arrogant, self-satisfied characters and would no doubt make a good marriage. She was probably just annoyed because if Anne had feelings for Archer, then why had she flirted with Digby, spiriting him away from her?

Jane dug her fingers into her palms; could it truly have been done with the best of intentions? Had Anne, in her proud way, seen through Digby, deduced that he had no moral fibre and would have married any girl as long as she had the surname of Darcy?

Well, at least Lady Goddard would be pleased if the match happened. It had been obvious to Jane that the old lady was anxious for her son to take Anne as wife. To her astonishment she found that tears were burning her eyes as she realised Archer could one day soon be her brother-in-law.

Just then the door opened and a footman announced, "Mr Archer Maitland."

The man who had so recently been in her mind strode into the drawing-room, brushing rain drops from his coat, his dark hair plastered against his forehead, his riding boots spattered with mud, bringing with him a gust of cold air and the scent of autumn woods.

"Miss Darcy - Miss Courtney - I apologise for bringing the damp weather into your snug surroundings, but the weather overtook me on my ride. I am sure that a countryman would have realised rain was imminent, but I am afraid I am too much a city dweller these days to heed the signs, hence my wet condition."

Susannah stepped forward, smiling, begging him to take a seat near the fire. She rang the bell and requested fresh tea for their guest. Having made a formal greeting, Jane retired into confused silence. This was the first time she had seen Archer Maitland since the night of the Green Man festival. Did he still harbour feelings of anger towards her for putting them in danger?

"We have missed seeing you, Mr Maitland. I trust your holiday has been a restful one." Susannah was making a valiant effort to keep the conversation alive, but her cough was troubling her.

"It has been interesting, let us say," Archer replied evenly. "But now it has come to an end. That is the reason for my visit - to pay my respects and say that I shall be returning to London tomorrow."

"So soon?"

"Yes, certain events have transpired that require my presence."

Jane bit her lip; to her it was quite obvious - Anne would be on her way to London by now, she had probably written to Archer telling him of her whereabouts and from the speed in which he was leaving Dorset, it was obvious that he was keen to be in the same general vicinity as her.

"Your grandmother will miss you." Jane forced the words out; she could not sit here in silence: he would think his leaving was of consequence to her in some way.

Archer's dark gaze turned in her direction. "Not for long - she is intending to remove to London for the winter season. The weather here by the coast can be very wild and cold."

"We, too, are heading for London," Susannah said, then stopped as another cough would not be denied. "I for only a few days on my way home to Derbyshire, but Jane will be in residence for some weeks. Goodness, they are taking their time bringing tea. If you will excuse me for a few minutes, I will see what is causing the delay and send word to the Colonel that Mr Maitland has come to pay his respects. I know he will be keen to speak to you, Sir."

Pressing her handkerchief to her lips she hurried from the room: there was silence, then Archer said, "Miss Courtney does not sound well. I hope she has not taken a chill."

Jane frowned. "So do I. That cough is worrying and she cannot possibly travel to London if she is ill."

"And the Colonel is still not back to full health?"

Jane nodded, aware of the concern in his eyes. "He keeps to his rooms for a large part of the day, but dines with us in the evening."

"He will miss you and Miss Courtney when you leave. But then he will have Signorina Celeste's company."

"No, Celeste is to travel with us to London, Sir. My parents are keen to meet her."

Archer stood up abruptly and walking to the window, stared out at the rain sodden gardens. "I had hoped to find Andrew here. I need him to know that we are leaving earlier than he anticipated. He needs to make his farewells to all his new found friends."

'So that is the reason for his visit,' Jane thought angrily. 'That makes sense. He could quite easily have sent a note with his compliments to say goodbye. He is alarmed at Dr Moore's obvious growing feelings for Celeste and does not approve of the connection. He obviously wishes to take him away from her influence. How I wish I could tell him that his fears are unfounded, that Celeste is promised elsewhere.'

"He has escorted Celeste into Dorchester, but I am sure they will be back soon."

Archer turned away from the vista of wet grass and trees and glanced across the room to where Jane was sitting, her loosely bound hair catching light from the flickering flames of the fire. "And are you looking forward to your time in London, Miss Jane? No doubt there will be much entertaining, meeting old friends, enjoyment of theatre and exhibitions."

"Our time in London is always busy. I know Bennetta is apparently determined to hold a winter ball. My younger sister is never satisfied until she has arranged a dance whenever she possibly can."

"It is always a busy time in town - country dwelling never seems so attractive during the winter months and people find their homes in London much more to their liking."

"We are, of course, lucky to have the choice in such matters. Most people do not." Jane hadn't meant to sound argumentative, especially to a guest, but as usual there was a hint of sarcasm in his voice that brought all her faults in manners to the surface.

"In that you are quite correct. We see the world from a position of privilege, our carriages carry us from house to house, but do we ever look out to see how those less fortunate than us survive during these difficult times. I think not."

"Well, Sir, my father pays good wages to all who work for him and our family does all it can to give aid and succour to those in the district whom we know have fallen on hard times. Why, Mama regularly distributes soup, bread, cheese and clothes and no beggar is turned away from the Pemberley door without a meal and a sixpence in his pocket!"

Archer smiled gravely at the indignation in her voice. "I am certain the Darcys do all they can, and while I honour them for it, it is but a drop in the ocean. I am fighting for things to change on a larger scale, for the basic wage of a labourer to be increased to a sum where he can afford to at least buy bread for his family and does not need to steal it."

Jane fell silent for a second or two, impressed by the passion in his voice. How interesting it was to listen to a man who had such views. Most of the men she met never talked of serious matters in front of ladies.

"I think it says in the Bible, does it not, that he who has two coats should give unto his neighbour one. Perhaps the world would be a better place if everyone remembered that."

Archer crossed the room and stood examining a chess set that was laid out in an intricate pattern. "Why Miss Jane, you sound quite the philosopher."

"And you sound surprised that I should have a serious thought in my head. I may not have had your depth of education, Mr Maitland, but I have been taught to think and consider as many aspects of the world around me as possible."

He bowed his head, then smiled across at her. "I stand corrected. And are you a lover of this game of chess. It is a splendid set, beautifully carved."

She shook her head. "No, Sir. I have never cared for the game but my godfather is, I believe an excellent player, as is my papa. They write their moves to each other by letter, so as you can imagine, one game takes many weeks to complete."

"This game is at an interesting point. The King is imprisoned on all sides. Only the Queen can rescue him." He stood gazing down at the game in silence, then seemed to recall where he was and turned back to Jane.

"Now I come to think of it, I recall that your sister mentioned that you are a great reader and spend many hours in the Pemberley library. I am sure there are books in that collection that I have not yet studied."

"Then I am sure that Anne will be only too happy to invite you to browse through them if you are ever in the neighbourhood."

"And you, Miss Jane, would you invite me to Pemberley?"

There was a silence: the room seemed to have grown very warm, Jane could feel a flush mounting her cheeks. She must push her chair back from the fire, must tear her gaze away from those dark eyes which held a message, that to her dread, she thought she understood. Oh, she must be wrong. His eyes said he had feelings for her that would not be denied by sense or logic, feelings that she was only too aware she was returning in her own expression.

She couldn't breathe. This man was to be her brother-in-law - she could not possibly be in love with him. She disliked him! He was arrogant, self-centred, opinionated and yet, with a flood of self-knowledge she realised what she had once felt for Digby was a pale ghost in comparison to what she felt for Archer Maitland.

Archer felt his head swimming - why wouldn't she reply, why wouldn't she see that he wanted her to invite him to her home, not Anne? Hell, this was madness, what was he thinking? He could not possibly be in love with Jane Darcy!

Then a log fell crashing into the grate, the door swung open bringing Susannah and a maid with a tea-tray and the moment was gone.

CHAPTER 11

The following morning dawned just as wet and windy; Jane felt tired and out of sorts. She had slept badly, unable to tear her thoughts away from Archer and her feelings for him. She was ashamed of herself. Only weeks ago she had been desperately in love with Digby - or so she had thought. Was she really that shallow or had she just mistaken liking, the unusual occurrence of being first in someone's affections, ahead of Anne for once, to colour her own?

She arose early, and with Tabitha's help, dressed in her travelling clothes; there was a lot to do before they set off for London where she was sure this flood of emotion for Mr Maitland would die down and vanish as quickly as it had arrived. No doubt she had not fully recovered from her experiences in the village the other evening. Back in the peace and quiet of their London house, all this would just be a dream.

Archer would marry Anne and she would attend her sister at the altar. They would make a splendid couple and she would dance at their wedding with great happiness!

"I expect you will be pleased to be going to London, Tabitha?"

Her maid paused in her task of tidying the room and gathering together all the items that needed to be packed. "Yes, Miss Jane, I will. There is so little to do here in the country, even less than at Pemberley. At home there is always something interesting happening, visitors and such like. The house is full of noise and bustle, especially when the young gentlemen are at home. And, of course, we travel to London at least four times a year."

"Well, you will no doubt enjoy the weeks we are about to spend at Matlock House."

"Yes, Miss. And I know someone else who will be pleased - that Luisa. She hates the countryside. As far as I can understand from her foreign chatter, she misses their life in Rome which seems to be as big a city as London, although I think she is likely to be exaggerating that."

"I think you must have misunderstood her, Tabitha. Signorina Celeste and Luisa come from Sicily. A long way from Rome."

Tabitha bit her lip: it wasn't her place to argue but she knew what she had heard. "Well, Miss, I'm sure it was Rome they lived in. But perhaps I misheard. She rattles on so, all about their life looking after some old lady who was very fond of Signorina Celeste and how exciting it was to travel to England."

"Well, we will find it exciting to travel to London! Now, if you have nearly finished in here, perhaps you could go to Miss Courtney and see if you can help her with her packing."

Jane sat quietly gazing at her reflection in the dressing-table mirror after the girl had left, gazing but not seeing. She was quite certain Celeste would be delighted to partake of all that London had to offer. When she and Andrew had returned from Dorchester yesterday, the Italian girl had been thrilled to hear of their forthcoming journey.

Andrew had hardly time to tell Jane that he would hopefully see them all in London in the days prior to his journey to Greece before Archer had called for their horses and with a swift bow over her hand, had left so fast that a splatter of muddy water doused the groom who had been holding the reins.

A knock at the bedroom door and Tabitha entered again. "Oh Miss Jane, I have just been to Miss Courtney, she is very poorly still. She begs your forgiveness but if you could step along to see her she would be grateful."

Within seconds Jane was at her friend's bedside. "Susannah - my dear - you are unwell. Let me call for the doctor immediately."

Susannah looked up from her pillow, her usually severely braided hair loose around her shoulders in a brown cloud. She coughed a little but her voice was quite strong. "No it is just a chill, Jane. A silly cough and a feeling of lethargy. I have had it before - it lasts a few days, maybe a week or two, and then vanishes. But I am afraid I shall be unable to accompany you and Celeste to London."

"I shall leave Tabitha behind to care for you," Jane said firmly. "And Mrs Oxley is most reliable. I am sure that my godfather will be leaving for his London home very soon so there will be no impropriety in your staying at Deerwood on your own until you are fully recovered. I will send our carriage back for you in a few days."

A flush that Jane hoped was not the onset of fever stained Susannah's cheeks pink. "My dear, at my advanced stage of spinsterhood, I think that the gossips would be hard pressed to make comments, even if the Colonel did stay here in residence."

Jane smiled: because Susannah had such a young spirit, she often forgot that she was very close to forty years of age.

Downstairs she found her godfather at the breakfast table, his face still drawn and grey with the pain from his old war wound.

"Jane, my dear girl, you are leaving so soon and I fear I have not been a good host to you. We do not seem to have had any time to speak quietly about our lives without interruption."

Jane sat next to him and patted his arm affectionately. "Dear Godfather, it is of no consequence. Pray do not trouble your mind about it. I have found the break away from home invigorating and educational."

"And Celeste is to go with you, I believe. She will enjoy London. Deerwood Park is very quiet for a young girl."

"But surely you will not be parted for long, Colonel. You will be recovered very soon and be able to venture up to London. We shall be all be able to meet up regularly - a happy party altogether once more."

"Yes, and hopefully Miss Courtney will be well by then and can travel with me."

Jane helped him to some slices of ham and beef and watched carefully to make sure he was eating. She dripped honey from a comb onto her bread and gestured to the footman for more coffee.

At last the Colonel spoke again, his voice diffident. "I suppose you think that I am too old to be considering an alliance with the lady in question? She is, of course, much younger than me."

"Too old? Not at all, Sir. Especially if you believe the lady returns your affections."

Colonel Fitzwilliam smiled. "Well, I think and pray that my instincts are correct in that direction. I have had my doubts, but our good friend, Mr Maitland, passed a remark the other day about seizing opportunities in life when they occur that made me realise I must not miss out on this opportunity due to cowardice!"

Jane reached up and kissed his cheek. "Dear Godfather. I wish you joy and I am sure everyone who knows and loves you will join with me in saying the same."

"That gives me great pleasure to hear. And you, my dear, you are looking in better health than when you arrived. Have you fully recovered your good spirits? You have been busy, walking and exploring, but you must not overdo things. Remember you are not as strong as your sisters."

Jane sipped her coffee and assured him that her stay in the country had done wonders for her constitution. She pushed aside the flicker of irritation that his words had caused her - once again she was being told that she was weak, must always take care not to exert herself, remain quiet and passive. A few weeks ago she would have listened and agreed, but now - now she felt as if she were a bird in a gilded cage, battering her wings against the bars. She was desperate to escape. Her time in Dorset had indeed changed her, although not perhaps in the way her family had hoped.

❦

Two weeks later, sitting with her mother, sisters and Celeste in the elegant drawing-room of Matlock House in one of London's most prestigious squares, Jane felt she was looking back at her time in the country as if it were a dream.

"I thought Dr Moore and Mr Maitland would have called to see us by now." Celeste was pacing around the room: she was obviously bored and sounded irritated, even a little anxious. "They surely are both in London. I am surprised at their lack of attention."

"I know nothing of any Dr Moore," Anne Darcy said smoothly, "but Mr Maitland is a very busy and important man in legal circles. Paying calls must take second place to his duties, especially as I know he wishes to make his mark in the world of politics soon."

"He sounds a very sober and proper gentleman," Bennetta said from where she was lying full length on a sofa, her shoes cast off on the floor, showing a great deal of stockinged leg. She was already bored with life in London - there was to be only one small dance held at Matlock House, not even a proper ball and she had met no new young men at all on this visit. She might as well have stayed in Derbyshire.

Sober and proper! Jane bent her head over her embroidery, so her expression should not show. Pictures flashed through her mind, Archer leaping off his horse when they had first met, his face when he stopped her from falling by the waterfall, the midnight escapade to the Green Man, his defiance of his grandmother's wishes in insisting on waltzing around the room. Sober and proper he certainly was not.

"Do sit up, Benny! I have never known a girl to slouch about the house as you do." Elizabeth Darcy's words were cross but she was smiling to take the sting out of her comments. "Did the gentlemen in question say they would hope to meet up with us all in London, Jane?"

"Er... yes... I believe something of the sort was mentioned by Mr Maitland, Mama. But I am not certain."

"You have said little about your meeting with his grandmother, Lady Goddard," Anne said suddenly, looking up from the table where she was reading. "Did she speak of me at all?"

"She mentioned that you had met in London," Jane replied quietly.

"I liked her very much." Celeste was wandering around the room again, idly fingering the ornaments, gazing at her reflection in a mirror, stopping every now and again to peer out of the window as if she was expecting visitors. "Except she asked me too many questions about Italy. I am from Sicily - I have never been to Rome or Florence."

"They are both beautiful places," Elizabeth Darcy smiled at her own memories. "Your papa and I travelled there after our wedding."

"But you have lived in Rome, have you not?" Jane was puzzled: Tabitha had been so sure of what Luisa had said. But Celeste was still occupied with the view from the window and did not reply.

"Lady Goddard's interest seems to be of great importance to you, Anne." Bennetta was still lying on the sofa, eyes closed, as if half asleep.

"She is his mother's mother," Anne replied. "A very clever, influential woman. I found her most interesting; I think we established a rapport when we met. Archer is devoted to her. It was good of him to take the time out of his busy life to invite you all to dinner, Jane. It must have been boring for him - after all, Celeste can not be expected to be able to hold a long conversation in a foreign tongue and you have never shown any interest in politics or law."

Elizabeth Darcy looked up and frowned. "You call Mr Maitland by his Christian name? Is that the modern practice nowadays? I fear your papa would not approve." She looked sharply at Anne - "Or is there more to your relationship than you have told us, Miss?"

Jane felt her breath catch in her throat as she waited for her twin's reply. Her hands that had been busy with the intricate embroidery on a linen runner for her dressing-table, were suddenly stilled. All she could think of was the candlelit room at Robyns, the pianoforte tinkling in the background and Archer's body against hers as they waltzed round the room. She could still see the expression in his eyes as he gazed down at her and was scared to think that hers had shown him how she was feeling too.

Bennetta's eyes flashed open to see a smug smile cross Anne's face as she said, "Mama, you can't possibly expect me to confess such a thing. Let me just say that I would be surprised if I still carried the name of Miss Darcy this time next year!"

As Bennetta watched, a bright drop of blood appear on Jane's finger as her needle missed the linen and with a gasp she pushed her work aside in case it suffered and bent her head to staunch the little wound with a scrap of fabric. Her fair hair fell across her cheeks, hiding her expression, but her younger sister had seen enough to notice how pale she had gone and how her eyes had suddenly filled with tears.

Celeste, who had not been paying great attention, suddenly said from her position by the window. "Goodness, what a surprise, here are arrived Dr Moore and Mr Maitland in a carriage, come to pay a call."

"Oh and I am still in my old morning gown!" Anne fled for the door and hurried upstairs to array herself in something more becoming. Jane followed; she felt no need to change her dress, she was not out to impress anyone, but the longer she could stay out of the company the better.

"Help me, Jane," her twin called imperiously from her room. "I've rung for my maid but I believe the wretched girl is deliberately slow when I most need her."

"You are wearing your best plaid?"

"Archer complimented me on it when we last met. It will send him a clear signal that I appreciate his admiration. Really, Jane, do you know nothing about how the game is played?"

"Game?"

Anne spun round so her sister could fasten the little hooks at the back of the dress. "The marriage game, you silly cuckoo. At our level of society, you must realise that who we marry is of consequence. I think that as Mrs Archer Maitland I will have a place in the world that will eventually be just as elevated, perhaps even more so, than life as Miss Darcy of Pemberley. Papa may enjoy a quiet life in the country, but I know Archer has far bigger ambitions and I intend to rise in the world with him."

She turned again, pulling a fine wool shawl across her shoulders. Tall, elegant and beautiful, it was difficult to see anyone stopping Anne Darcy from getting her own way.

Jane stared at the face that was, supposedly, so like her own, and once more felt like a pale shadow. All the confidence that her stay in Dorset had given her began to drain away and, taking a deep breath, she struggled to retain the self-worth that she had gained over the past weeks.

But as hard as that was, even worse was the pain that Anne's words caused. She seemed so sure of Archer, so determined to have him as her husband. Jane fought back her own feelings - she must see him only as a brother, for that was what he would be.

Hopefully, once they were married they would live most of the time in London and she could return to Pemberley and only have to see them maybe once or twice a year. Then another blow fell. Deerwood Park, her beloved sanctuary, would be denied her; Archer would be certain to visit Robyns regularly with his wife and if it so happened that she was visiting Dorset at the same time, there would be no way of avoiding his company.

She left her sister and returned to her own room to tidy her hair and pinch her cheeks hard to bring up some colour. There was no way she was going to allow Archer to suspect that she was upset at seeing him once more.

Bennetta swung her legs off the sofa and hunted for her shoes as the drawing-room door opened and the footman announced two gentlemen. This was the first time she had seen them and she considered both critically from under her lowered lashes as she was introduced by her mother - Dr Moore had a pleasant, kind face, untidy brown hair and a jacket that needed a good brushing. Mr Maitland - tall, dark, was he good-looking? His face, she decided with all the critical ability of eighteen years, was to taste.

Archer Maitland, who considered that there was nothing in could disturb him, didn't understand his own tumultuous feeling. .. ..e entered Matlock House. He knew he was tardy in paying his respects to the Darcys; he should have come days ago. Andrew had urged him to do so and had been irritated when he had made various excuses.

He felt as if he had reached a crossroads in his life - one path was pulling him towards a glittering career with a beautiful, witty woman at his side and the other.... But this was ridiculous, there was no other path. His grandmother had made it quite clear to him that his duty was to propose to Miss Anne Darcy and thus establish himself in everyone's eyes as an up and coming man.

Now there was Mrs Darcy, smiling and charming, Celeste Fiorette, exclaiming how much she had missed them both and a young girl with long dark ringlets and an innocent expression he didn't believe for one moment, murmuring that she had heard so much about him and surely it couldn't all be true.

Impatiently, he glanced round the room as Mrs Darcy continued to speak, apologising for her husband's absence, asking after his grandmother, enquiring of Andrew as to when he was going to set off for his archaeological dig in Greece.

And then the door swung open again and Anne stood there, holding out her hand in welcome, her golden beauty lighting up the room like a flame, her bright blue gaze giving him a message he could not deny.

He bowed and bent over her hand and as he raised his head, over her shoulder he saw Jane - no hard golden beauty, just a slim, pale pearl whose downcast gaze told him nothing whatsoever!

Bennetta was intrigued - this was interesting - as greetings were exchanged, she noticed several things: that Dr Moore kept Celeste's hand in his far longer than was proper and that although Archer Maitland bent over Anne's with polite elegance, his smile did not reach his eyes. Yet when Jane stepped forward, head bent and whispered her greeting, his gaze was warm and friendly. Bennetta felt a quiver of anticipation - perhaps these weeks in London were not going to be as boring as she had imagined?

Elizabeth Darcy received the gentlemen's compliments with a smile. "It is good of you to call, Sirs. Jane and Celeste have told me of your kindness owards them down in Dorset. Your attentions made their stay even more agreeable."

Archer bowed in reply. "We were only too pleased to meet Colonel Fitzwilliam's extended family and must apologise for not calling here as soon as we reached London, but Dr Moore is shortly to leave on his expedition to Athens and I have been assisting him with his preparations."

Elizabeth raised a mental eyebrow! This was a very weak excuse; she couldn't see how Mr Maitland's help could possibly have been required. Surely, if he had been keen to see Anne again, he would have called earlier? Was her daughter wrong in her belief that she had caught this man's attention? She was usually so sure of herself; could she have mistaken his friendship for something more?

"Has your grandmother joined you in residence in London, Mr Maitland?" Anne smiled at him, admiring the breadth of his shoulders and general appearance. There was nothing for her to find fault with in the way he looked and dressed. So many other young men who had courted her attention had fallen short in that aspect.

"Indeed she has, Miss Anne. She has many friends in town and is, in fact, busy this morning returning calls."

"Do, please, I beg of you, remember me to her."

Archer bowed. "I am sure she recalls your meeting with pleasure."

Anne turned away for a second as Dr Moore had picked up her book and was asking her a question about it. Archer crossed the room and sat down next to Jane who had chosen a chair as far away from the other group as possible.

"I find you in good health, Miss Jane? Fully recovered from all your Dorset-shire escapades?"

Jane felt heat rising in her cheeks and pretended to study her embroidery. She could not, would not, look up into those dark eyes. If she did she would be lost. And how terrible that would be - she could not possibly be in love with her future brother-in-law! It was unthinkable.

"Quite recovered, thank you, Sir. And yourself? I am sure you are glad to be back in the hustle and bustle of the law courts."

"Indeed. I have new offices. I am extremely busy, which keeps my mind from wandering down other, more pleasant paths."

"Escapades? I know you must be joking, Sir. Please tell." Bennetta had overheard the one word. She joined their group and Archer immediately vacated his chair for her. "Jane is never involved in escapades. She is the quietest and most sensible of all us Darcy children and, indeed, of all our many cousins too."

Archer's mind flew back to an angry girl, her hat crooked, the feather askew, glaring at him from a carriage window, the same girl perched precariously on a steep slope, about to plunge to her death, the warmth from her body as he waltzed her round the room at Robyns and her bravery as she shouted down the drunken revellers at the Green Man.

"Sometimes we surprise even our nearest and dearest, Miss Bennetta."

Jane glanced up - she had heard a tone in his voice that made her tremble. Nearest and dearest? What was he really saying? Oh why didn't he just ask Anne to marry him and be done with it? He should not look at her with that expression in his eyes. Bennetta was as sharp as a tack; she noticed everything.

"Bennetta, have you told Archer of our plans for a dance?" Anne had crossed the room to stand at his side. "We have a beautiful ballroom here at Matlock House, Sir. Not as grand as that at Pemberley, of course, but it does very well for a small dance. I do hope you will be able to attend. And Dr Moore, of course."

Jane looked to where Andrew and her mama were in deep conversation with a laughing Celeste. There at least was one man who seemed not the slightest bit affected by Anne's charms. She just hoped he wouldn't be too disappointed when he heard of Celeste's attachment to Colonel Fitzwilliam. He was such a kind man; it was sad to think of him being anything but happy in life.

"I shall be delighted to attend." Archer bowed in Anne's direction. "As to Andrew, I am not sure. He leaves for Greece any day now and with the trip already sadly delayed, I know he will not wish to tarry any longer, even if it means giving up the delight of a dance with you charming ladies."

Anne laughed and tapped his sleeve with her fan. "You turn a pretty compliment, Sir. I shall be delighted to dance with you."

"And you, Miss Jane. Will you write my name on your card for a waltz? We both know that you are proficient at that particular dance."

There was a silence. Jane knew her face had gone red and she struggled to keep her composure and answer sensibly, all the time remembering that magical night at Robyns.

"Oh you will be very lucky if Jane can spare you a dance," Anne, irritated at losing his attention for even a moment, broke in with a light laugh. "A certain

Mr Frobisher is back in town. A particular friend of Jane's. La, there is no need to look shy and silly, Jane. You know Digby is your greatest admirer and, if I am not mistaken, you were broken hearted during the summer when you had that little argument."

She tossed her head, her gold and garnet earbobs jingling merrily - "Really Archer, you have no idea what Jane put us all through this spring and summer. I have never seen two people so well suited who found it so difficult to admit the fact. But Jane, dear, you must let the poor boy know your true feelings. Being reserved and silent gives a suitor no indication of how he is to proceed. Why, as a jest, I once completely confounded Digby by pretending I liked him more than you!"

Jane stared helplessly at her twin. She had said earlier that she had encouraged Digby, because she had been certain he was fickle. Now, apparently, she had changed her mind.

There was another silence. Bennetta broke it by chatting aimlessly about the dance but she was hardly concentrating on what she was saying. The last few minutes had been so interesting: Anne was being annoyingly bright, Jane was obviously deeply embarrassed and unhappy and Archer Maitland, having gone very pale, shortly made his apologies to her mama and left.

Bennetta picked up her embroidery and frowned down at the rumpled material. She sighed; no matter how hard she tried, her stitches were too big or pulled too tightly. Mama would frown and ask her to try harder, but plying your needle in and out, over and over again was so boring.

Now Anne's news was far more interesting: so Digby was in town. Would he ask for Jane again? Would she accept him this time? Her heart had been broken so badly months before when he proposed to Anne, but a broken heart might easily be mended if you were being pursued by an ardent admirer.

As soon as she could, Jane stole away to her room, flinging herself down on her bed, regardless of her dress. She had seen the look of disdain on Archer's face when Digby's name was mentioned in connection with herself. He had obviously heard the gossip about that young gentleman's proposal to Anne. He would no doubt think her very shallow if she herself would now accept him.

Did it matter if her future brother-in-law thought her morally weak? Did he really believe she would marry Digby if he proposed? She sat up, pulling the pins from her hair, letting it fall in a fair cascade around her shoulders. Only a few months ago the thought of becoming Mrs Frobisher had filled her with joy.

How could she have been so stupid, believing that what she felt for Digby was true love? She had been flattered at being admired, at being put before Anne in someone's affections, that was all.

"And what if I had accepted him," she murmured to her reflection in the mirror as she brushed her hair. "If I had married, thinking that was love and then I had met Archer! What heartbreak that would have caused. How could I have been such a silly, green girl!"

Love, she now knew, was nothing to do with being admired, or being put first before her twin. Love was a consuming fire that burned inside you. Love was what she now knew she felt for Archer and was afraid she always would.

Leaving the carriage for Andrew, Archer strode away from Matlock House, fighting to keep his temper under control. He cursed himself for being a fool. Jane's beau had returned; she would be happy, accept him and go to live up north in Cheshire on the Frobisher estate. He would never need to see her again, never have that desire to push those ridiculous curls back from her cheeks, hold her in his arms as they danced. She could have that stupid puppy, if that was what she wanted, if she was the type of girl who could be satisfied married to such a man. He had thought her more than that; believed she had principles, a belief in what was right. He was wrong.

And he would propose marriage to Anne just as soon as he possibly could! He remembered the dance that young Bennetta had mentioned. That would be the perfect opportunity. He strode on into the bustle and noise of London, his expression oddly dark for a man who had just decided to marry a beautiful young woman.

CHAPTER 12

"Ah, this is a part of London that I would never tire of seeing!" Celeste stood at the entrance to the Burlington Arcade, her eyes gleaming from under the brim of her extravagantly decorated hat. She was wearing an elaborately embroidered cloak over a fashionable dress with vast puffed sleeves of darkest pink, her waist pulled in tightly under a belt above the billowing silk skirts.

Next to her, Jane in a simple green plaid dress whose sleeves were half the size of Celeste's and a hat with only two feathers and a ribbon on top, felt she must look like a sparrow alongside a splendid peacock! She was quite unaware that the beauty of her face and the elegance of her walk far outshone that of her more robust companion.

A fine October day had drawn Jane and her Italian cousin out into London: Jane had been instructed by her mother to show Celeste interesting historical sites such as the Tower and St. Paul's Cathedral. Accompanied by James, one of the Pemberley footmen who had accompanied them down to London, they had dutifully set out that morning.

Celeste had looked, listened and yawned. She had no interest in history or buildings and was more than happy when their carriage deposited them in the fine shopping parade called Oxford Street where they had visited several establishments.

James was now carrying a quantity of bags and hat boxes, all of which belonged to Celeste whose purse had been full of golden guineas - a present, she whispered to Jane, from their dear Colonel Fitzwilliam.

Jane had smiled in reply: it was only fitting that the future Mrs Fitzwilliam should be dressed with all the style and pomp her place in society would demand.

As the morning wore on, Celeste suggested they end their outing by visiting a place she had heard of recently, although she couldn't quite remember who had mentioned it to her. Here in Burlington Arcade, the finest glass-covered walkway in all London, where well-dressed ladies and gentlemen paraded past the shops, trailed by their maids and footmen, Celeste was suddenly wide awake, her black eyes sparkling, anxious to look, admire and spend even more money.

She had no sense of regret about how she had spent her time since arriving in England. Celeste had learnt at a very early age that there was no one who cared or worried about her, that if she wanted to achieve anything in life, it would be down to her own efforts.

Admittedly she had never thought of marrying Colonel Fitzwilliam when she arrived unannounced on his doorstep, but she had soon seen that the man was rich but lonely and that instead of being just his poor cousin whom she helped in a modest way, she could be his very rich wife.

Then her plans had all come to grief when she met Andrew Moore. Did she love him? Celeste wasn't quite sure what love should feel like, but she did know that she wanted to be his wife more than becoming Mrs Fitzwilliam, even if Andrew had no titled family in the background! He was young, good-looking, with enough money in his pocket and the prospect of making much more in the future and she was tired of playing the role of poor relation. She also had no desire at all to meet the head of the Fitzwilliam family, the Earl, when he recovered from his bout of ill health. No, it would be far better to leave England as Mrs Moore.

She disliked the weather in England, longed for the sun on her face all day long. She was well aware that winter in Greece would be cold, but come the spring, it would be heavenly warm.

Glancing at her companion, she sighed - poor Jane! Celeste did not care for Anne Darcy, but she could see which twin was the better catch and, from her experience, gentlemen were impressed more by wit and elegance than softly spoken words and a demure manner.

She loved this Burlington Arcade: so many wealthy people, so finely dressed, but none of the ladies were as beautiful as she was herself and she could not wait to spend even more of the Colonel's guineas on adorning herself. You could take jewellery with you anywhere in the world and if, by chance, her life with Dr Moore did not turn out exactly as she hoped, well, she would have plenty of portable wealth to carry her on to her next adventure.

"That is certainly a beautiful piece," Jane said as they bent to consider a ruby necklace displayed on a white silk sheet.

"I prefer diamonds!" Celeste had turned her attention to a side window where several rings could be seen. "Why Jane, perhaps your beau, Mr Frobisher, will buy you such a ring when you marry. Although I suppose your papa will have given you many such things already."

Jane winced at the mention of Digby, then smiled, trying to ignore the touch of envy in the girl's voice.

"Indeed, he is not my beau and mama and papa do not care over much for young girls wearing expensive jewels. Mama says they detract from our natural appearance. Anne, Bennetta and I all received a pearl necklace on our eighteenth birthday and we have small pieces - garnets, peridots, amethysts for wearing in the evening. Anne likes to borrow Mama's emeralds when she has the chance, but I fear they do not suit my personality."

She glanced back to make sure James was still in attendance as the crowds parading through the Arcade were growing larger, and frowned as she saw him stopping to talk to a young woman, wrapped in a vivid red cloak, standing in a doorway. She beckoned him and he hastily took up his position once more but before she could reprimand him, Celeste said,

"Oh, emeralds would look wonderful worn with a dress made from this white silk with this beautiful silver embroidered pattern!" She had moved on to the next store where quantities of rich materials were for sale. "Look at the intricate work, Jane."

"It is indeed quite beautiful but I wonder how long it took some poor girl to produce such a fine piece of material. Can you imagine the strain of embroidering with silver thread for hour upon hour?"

"My dear Celeste, with your dark eyes and hair, you would look like a princess in a gown of white silk!"

The girls spun round, dropping hasty curtsies as they realised Andrew Moore and Archer Maitland were standing behind them, bowing, their hats in their hands.

"Andrew! Dr Moore, why what a surprise to meet you here."

Jane flicked a quick sideways glance at her cousin. Her voice sounded odd; almost as if she was acting the part of being surprised and she suddenly wondered if Dr Moore had been the person who had mentioned the Burlington Arcade and that he could be found there shopping at a certain time of day.

"I am here to purchase another trunk for my journey out to Greece," Andrew said with a beaming smile, offering Celeste his arm. "Please, do come and help me choose which one to buy. A lady's opinion is always of great value. I have a perfectly good suitcase but Archer says it is a disgrace and will fall apart before I reach the ship that will carry me to France and overland to Greece."

They walked further down the Arcade and Jane could do nothing but follow with Archer at her side, James following a discreet distance behind them. Jane waited for her companion to speak but he was silent and at last she could bear the silence no longer. A few months ago she would never have spoken first, but that timid girl seemed to have disappeared since her stay in Dorset.

"I am surprised to see you indulging in such a frivolous pastime as shopping, Mr Maitland. I thought you would be hard at work in your office, righting wrongs and making laws."

"I am not yet in a position to make laws, Miss Jane, and believe me, I have nothing against shopping when there is a purpose to it, a goal to be achieved. I fear that like most men, I do find the endless gazing into windows with no intention of purchasing any of the items on display very irritating."

Jane tried to suppress a smile but felt her lips twitching. She had so often heard her dear papa say exactly the same thing to her mama when they were out and about in town.

"You laugh at me, Miss! How unkind."

"No, no, I assure you, I am not laughing. Well, perhaps a little. I suspect most gentlemen have the same attitude as you do yourself, my father for instance. But you must admit you are all very useful for carrying packages and parcels. Poor James, here, has had to follow us around all morning without expressing a moment of annoyance, although I know he would much prefer to be back at Matlock House about his other duties."

Archer sighed and ran his fingers through his dark hair. "And I should be in my new offices, dealing with a several legal cases. I would be happy to show the place to you, and your sisters, of course, if you would care to call round one day. The rooms need attention, as does the furniture. You may have ideas that would be of help."

Jane hesitated: she wanted to say that surely it should be Anne alone he was inviting to see the place where he worked. It was Anne who would probably furnish and decorate it in a suitable elegant style. But, rightly or wrongly, she wanted to go, to have just this little part of his life entirely to herself, a memory she could bring out and savour in the dark days that lay ahead when he had married her sister.

Jane was just about to reply when - "Archer, pray come and give us a moment of your valuable time, my friend!" A shout from Andrew who was waving his hat above the heads of the crowd further down the Arcade: Celeste was hanging on his arm, laughing up at him with a smile that could only be called inviting. Several passers-by looked at the couple and walked on, seemingly shocked by her behaviour.

The Italian girl looked happier than she had done for days and Jane felt a quiver of disquiet. Why was Celeste behaving in this flirtatious way with Andrew when she was already spoken for by Colonel Fitzwilliam? It was scandalous and the Colonel would be so upset and hurt by his future wife making such an exhibition of herself.

Why, only that morning she had received a letter from her godfather, stating that he was making a good recovery, as was Susannah, and that they were planning to travel up to London very soon where he would tell the whole family his good news. How dreadful it would be if he arrived to find Celeste and Andrew involved in a flirtatious fashion.

"It pleases me to see Andrew so happy," Archer murmured. "He is a good man but sometimes I feel he is lonely and deserves a companion to accompany and care for him through life."

Jane came to a sudden stop. "A companion? Through life. Marriage? Can you possibly mean Celeste, Sir?"

Archer shot her a sharp glance. "Indeed I do. Surely it is obvious to you that Andrew has strong feelings for your cousin?"

"But that cannot be! It is impossible."

His face darkened. "I am aware that Signorina Celeste is a member of the Fitzwilliam clan, albeit a distant one, but even if Andrew does not carry a title, surely your family would not treat him with disdain? He is a clever man with prospects to climb to the top of his profession, a man held in great esteem amongst his peers. It is rumoured that one day soon he will receive a knighthood for the work he does. He is to give a lecture at the Royal Society next year when he returns from Greece. That will bring him into even greater prominence."

Jane did not see his expression as she shook her head impatiently, unaware that her usually pale cheeks were now pink and flushed. "But they cannot marry! Celeste and Andrew? No, he must be dissuaded of such an idea."

Oh, how could she possibly explain the situation to him without breaking a confidence? How could she make Archer understand that she was more bothered about Andrew having his heart broken than Celeste. Once Colonel Fitzwilliam was in London, claiming her as his intended, the Italian girl would stop this silly behaviour. If she did have certain feelings for Andrew, Jane was quite sure that her cousin would deal quickly and firmly with any emotional upset. She was not a girl who would let heart ache linger for too long.

"Are you concerned that living in Greece in difficult conditions might prove too much for Celeste?"

"No, no, of course no." Jane was hardly listening to what he was saying: all she could think of was how upset her godfather was going to be if this turned out to be true.

"Then I can only surmise that you have more than your fair share of the Darcy pride that your sister talks of so eloquently. Andrew Moore might not be as socially acceptable as Archer Maitland but he is far the better man. I must admit I am disappointed in you, Miss Jane."

"Oh please, you do not understand."

"No, I don't. What is there to understand except the spectre of snobbery raising its head, just as it used to do when we were at school." He laughed, but it wasn't a happy sound. "I used to fight the boys who bullied Andrew because he was from a family they considered to be beneath them. As that is not an option here, I will just say that I fear we have nothing else to say to each other at this time, so I will bid you good-day!"

He bowed then walked swiftly along the Arcade, pushing though the crowds to where Andrew and Celeste were standing in a doorway conversing with the owner of a shop selling a variety of leather items.

Jane stood staring after him, realisation dawning as to what he thought she meant. Oh this was dreadful. That Archer should think she was the type of girl who put wealth and social standing before everything else that was important in life! For him to be disappointed in her was almost more than she could bear. She started after him, determined to explain, to beg Celeste to free her from her vow of silence when James spoke her name.

"Miss Jane." The young red-headed footman was looking anxious.

"James?"

"Miss Jane - look - this girl here - well, Miss, it is Grace Frost, Miss! You remember Grace, surely, Miss. She was a maid up at Pemberley. She begs a moment of your time, if you please."

Jane cast a despairing glance after Archer, to find that he had obviously made his farewells to the others and was disappearing at a fast stride towards the entrance of the Arcade. There was no way she could reach him now.

She turned her attention to the girl leaning against the pillar between two shops. James was quite right, the dark hair might be hidden under the hood of her red cloak, but Jane recognised the bright blue eyes of their former maid whom she had known for years whilst she was growing up.

Why Grace had left Pemberley so quickly a few months ago was a question that had once intrigued her. Working for the Darcy family was considered the pinnacle of achievement for most servants in Derbyshire and the surrounding counties. She had idly inquired once and her mama had told her that Grace had taken a position in the London household of the great artist, Edmund Avery, who had spent a few weeks in Pemberley that spring, painting a portrait of the Darcy children.

"Grace Frost! My goodness, to see you here in London. How are you keeping? I trust I find you well?"

"Miss Jane." Wrapped in the red cloak, the girl dropped a small curtsey. She looked - Jane frowned - if she hadn't thought she was being over dramatic, she would have said the girl looked scared. Her face was very pale and the plump rosiness of her cheeks that Jane remembered had quite vanished.

"Are you enjoying working for Mr Avery? Such a clever man. The portrait he painted of us children was remarkable. It is not yet on show at Pemberley - I think Papa is still deciding where it should be hung. But tell me, are you enjoying your life in London? I imagine you must see a lot of interesting and important people coming to his studio?"

"I'm... I'm not working for Mr Avery any more, Miss Jane."

"Oh! You didn't stay there very long, Grace. Is it wise to move around from position to position so quickly? Or perhaps that is what happens here in London? I must admit it is a long way from Pemberley and our quiet country ways."

"I was hoping.... that is... I was hoping..." She cast a glance towards James who was gazing at her with disapproval. People were pushing past and the mid October day was beginning to feel colder as the sun dropped lower in the sky.

Jane suddenly realised that the girl was reluctant to talk in front of James. She could understand that: the footman was not yet eighteen and Grace was probably worried that he would gossip about her once he returned to Pemberley.

"James, there is no need for us all to stand here, blocking the Arcade in such a fashion. I wish to speak to Grace, so take the parcels and accompany Signorina Celeste back to the carriage, then return here. I will wait for you. I know you have strict instructions not to leave me alone on the streets of London, although I am not sure exactly what Mama thinks will happen to me!"

James hesitated, then nodded and hurried away up the Arcade. He had a very good idea what Grace was going to say to Miss Jane and, if he was honest, he didn't want to be around to hear it. He'd never had any time for the arrogant young maid when she worked at Pemberley, but he hated to see how far she had fallen.

"Now Grace, what is it you want to say to me? Do you perhaps have messages for your family and friends back home? I will soon be returning to Derbyshire so when I do - " She stopped, startled into silence for Grace, unable to put her plight into words, had let the cloak fall back from her shoulders and Jane could immediately see the swelling of her stomach.

"Grace! You are married - no! - you wear no ring - oh Grace. Whatever has befallen you?"

The girl hastened to pull the cloak back around her, almost glaring at the pity in Jane's voice. She had been reluctant to approach any of the Darcy family once she heard they were in London. The same pride that had led her to believe Edmund Avery's honeyed words during the weeks he stayed at Pemberley, that she was as good as any of the cousins who visited the family, that had

let her think that allowing him to use her as model for some of his more sala-
cious paintings would guarantee her a place in his heart, had almost stopped
her from asking for help, now she needed it so badly.

She had been begging on the corner of Oxford Street when she had seen
Jane and another young lady step down from the Darcy carriage, with James in
attendance. If it had been Mrs Darcy or the horrible Miss Anne, she would
have walked in the other direction, but Miss Jane had always been kind, a soft-
hearted girl, only too happy to pass on little items of clothing she no longer
had a use for. Surely she would offer some help.

"It's a long story, Miss Jane. Life has struck me a cruel blow. I thought I was
secure in a certain gentleman's affections, but when I told him about - " she
gestured at her stomach - "this, he laughed, said it was nothing to do with him,
that I was no better than a common.... person.... and threw me out of the
house."

Jane closed her eyes as the Arcade spun around her: she felt faint and would
have given a gold guinea for a glass of water. Then she forced herself to look at
the poor girl in front of her, defiantly clutching the edges of her cloak together
to hide her shame.

But why was it just her shame, she found herself thinking? Surely Mr Avery
must take his share of responsibility? Jane was not completely sure exactly
what happened between two people to make a baby, but having lived in the
countryside all her life, she was more aware of the facts involved than many of
her town bred friends.

"Mr Avery must listen to reason," she began, "perhaps I can get my papa to
speak to him, to provide for you and the child."

"No! I want no one else to know what has happened. It is enough to bear as
it is without knowing that everyone at Pemberley, people who think that I am
living a good life here in London, would know it has all turned to dust and
grief."

"But Grace - " Jane hesitated, bewildered. "Money - is it a question of
money? But where will you go? Where will you live until... until..."

"The baby comes?" Grace laughed bitterly. "You can say the word. That's
the one thing that I do know is going to happen. There'll be a baby. And yes,
Miss Jane, it is a question of money. I have an aunt who lives on a farm down in
Devon - she has agreed for me to go there but she wants twenty guineas. I have

saved ten, but there is no way I can find the rest before I am unable to work or beg in the streets."

"Twenty guineas!"

"We will need to pay the midwife when the time comes, and then there's my keep when I can't work, but I will gain a position as soon as I possibly can. There is a very fine family who live in the same valley as my aunt's farm. I am sure they will have use of a good maid."

"Grace, surely it will be far better if you go home. If I remember correctly, you have a family in a village near Pemberley. Go to them, explain what has befallen you, they will surely take you in."

Grace shook her head. "No, I will never shame them in that way. That is one thing I can do right. No, I'm going to Devon and only hope you can see your way to letting me have some money from your own funds, Miss Jane. And to promise me not to tell your parents or sisters what has occurred."

Jane hesitated: she knew she should not promise anything of the sort, but Grace looked so unhappy. As an unmarried mother she would now be cast out of decent society. "Do you intend to keep the child or give it up?"

Grace tossed her head and for a second, the old, arrogant expression she used to wear crossed her face. "I am keeping it, Miss, I'm not putting it in some workhouse orphanage. We'll manage somehow. My aunt will care for it whilst I work, but only if I can give her the twenty guineas now."

Jane nodded reluctantly, torn as to what was the right course of action. "I'll keep your secret, but I do not think that is the right thing to do. I wish you would let me tell my mother - no, do not get distressed, I can see you would rather I didn't. But I do not have that amount of money with me. Where are you living, Grace? I will send it round to you within the next few days."

Grace's hand shot out and clutched Jane's arm. "No, tonight, I must have it tonight. There is a fruit wagon heading down to Devon from Covent Garden tomorrow and I can travel free if I'm there early enough. Here!" She pushed a grubby piece of paper into Jane's hand. "I share a room in this boarding house. 'Tis the other side of Westminster Bridge. Not far. Please, Miss, please try and bring me as much as you can spare. For the baby's sake."

And with a swirl of scarlet cloak, she turned and vanished into the crowds of passers-by.

CHAPTER 13

A rcher Maitland was cursing himself for a fool, a mutton-headed idiot of a fool! He tossed a coin to the small boy holding the horses, told him to wait with Andrew's mount and swung himself up into the saddle. He had stormed away from Jane Darcy, in great danger of losing his temper and saying words he would later regret.

But her reluctance to see Celeste as a suitable wife for Andrew had upset him. His friend was a good man, clever, kind-hearted, generous. So he was not from some titled or rich family, but would one day no doubt be honoured in his profession with a knighthood. But obviously that was not enough for Miss Jane Darcy to welcome him into her family circle!

As he trotted through the crowded streets, back to his offices, he realised he would not have been surprised if Anne had similar views - that was part of her damnable Darcy pride and vanity - but he would never have believed Jane could feel the same way.

Well, it was a hard lesson for him, well learned. Women were impossible to understand and in future he would keep his emotions under control. Because he knew he had been in danger of losing his head, forgetting that it was Anne his grandmother wanted, indeed insisted he marry, and picturing himself in the future with Jane at his side as his wife.

Which was ridiculous! How could he have fallen in love with a quiet, unassuming girl, a delicate creature, who expected to be cared for? Anne in comparison was all elegance, energy, wit and beauty - Jane was...

Jane had stolen into his heart and mind! And he refused to accept it! He would not give in to soft emotions such as love. His dear mother had married for love: a lowly lawyer who hardly made enough money to keep them in food and shoes. She had been cast aside by her very own family and even though she had seemed extremely happy with his father, as a young boy Archer had seen how she struggled to manage without all the comforts and servants that had surrounded her since she was born. And he had also seen how distressed his father had been as the years passed and his situation and salary did not alter.

It wasn't just the material things in life that had sometimes lowered her spirits. Mr Maitland had been a well-read, sensitive man, with a great love of poetry and music. But there was no meeting of minds between herself and the rest of his friends and colleagues. By self-education he had elevated himself above the social position he had been born to but, on his death, there was no one in their circle to whom she could turn for emotional and spiritual support.

Violet, his dear mother had been born a Goddard, with two very determined and opinionated parents. When his father had died, she could have returned to their home, if she had apologised for her marriage, but Archer knew she had stubbornly refused, although she had never prevented his contact with his grandparents. He had watched her wilt and fade away, missing his father more and more with every passing week until she joined him in the graveyard.

Archer was left knowing that marrying for love was a very dangerous thing to do. He would not make the same mistake: no, he would marry for convenience, marry the right woman, the type of woman everyone expected him to take as a wife.

He urged his horse forward, ignoring the shouts of pedestrians who were spattered with mud as he passed. Enough of this nonsense! He would propose to Anne Darcy just as soon as was possible and end this nightmare of roaring emotion.

❀

JANE WAS SORELY TEMPTED TO BREAK HER PROMISE TO GRACE AND CONFESS everything to her mother when she returned to Matlock House with Celeste.

She could hardly listen to her cousin's chatter about her many purchases, of how lucky they had been to meet with Andrew and Mr Maitland, of how exciting the good Doctor's expedition to Greece sounded, what a kind, clever gentleman he was. At last she vanished upstairs, vowing to try on all her purchases before dinner.

All Jane could think of was the terrible position in which Grace found herself. Whether the girl had brought this on herself was, at the moment, of no importance. Grace had been a servant at Pemberley for many years: in Jane's eyes that meant the Darcys were responsible for her. She would never have met Edmund Avery if she had not been a maid in their household whilst he was a guest.

If Mr and Mrs Darcy had been at home, Jane would have found it difficult to have kept silent, but they had gone with Anne to call on Mrs Caroline Tremaine, whom having lately been staying with Jane and Charles Bingley, had letters from them to distribute.

Bennetta was practicing her piano playing in the drawing-room and smiled mischievously at Jane when she asked why she had not gone with the rest of the family.

"La, you would never believe the headache I had after luncheon. I fear I was quite laid flat on my bed with a lavender compress on my temples and could not possibly have entertained the thought of visiting Mrs Tremaine!"

"You look quite well now!"

"Yes, it is amazing how quickly the pain went after the carriage left. I do believe that Mama would have joined me in my prostrate state, but she has too keen a sense of duty. I am quite sure she doesn't care greatly for Mrs Tremaine, but feels she must not offend dear Uncle Charles' sister and the thought of receiving a letter from Aunt Jane settled the matter."

"What time will they return?"

Bennetta idly picked out a little tune with one finger. "I believe they are asked for early supper, so not before eight, I imagine. Do go and take off your hat and cloak. I want you to help me with the guest list for the ball. Mama says we cannot have twice the number of men than women, but I think that is very unfair. You are certain of dancing every dance if there are more men than women.

"Anyway, I need your help to think of more girls to invite. I do wish Cassandra and Richard would come down from Derbyshire, but I cannot persuade them. Richard is always so busy with his patients and Cassie will not be parted from Victoria even for a few days."

"Anne will surely know a great many suitable young ladies. She is so often in town."

Bennetta banged several keys together in discord. "All Anne wants is Archer Maitland's acceptance of the invitation we sent him. Our sister is, I believe, more than interested in that gentleman. She told me this morning that his grandmother let slip a secret - she believes it probable that he intends to propose to Anne at our ball! So that will make a suitable climax to the proceedings."

"So it is all settled. They are to marry." Jane could hear her voice as if it came from a long way off. Bennetta glanced up at her sharply. She had long suspected that Jane cared a great deal more for Mr Maitland than his intended!

"Who knows? His father, I believe, was a gentleman, but of no account socially. But on his mother's side, the Goddards are an old and respected military family. His grandfather was an Admiral and there are generals and colonels going back generations. At least Archer has turned his back on becoming a soldier or sailor. He is ambitious, determined and, I imagine, a little ruthless."

She giggled. "You have to admit that sounds just like Anne, so I suppose they are a good match. What do you think of him? You were in his company a great deal down in Dorset, I believe, or so Celeste tells us. Do you find him handsome? I admit he is tall and broad shouldered but sometimes his expression is so very dark. Is he a worthy husband for our sister?"

Jane muttered something under her breath, then said she had to change her shoes and left the room, blinking back tears she refused to shed.

Bennetta returned to her piano practice and moodily played a little waltz tune. She didn't like to see Jane upset but surely she could not have feelings for Archer Maitland. Only weeks ago she had been head over heels in love with Digby Frobisher! It was all very confusing.

She sighed: sometimes she wondered if this was all life had to offer her. She was eighteen years old and did nothing except enjoy herself, arrange balls and watch as those around her got married and began new lives.

She thought of her cousin Miriam, sailing away from England with Nicholas, her sea captain. They could be anywhere in the world by now, having all sorts of adventures. And all she had to think about was the order of dances for her next entertainment!

Bennetta pushed her hands through her dark curls, absently pulling out her pins and ribbons. She wanted to do something dramatic, wanted to make a difference in the world about her, but she had no idea how.

Thoughtfully, she crossed the room to a desk and perused the list of possible invitees to the ball. She had always prided herself that she had been partly responsible for her cousins, Cassandra and Catherine, finding happiness with their husbands. Well, if she was doomed to spend the rest of her life making sure the right people married each other, then she might as well do her best for her favourite sister.

Bennetta had noticed that sometimes gentlemen reacted well to a touch of jealousy. Her parents would not be pleased; but as the list had already been approved, they would not know until the night in question. She picked up her pen and carefully added the name Digby Frobisher to those to be invited.

Jane hurried up to her room, pushing all thoughts of Anne and Archer to the back of her mind. She had the rest of her life to grieve for a love she could never have. Grace Frost had to be her main concern at the moment.

Luckily, she had a small amount of money put safely away in a drawer. There was certainly not the twenty guineas that Grace had mentioned, but it was all she had. Wrapping it carefully in a silk square, she sat on her bed for a moment, trying to gather her thoughts into some sort of semblance.

If her mother had been at home she would have gone to her and explained. She had often heard Elizabeth Darcy discussing the plight of unmarried mothers with her Aunt Jane. They both felt strongly that it was wrong when all the blame was placed on the shoulders of the poor girls concerned and none on the men who had obviously played their part!

Why, only this August, when an Act had been passed in Parliament, forbidding the keeping of slaves in parts of the British Empire, she had heard her mama say to her father that it was a pity that the same sense of care could not be offered to young women who fell from grace.

Yes, her mother would have gone with Jane to find Grace. She might not have given her money, but she would have had a plan to make her life easier. Well, she wasn't here and tomorrow would be too late because Grace would have vanished into the depths of the country to an unknown fate and future. No, it was up to Jane to at least pave her way with a few miserable guineas.

Hastily, she changed her embroidered velvet cloak for the plain, sensible one she wore when visiting the poor, donned a pair of sturdy boots and casting aside her blue feathered hat, she found a disgraceful, squashed, old bonnet that had been left on a shelf for many years.

There was no doubt in her mind that her parents would be horrified if they knew what she was about to do and, even more importantly, they would be distressed. To venture out into town without anyone knowing where she was going - she could not think of another time she had ever done such a thing, could not remember a time when she was growing up when she would have even dreamt of doing anything so foolhardy.

She fastened the bonnet strings tightly under her chin. The days of her being scared and compliant had vanished when she had gone to the Green Man to rescue Tabitha without asking anyone's permission!

For a moment or two she was tempted to ring for James and require him to accompany her, but she resisted. Even if she made it clear to her parents that she had ordered the young footman to do her biding, she knew they would see it as a dreadful dereliction of his duty. They would expect him to refuse, to at least tell the housekeeper what had transpired. And if he did go with her, then he could easily lose his position as a result.

No, it was best that she and she alone took on the responsibility of her actions.

Matlock House lay peaceful and quiet as Jane crept down the stairs. The servants were using the Darcys' absence for several hours as a chance to rest, so the footman who was usually on duty in the hall was sitting contentedly drinking tea in the kitchen. From the drawing-room she could hear the sounds of Bennetta's piano playing. In seconds the latch to the front door was lifted and she was out on the street.

Archer Maitland had no idea why he had ridden back to his offices, dismounted, handed his horse over to the groom in charge of the nearby stables, then immediately taken the reins back and swung himself into the saddle once more.

He had headed back across the city in the late afternoon towards a quiet square which seemed far away from the noisy, bustling streets full of carriages, carts, hawkers crying their wares, muffin men, hot chestnut sellers, beggars, ladies of dubious intent and pickpockets lurking, waiting for opportunities to come their way.

Dusk was falling - mid October and it was already nearly dark. He had no plan of what he intended to do once he reached Matlock House. He would call on the Darcys, perhaps repeat the invitation to Anne and Bennetta that he had already given Jane - to inspect his new offices and suggest improvements in furnishings and fittings.

If he saw Jane - he would apologise for leaving her so abruptly in the Arcade. He was anxious that they remain friends, even if they could never be anything more.

The pale perfection of her face, her eyes the blue of the sky in early morning, the fair hair that fell like spun gilt across her shoulders, all cascaded through his mind until he realised with a jolt and an automatic tug on the reins that brought his mount to a halt that the reality was within his view.

Jane Darcy was hurrying down the steps outside Matlock House and, pulling her cape hood over her head, she walked swiftly towards the hansom cab rank that stood in one of the streets leading into the square.

Archer stared after her in consternation. Of course there was no reason she should not be out on some perfectly acceptable errand. It was only late afternoon - an appointment with a dress-maker, perhaps - a sudden shopping trip to buy more embroidery silks, or paints for her landscapes? But if so, where was her maid or footman?

He knew only too well, from all Anne had told him and from what he had gathered from his own observation of the situation amongst the Darcy family, that Jane was cossetted and guarded in a way that neither of her sisters would ever have countenanced.

Inadvertently his spurs touched his mount's side, and it bucked and circled crossly, as he realised she might well be on her way to some assignation! He knew Frobisher was in town, had heard him mentioned in his club only the other evening. Could Jane possibly have an appointment to meet the man who had broken her heart?

He urged his horse forward, his hooves silenced by the sand laid down on the roadway to deaden the noise of carriage wheels. A hansom cab pulled out of the rank and Archer urged his horse into a trot to keep it in sight, a grim expression on his face. He knew it shouldn't matter to him where the wretched girl was going but also knew that it did and that he could no more turn round and forget about her than fly through the air like a bird.

The traffic in the streets was heavy and Jane's hansom made slow progress down to the river but eventually as dark was falling, she was glad to see they were crossing Westminster Bridge, the dark river flowing deep and silent beneath them. There were still plenty of small boats out on the water, lanterns beginning to show green and red, pointing their position and speed.

She peered out from under the canopy and looked back to where the bulk of the Houses of Parliament, Lords and Commons, were outlined against the dark blue of the October sky. It was a magnificent sight and one she had never seen before from this side of the Thames. Little wisps of cloud seemed to float across her vision and then they turned off the bridge and the view was lost.

The horse picked up speed on the other side of the bridge and it only took minutes until they turned down a street running parallel to the river bank where old boarding houses leant against each other, looking dirty and run down with several of their windows broken. The street seemed to be empty, but it was hard to tell because the shadows around the houses were so deep.

With shouts to his horse, the cab driver pulled up in front of one. "This 'ere is the address you showed me, Miss. But it's no place for a lady, especially not one on her own."

"Thank you for your concern, Sir, but I shall be quite all right. If you would kindly wait for me." She didn't wait for him to dismount from his box and help her down, but turned impatient to reach Grace, feeling for the step with her foot.

Then Jane felt hands grip her waist and with a shriek of fear, she was lifted clear of the hansom and, struggling and kicking, found herself clasped in Archer's arms that were holding her so tightly she was sure she would never breath easily again.

"Miss Darcy! Jane! What in God's name are you doing here in this place? Are you mad?"

"If you will unhand me, I might be able to reply," Jane gasped, gazing up into the face she loved so much that was now dark with anger.

He loosened his grip, although slowly, as if reluctant to let her go.

"Oi! Are you all right, Miss? Is the gent bothering you?"

A flicker of a smile twitched Archer's mouth. It seemed that even a hansom cab driver would protect this girl.

"Thank you, I am quite all right. I know the gentleman. I am quite safe in his care."

Archer handed over a pocketful of silver to the man who was still gazing down at him, his expression doubtful. "I thank you for your concern. You need not stay. I will convey the young lady home on my horse."

With muttered thanks, the driver flicked his whip and the cab took off down the street.

"Miss Jane?" A hoarse whisper sounded from the shadows at the side of the house. "Who's that with you? Not the Peelers?"

"Grace? Yes, I have come as arranged. Don't be alarmed. This gentleman is certainly not a policeman. I promise he will not harm you."

The girl stepped out into the street, still wearing the scarlet cloak, gazing apprehensively at Archer.

"This is Mr Archer Maitland, a friend of our family - this, Sir, is Grace Frost who used to be in our employment at Pemberley. She came to London, having been promised a good life by a certain gentleman but, alas, was lied to, misled and treated ill. I have brought her a little money so she can travel down to Devon, to her aunt."

She held out the parcel of guineas and with a soft thank you, Grace shot out her hand to take it.

Archer understood immediately what was happening. He could not but admire Jane for her good intentions, her lack of condemnation and her bravery in coming to this dubious part of town on her own.

"Can we help in any other way, Miss Frost."

Jane bit back a gasp at the use of the word "we". He was allying himself to her and she was almost overcome with the joy that gave her.

"The - man - concerned. Do you wish us to ask him for support for the child in the years to come?"

Grace fingered the guineas that were now deep in her pocket. She coughed and her eyes watered, something was stinging them. She stared into the gentleman's face: did he really believe that the famous artist, Edmund Avery, a well-known, popular figure about town, would admit to being the father of her child?

She coughed again, thinking bitterly that if this had happened to her whilst they had been together at Pemberley, then perhaps a case could have been made. But even then he would probably have sworn his innocence and insisted that she had lain with Archie Biggs, the head groom she had been walking out with or one of the footmen or even his own valet. It wasn't, after all, an action that usually had many spectators!

"It is mortal kind of you, Sir, but I think not. I want nothing more to do with the devil and me and my child will do better without any connection to him. Now, you had better take Miss Jane home. It grows dark." She coughed again and suddenly all three of them were coughing as the air seemed to swirl with acrid smoke.

Archer was about to reply that yes, it was getting dark, when he realised that was a lie. Above the rooftops, the sky towards the river was no longer dark blue but tinted with red and orange light that reflected up against the clouds. And now the air was thickening even more as thicker smoke blew towards them and faintly he could hear a weird rumbling thunder.

"There's a fire! A big one, I fear, but it's on the far side of the river, I think. You should be in no danger, Grace, but stay outside, just in case it spreads. Quick, Jane, put this across your nose and mouth. I need to get you home. Your parents will be distraught that you are out."

He tore off his cravat and Jane buried her face in the soft material. Then, with a gasp, she realised he had mounted his horse and was bending to pluck her off the street and swing her up behind him in a flurry of petticoats. Automatically she wrapped her arms round his waist as he urged his mount into a trot and headed back towards Westminster Bridge.

But even as they reached it, Archer realised they couldn't cross: soldiers were already being stationed to keep people away. Hundreds were gathering along the river's edge, staring across the Thames to where it seemed the end of the world was happening.

The crowd was oddly quiet, disbelieving what they were witnessing. On the far bank of the Thames, the great ancient buildings of the Houses of Lords and Commons that had been there for all their lives were ablaze in an inferno of dreadful heat. Vast spirals of angry orange and yellow flames leapt into the dark sky, smoke billowed, sparks flew in showers of gold and crimson and you could hear the ominous roar of the fire sounding like some evil dragon even with the breadth of the river between them.

The rapidly flowing water was stained with all the colours of the flames above, so that the shiny black ribbon changed into a kaleidoscope of gold and scarlet, orange and brown.

Archer dismounted and swung Jane down to stand beside him. Without thinking, he wrapped his arm round her shoulders, to hold her tight, scared that in this crush she could well be trodden under foot if people suddenly decided to move forward and he was scared she would be pushed down the embankment towards the water.

"It's the Houses of Parliament!" Jane whispered, her voice muffled by his cravat that she still wore over her nose and mouth. "Oh what a tragedy! I have never seen anything so dreadful. What can possibly have caused this?"

There was a long rumbling sound, distant thunder as another part of a roof gave way and great timbers, already blazing, were hurled into the sky, some of them crashing down to sizzle in the river below. There were shouts and screams as some of the small boats that had foolishly been rowed close to the bank for a closer look, caught fire from falling brands and their occupants were forced to leap into the water. Their screams as they splashed, some swimming for safety, some drowning in plain sight caused Jane to hide her face against Archer's shoulder. It was a scene straight from a picture book of Hell.

Even from a distance, Jane could feel the searing heat and Archer's horse moved restlessly, anxious to be away from the inferno that was hungrily consuming all that lay in its path.

"I need to get you home, Jane," Archer said at last, tearing his gaze away from the dreadful scene. "We cannot cross the river here, we need to head upstream. Eventually we will find another bridge open."

"If you can just accompany me to the other side of the river, Sir, I am sure I can get a cab to take me home. There is no need for you to worry."

"Jane! If you think for one moment that I am going to allow you to roam around London on your own again, then you are very much mistaken. I'm sure you thought you were doing the right thing for that poor girl, but it was incredibly foolhardy. Anything could have happened to you in that part of town and no one would have known where you were. What would you have done when you saw the fire? You could have been trampled in the crush. I am sure many people suffered that fate tonight."

He helped her back onto the horse and she silently accepted his assistance, aware that he sounded angry. She was well aware that he had every right to be so. This was the second time he had rescued her from danger - well, the third, she cautioned herself honestly, if one counted the time on the top of the cliffs!

She supposed that he was thinking that Anne would not have acted in such a way. That she would have consulted their mother and let her deal with Grace Frost. But Jane knew Anne would have done no such thing. She would have completely ignored Grace and the terrible situation she was in. Jane had no doubt that her twin's reaction would be that the girl had caused her own downfall by being wanton.

That might have been the case, but it was not up to Jane to judge. She remembered an old saying of her dear Nanny Chilcot who had looked after them for so many years. "You can't put the honey back in the comb". That was the situation with Grace. There was a baby on the way and what happened next to the girl was in some aspects more important than what had happened to cause the child to exist in the first place.

Her own feelings of anger began to surface. She wanted to say that she had not asked him to follow her to Grace's home tonight or to rescue her from the crowd at the Green Man. Archer was here of his own volition, so blaming her was wrong. Surely there was no need for him to be so irritable, especially when such a tremendous tragedy was taking place in Westminster.

She could only hope that no one was hurt but she knew that was not a realistic thought. With such crowds, excited and scared, all sorts of crimes could have been committed. Pickpockets and cut-throats would use the fire as a perfect cover for their heinous activities. She prayed that Grace had had the sense to stay back from the crowd. It would have been most inadvisable in her condition to be pushed around by a mob of people.

Archer was fighting down his temper, trying to stay calm, to concentrate on getting the girl away from any danger and safely home to her parents. When all the while he wanted to shake her, to demand to know why she insisted on putting herself into these alarming situations. He wanted to make her see that she could have been attacked by footpads, robbed, injured - his imagination had her bound hand and foot and taken on board ship, a victim of the white slave trade! He wanted her to promise him most faithfully that she would never, ever do anything like this again.

Whispering at the corners of his indignation was a voice that told him her future behaviour was not his concern. Jane Darcy was to be his sister-in-law, she would owe him nothing but family affection and that was all he would be forced to show her in return. He felt a twist of pain in his stomach, caused no doubt by the thick smoke that still billowed around them.

The journey back to Matlock House was slow, so many people were hurrying in the other direction, all noisy exclamations, crowds anxious to see the fire. But at last they were trotting under the trees of the Square and there was the house in front of them, every window ablaze with light.

Jane winced with weariness and aching limbs as she half slipped, half fell from her perch behind the saddle onto the ground. Once more Archer's arms held her and for a long moment they stood, silent, in the shadow of the trees. She lifted her face to his and he traced a line across her cheek to her lips.

"Soot!" he muttered hoarsely. "But still beautiful." And then he was kissing her, at first softly, then with a terrible hunger that brought her hands up to his head, tangling her fingers in his hair as she returned his embrace, straining against him, wanting nothing more but to be as close to him as she could.

At last they broke away and with a shudder, Archer pushed her away. "Go indoors, Jane. Quickly. I will not apologise for kissing you, although I know it was indefensible. Let's just call it a fitting end to a nightmare evening."

CHAPTER 14

B y the end of October, the excitement caused by the great fire had faded a little, although the vast ruins were still being inspected and removed. Blame and recriminations were bandied about but nothing would bring back the wonderful old buildings. Speculation was rife as to how the Houses of Parliament would be restored and it was rumoured that a competition was to be announced, so that architects could submit their plans.

In all the upheaval of that dreadful event, Jane's arrival home that night, minus bonnet, her hair tangled, eyes reddened by tears that had mingled with the black streaks across her face, had gone almost unnoticed. Yes, she had been missed, but when reports of the fire had reached Matlock House, all the servants who were not on duty had rushed out to head for the scene, gaze and exclaim and somehow it had been accepted that Jane had gone with them, unnoticed, to view the fire for a short while.

She was glad that she hadn't had to give an explanation of her absence. She had never been good at twisting the truth to her own advantage. But luckily her parents had been engrossed by the tragedy. Anne had not the slightest interest in what she was doing and only Bennetta looked puzzled when Jane said the following day that she was very tired and would keep to her room and have her meals sent up on trays.

"A nightmare evening!"

All Jane could hear ringing in her ears as she paced her room were those words that Archer had spoken. All she could feel was the warmth and pressure of his lips on hers, and the look on his face as he had pushed her away. Almost an expression of despair, which was ridiculous. He had kissed her out of anger, out of the emotions the fire had raised in him.

She didn't blame him for one second. Obviously he felt despair: as a gentleman who was apparently in a close relationship with a young lady, kissing her sister in such a fashion would be unthinkable to his sense of honour.

No, she did not blame him, she blamed herself for responding! She burned with a shame, as hot as the flames she had witnessed, to remember the wanton way she had curled her fingers into his hair, pressing herself against him so tightly that she could feel his heart thundering through the silk of his shirt.

What must he think of her? The shame was great, but linked with the shame was the appalling realisation that if she had the chance, she would kiss him again! She loved him with every fibre of her being, she was burning up with the pain of a desire that she knew was a consuming love.

She buried her face in his cravat - she had clutched it in her hand all night long. What would he say when next they met? Did he realise how much she cared for him? Oh, she hoped not! To think of him as her brother-in-law, having to visit them in their home, sit with them at meal-times, engage in all the little intimacies of family life - it would have been hard to do if he thought her indifferent to him, but knowing she loved him, it would be intolerable.

No, the first thing she had to do was make it quite clear to him that she had no feelings of great affection for him. Once he was convinced of that, then her life would at least be a little easier, although the thought of having to stand for her sister at Anne's wedding to Archer brought her to the point of despair.

It was one thing to make a decision as to her course of action but it was another to carry it through. Although Andrew often called at Matlock House in the last days of October, by early November there had been no sign of Archer.

Jane finally plucked up her courage and casually asked Anne why they had not had the pleasure of his company. Her sister had shrugged and said he was extremely busy with different cases going through the law courts and not a man of leisure such as Dr Moore seemed to be.

Andrew's journey out to Greece had been delayed once again. An outbreak of cholera in Athens had stopped work on the ruins of the temple he was interested in exhuming and it had been decided he would not travel out there until the early Spring.

Celeste was delighted and made no effort to hide how she felt about the archaeologist, how delighted she was that they could spend more time in each other's company.

Even amidst her unhappiness over Archer, Jane found time to worry about her poor godfather. Colonel Fitzwilliam had written to say that he was now fully recovered and would be travelling up to London any day, before the bad winter weather set in. He was pleased to say that Miss Courtney was also in extremely good health and would be accompanying him.

"Poor Susannah, she has been away from home for far longer than she imagined," Elizabeth Darcy said as she read the Colonel's letter at the breakfast table.

"So have we, my dear." Mr Darcy folded *The Times*, laid it next to his plate and began examining the pile of letters that had just been brought in by a footman. "But I suppose we cannot go home until the girls have given this dance they are so excited about. Would cancelling it be an option?"

"Papa! I know you are joking, but please do not even say such a thing." Bennetta waved her knife in her father's direction, oblivious to the honey dripping onto the tablecloth. "The invitations have all been sent and everything is arranged. It will be my last excitement until you force me back to the quiet of Pemberley."

"Really, Bennetta, you make it sound as if your home is some dark and dismal prison," Elizabeth said crossly.

Celeste looked up from a letter she had received, smiling. "Oh, I am longing to see Pemberley, Cousin Elizabeth. I cannot wait until we go north - although I am looking forward to the ball as well, naturally."

Jane couldn't help but say, "But surely you are most anxious to see Colonel Fitzwilliam once more. Do you not long to be back at Deerwood Park?"

Celeste looked surprised. "But of course I wish to see the dear Colonel. He has been so good to me. No one could have been more welcoming when I arrived in England."

Jane fell silent. She wished Celeste would not look at her with that innocent expression. She must know that flirting with Andrew, giving him the impression that he meant a great deal to her, was wrong when she was still engaged to the Colonel? Perhaps in Sicily they managed their relationships in a different fashion, but no matter why she acted as she did, the Colonel was still going to be hurt.

"Oh, this is a surprise indeed - an invitation from Lady Goddard!" Elizabeth had opened another envelope and smiled round at her daughters. "Well, Anne, I am sure we have you to thank for this. Lady Goddard asks us to take tea with her this afternoon, if we are not otherwise engaged."

"Yes, Mama," Anne said complacently. "I called there a day ago and found her everything kind and obliging. She was very sorry not to see me in Dorset when she met Jane. I don't think you made a particularly good impression, Sister. Lady Goddard had no compliments for you, although she did say she had had an interesting conversation with our Italian cousin."

"Then I shall be quite happy not to go to tea with her," Jane replied with spirit.

Her mother glanced up at her tone. "The invitation is for all us ladies, and so yes, we will all go, you too Bennetta, so stop wrinkling your nose in that annoying fashion. Although I must admit I am very surprised to receive such a request. As far as I can recall, Lady Goddard was a great friend of your great-aunt, Lady Catherine de Bourgh and, as such, was heartily against my marriage to your papa! For over twenty years she has ignored the Darcys. Now we are invited to tea. It is all very mysterious but I imagine that a certain young lawyer is at the bottom of it all, although Anne keeps very silent on the matter."

"Mama, I cannot speak of it just yet, but believe me I do not think I will be sitting at *your* breakfast table this time next year."

"So has he asked for your hand or not?" Bennetta was getting tired of all the innuendo; she didn't know why people couldn't speak plainly about such matters.

"You are too young to understand," Anne replied in her usual haughty style, glaring at her sister who kicked her under the table.

"I am surprised, Mama, that you wish to have any contact with someone who thought your marriage wrong." Jane was trying desperately to think of something to take her mind off Anne and Archer becoming engaged.

Elizabeth smiled. "My dear Jane, your father and I had the few friends and acquaintance who wished us joy. The rest were of no consequence to us. Time passes and we must all forgive and forget. And, my dear," she turned her brilliant smile on her husband, "the esteemed lady is well aware that gentlemen find taking tea rather a waste of their valuable time, so she does not include you on the invitation."

Mr Darcy looked up from a letter he was reading. "I cannot say I am sorry, her lack of respect towards you still rankles, even after all these years. Perhaps I do not have such a forgiving nature as you. More news, Lizzy. Henry will be coming home on leave whilst his ship undergoes work at the docks in Portsmouth. He should be with us for Christmas, although his handwriting is so bad that it could be Easter! I fear the money we spent on that boy's education was completely wasted. I only hope the Navy will have instilled some sense into him. But it will be good to see him again. And Fitz will be home from college so all your chicks will be together in one roost for a few days."

"Really, Papa, I think comparing us to chickens is rude!" Bennetta said crossly. "But it will be good to see the boys again, especially Henry. He will have such a lot of news to tell us about life in the navy."

Jane was only half listening to her family's conversation. Tea at Lady Goddard's! Would Archer be there? Surely not. He would be at work in his law offices, or at the courts themselves. She wondered why the old lady had invited the Darcys after ignoring them for so many years? There was no avoiding the fact that it could only be because of Anne and Archer's forthcoming engagement.

'Lady Goddard probably wants to have a private conversation with Mama, to make sure that she and Papa are happy for the alliance to be announced.' Her thoughts were as heavy as her heart.

Oh if only it was over and done with! If only this dreadful ball was in the past and she could return to Pemberley and the quiet seclusion of the library and her beloved books.

But even as she thought that, she felt a surge of restlessness. She was no longer the same girl who had left Derbyshire for Dorset, who thought her heart had been broken because that ridiculous Digby had turned her head. She realised she had no desire to return to that quiet life where she was protected at every turn, kept away from the harsh realities of the world.

Jane glanced across the table at Celeste, who was re-reading a letter that had arrived that morning, a secret smile curving her dark red lips. How could she possibly stay for weeks with Colonel Fitzwilliam and Celeste when they married, knowing that Archer and Anne might arrive at his grandmother's house at any moment and she would be forced into their company, have to witness their happiness together?

But there was no avoiding the invitation to take tea; what possible excuse could she give? She was terrified that Anne should guess her feelings for Archer. How could they possibly have a happy family life with that secret between them? Anne might laugh: she might even tell her husband that his sister-in-law was in love with him. And that was not to be born. No, she would go to Lady Goddard's, she would smile and congratulate and lock away, deep inside her, all the passion and love she felt for Archer Maitland.

◈

LADY GODDARD'S LONDON ABODE WAS SITUATED NOT FAR AWAY FROM Matlock House in Mayfair. It was a smaller establishment than Robyns, set in a street of elegant little houses, well lit in the gloomy November afternoon by the new gas lights that had been fitted along the pavements.

She had ordered a fire to be lit in the drawing-room and was sitting, waiting for the Darcy party to arrive for tea, watching her grandson kick moodily at the smouldering logs.

"Do leave the fire alone, Archer, you will ruin your boots. Sit down and talk sensibly to me before our guests arrive. Andrew is tardy, as usual, but this gives us a chance to talk alone. We have important matters to discuss and you have been avoiding me of late."

He threw himself into a chair opposite her, his expression stern and remote. With his dark hair and eyes he reminded her, painfully, of the daughter she had disowned: that stubborn set to the mouth, the air of intransigence, all brought back bitter memories of Violet to the elderly lady.

"So, have you decided when you will propose to Miss Anne Darcy? If you are not careful, some other ambitious young man will come along and sweep her off her feet."

"Anne is not the sort of girl who would allow herself to be swept off her feet, Grandmama. She is far too sensible."

Lady Goddard sighed silently. "Very well then, she might think that she could do better with someone else. I like the girl, she is ambitious and clever, all qualities you will need in a wife when you go into politics."

"I am not sure if I still wish to enter politics, Grandmama. There is so much good I can achieve in the legal profession, people I can help, people who do not have the advantage of money and education. I feel that is where my future lies and I certainly do not wish to marry someone just because they are ambitious and clever."

Lady Goddard caught hold of her temper before she said something she would regret. "It has always been decided that your law career would lead you to the political arena where the real power lies in this country. The House of Commons is your destiny. Anne Darcy is elegant, beautiful and witty. I like her very much."

"I like her, too."

"Well, then...."

"But Grandmama, I do not love her."

"Love! What part, pray, does love play in your decision?"

"It should surely play the most important part."

Lady Goddard felt suddenly very cold. She was seeing and hearing a young woman, standing in this very room, many years ago dark eyes flashing, saying "But Mama, I love Mr Maitland and I intend to marry him whatever you and Papa say."

"Your mother married for love and lived a life of poverty and hardship. Remember, you would not have had the good education you had if your grandfather and I had not stepped in to help."

Archer bowed his head; sometimes endless gratitude could be very galling. "Believe me, I appreciate how kind you have been. And I know how much you like Anne."

Lady Goddard played with the long jet necklace that hung around her neck. "Perhaps there is another young lady who has come to your attention. To be sure, the girl Celeste is pretty, if flamboyant, and related to Earl Fitzwilliam. However, from what I have seen, dear Andrew has already made his feelings towards her clear and I cannot see you hurting him by taking her away."

"Celeste!" Archer almost shouted with laughter. "Dear Grandmama, please put that idea out of your head at once. I have no feelings towards Celeste at all."

There was no way Lady Goddard was going to mention Jane Darcy. She had spent too many years believing that if you ignore a problem it goes away. And she intended to ignore the possibility that Archer might prefer the younger twin. She would be so unsuitable as his wife, a pale shadow of her sister, a delicate creature who would probably die giving birth to any child they might breed.

She stood up in a rustle of black silk. "Archer - I can hear voices in the hall. Our guests have arrived. But let me say one thing more. I want you to be quite clear before you make any hasty decision. I wish you to marry Anne Darcy - I believe she is the right wife for you and will be of immense benefit in your future career. You are, of course, at liberty to choose someone else, someone of whom I do not approve. No - let me finish - " she said, holding up her hand as she heard the sound the footman outside the door. "In that circumstance, you will not be surprised to learn that I will withdraw all my monetary support for you. You will always be my beloved grandson, but I will not be party to you ruining the brilliant career I know could be yours."

Archer had no time to reply - which judging by the angry words that he wanted to speak, was probably a good thing. During the past few weeks he'd begun to realise the truth in Andrew's words - that for years, he had lived in a prison - oh a velvet one, no doubt, but still a prison. His life was easy and productive, but only as long as he agreed with the person who held the key to his cell.

He felt as if the very foundations of his world were cracking when a footman announced Mrs Darcy, Miss Darcy, Miss Jane and Miss Bennetta Darcy and Signorina Celeste Fiorette.

The room suddenly seemed full of bright colours that swirled and fluttered before him like so many butterflies as he bowed. He was aware of Anne in deep red with wide diaphanous sleeves, her hair style in the latest fashion with rolls of fair curls over her ears. She looked charming and beautiful, reaching out her hand to his, her eyes sparkling in the firelight.

Mrs Darcy was smiling at him and he could well see the attraction that had ensnared one of the richest men in the country twenty or more years before. Celeste greeted him like an old acquaintance and then there was Bennetta, pretty in dark green velvet, with shining black ringlets who looked up at him under thick lashes and whispered that she was so pleased to meet him once more in such a flirtatious tone that he found himself grinning. He could see that everything Jane had told him about her younger sister was probably true.

Then the doorway into the hall stood empty. Jane? She had been announced, so surely she had come with the others?

Two strides took him out into the hall, pulling the door shut behind him. A maid had taken her cloak but Jane had stopped to talk to Miss Purkiss, his grandmother's companion, who had been told her presence was not necessary at the tea party and had been heading for the sanctuary of her own room when the Darcys had arrived.

"Jane."

She spun round, colour flaming into her cheeks, remembering that the last time she had seen him, they had kissed with a passion that was outside her understanding. "Mr Maitland."

"Archer, please. I think we are long past the polite niceties of society."

"I am so sorry to have kept Miss Jane talking. I do hope I have not delayed tea. Lady Goddard will not be pleased." Miss Purkiss pulled worriedly at her necklace and then squeaked in horror as the thread broke, sending beads scattering across the hall floor.

"Oh dear, oh dear! No, no, dear Mr Archer, Miss Jane, please do not bother yourselves to pick them up... only a silly old necklace... no value... no value at all... one of the maids will help... oh, please, Lady Goddard will be wishing your attendance immediately... she will blame me for delaying you..."

Ignoring her, Archer scooped up a few beads and pressed them into her hands, remembering with a jolt how he had thought moments before about the pain of having to be continually grateful. Thanking him profusely, she turned and hurried up the stairs, still apologising as she went.

Jane was on her knees, groping for an errant bead that had rolled under a marble table. She gasped as Archer's hand fastened on her arm and he drew her to her feet. To her surprise she found he was smiling, his eyes full of humour.

"Jane, Jane, Jane. It must be your influence. No one else I know can cause such chaos in my life so easily!"

She felt her lips twitch in a smile against her will. "I assure you, Sir, it is not intentional." She realised his fingers were still grasping her bare skin - she felt they were burning, that she would bear the mark for ever. But she couldn't pull away. He was standing so close, the humour was dying from his gaze and she felt her head swim at the passion and love she read in his eyes. She longed to return it, but knew she had to hide how she felt. He must never know. Never!

"Jane - listen - I want to explain - you must realise that - I must know if you - "

The front door was flung open and Andrew strode in, bringing a gust of chill air and a scutter of dried autumn leaves.

"Archer! Miss Jane! I am damnably late. My most abject apologies. Is everyone in the drawing-room? Celeste, too, I hope." He flung his riding cape at a footman who had appeared from the back of the house. "Come, I must make my apologies to Lady Goddard and all the Darcy ladies."

He led the way into the drawing-room, just as Lady Goddard was ringing the bell for tea to be brought in. She accepted Andrew's apologies for his late arrival, nodded briefly in acknowledgement of Jane's curtsey, and gave Archer a long, considering stare.

"Andrew, I am sure Signorina Celeste would be delighted to see my collection of little miniatures in the cabinet. Pray show them to her. Archer, come and sit next to Miss Darcy. She wishes to hear all about what is planned for the rebuilding of the Houses of Parliament. A competition, it is rumoured. Seems like a waste of time, but then it will be a mammoth undertaking. Such careless-ness in allowing such destruction. I do hope someone will be severely punished."

Anne held out her hand, smiling as Archer took the chair next to hers on the far side of the room. Jane was only too aware of Lady Goddard's keen appraisal of her face as she found room on the sofa next to Bennetta. She had seen her expression harden as she and Archer had come into the room.

"You look quite flushed, Miss Jane," the old lady said. "I hope you do not have a cold coming. Is this daughter of a delicate disposition, Mrs Darcy?"

Elizabeth took a cup a footman offered her and waved aside the plate of little cakes. She frowned slightly: it was extremely impolite for a lady - even one with great age on her side - to ask such a personal question of a guest, especially with the object of her question sitting within hearing distance.

"She was perhaps not quite as robust as her sisters, Ma'am, when young, but she suffers no more from ill health than any other young lady of my acquaintance."

"Mama! How can you say such a thing. Jane is always the first to take cold and she suffers from bad headaches very often. I feel for her, indeed I do." Anne sounded as sincere as any sister should be.

"It is good of you, Lady Goddard, to be concerned for my health. I assure you, I am quite well. I was, perhaps, prone to childhood complaints more than my brothers and sisters," Jane broke in quietly, "but coming up to my twentieth birthday, I am no longer a child."

Archer gripped the handle of his teacup so hard he feared it would snap.

He quite well understood the undercurrent of his grandmother's question to Mrs Darcy. She was determined to point out that he needed a wife who was strong and Anne with her high colour and brilliant gold hair looked every inch the sort of woman who would shine at his side.

He glanced across the room to where Jane sat. Their eyes met and he felt the room tilt. She loved him! He could not be wrong. Every time she looked at him, he knew in his heart that his feelings were reciprocated. He found himself smiling. Strength came in various ways - the girl on the cliff top, admonishing the ruffians at the Green Man, travelling alone across London to help a pregnant maid - this was a quiet strength that Anne did not have.

"And do you have many beau, Miss Jane?"

"No, Ma'am, I do not."

Anne caught the question, turned from Archer and laughed. "Why Jane, there is no need to be so shy. We are all friends here. My sister has indeed a very faithful follower, Lady Goddard. A handsome gentleman from Cheshire. His name is Digby Frobisher."

Lady Goddard's stern features relaxed slightly. "And do you, Mrs Darcy, approve of this liaison? In my day, a young girl would never strike up a relationship without her mother's approval."

Elizabeth put down her tea cup. "I hope to approve of all my children's future wives and husbands, but it is their feelings that are important, not mine."

"What a very odd way of looking at the world. But I suppose, when you married Fitzwilliam Darcy, your own mother must have been delighted. She could never have expected such an advantageous match. My good friend, Lady Catherine de Bourgh, related the story of your pursuit of her nephew. I truly believe the horror of the match hastened her sad demise."

Jane never knew what her mother would have replied because Bennetta took a fit of coughing at that precise moment, gasping that she had drunk her tea too quickly. By the time she had been exclaimed over and made comfortable once more, the subject had luckily passed. But sitting next to her on the sofa, Jane knew quite well that her little sister had finished her tea many minutes before and that her cup had been quite empty.

Archer, who had come swiftly to Bennetta's aid, helping her to her feet and bringing her to cooler side of the room, returned now to sit down beside Anne again. In a low voice that could not be heard by the rest of the party he said, "You seem very sure of your sister's attachment to Mr Frobisher?"

Anne smiled. "Why yes, I am. I know my sister, Sir. We are not alike, except in looks in some degree, but as her twin I know when she is happy or sad. She and Digby had a silly falling out a few months ago, which I must admit, to my sorrow, was partly my fault.

"I was desperate that she wouldn't be hurt and so tested his feelings for her in a clumsy fashion. She was broken-hearted when they quarrelled. Her health suffered – why you must have seen that when you met her in Dorset. But since he has returned to London, she is happiness itself. I am quite sure we will be hearing of a proposal very soon. A quiet home in the beauty of the Cheshire countryside is just the style of life that Jane will enjoy. She is not a girl for cities and towns."

"She has seen him since his return?" Archer tried to sound as if he was just making polite conversation. Was this why Jane seemed to glow? He had thought.... hoped.... it was her feelings for him that caused her eyes to shine so brightly, but perhaps he had been deluding himself.

Anne hesitated. She thought Digby a stupid young man, whose only aim in life was to marry a young lady with her own fortune: the very fact that he had proposed to her instead of Jane proved that he was not constant in his affections, but if he was what Jane wanted, then she would do all she could to help the relationship prosper. Once she was married to Archer and they had a suitable London establishment, it would make no difference to her if her sister was living up north in faraway Cheshire.

"Not to my knowledge, but then Jane can be very secretive. I am sure they have been corresponding." She smiled and touched him lightly on the arm. "I myself have no time for the games that some lovers play, but I fear Jane is of a different disposition. She reads a great many romances – why she is hardly ever out of our library at Pemberley! She may well have mentioned to Mr Frobisher that she had met you and Dr Moore in Dorset, believing that a little jealousy can galvanize a gentleman into action."

"I see." Archer was silent for a minute or two, then with a bow, left the room, desperate for fresh air, trying to force his thoughts into order. Anne could surely not be wrong about her twin: she must know her better than anyone. Was he preparing to jeopardize his whole future for a girl who was not whom she appeared to be?

CHAPTER 15

L ady Goddard beckoned Jane to her side. "Your arm, if you please, Miss. I would take a walk around the room. At my age one grows stiff if you sit in one position for too long. No, do not disturb yourself, Mrs Darcy. Finish your tea. I myself do not eat a great deal, but I am sure your youngest will find those little lemon cakes enjoyable."

She cast a sideways look at Bennetta whose innocent glance from under her eyelashes did not fool her for a moment. The minx had pretended to choke so her mother had had time to regain her composure.

Lady Goddard admired the quick thinking and decisive action. She could see that at eighteen, the chit was already astoundingly pretty and was only grateful that she was not any older. She could tell that in lots of ways she was still a child, but one day, some poor man was going to have to deal with her. Lady Goddard was only grateful it would not be Archer.

Leaning on Jane's arm, she walked slowly to the far end of the long room where the windows looked out onto a small wilderness. It was dark outside now and only a few solitary lanterns lit the pebble paths that wound their way through the shrubbery.

"So your future may lie in the county of Cheshire, Miss Jane?"

Jane did not know how to reply. Yes or no - both sounded wrong. "None of us can see the future, Ma'am."

"Too true, girl, too true. Of course, we can always make an informed guess. Take my grandson, for example." She flashed a swift glance at her companion and saw the colour wash up and then down in her cheeks. "As you know he is a very successful lawyer."

"So I believe."

"But politics has always been his first love. I think once he enters Parliament, his career will soar. Why, you may even be able to boast in a few years' time that you took tea with the Prime Minister!"

"Indeed, I am sure all his many friends would be proud if that day should come."

"Yes, but I wonder if you are aware how difficult the path is that he has chosen to walk. Powerful men can be very lonely. Archer will need a certain type of woman at his side in the future. One who is as ambitious as he is himself. A woman who can charm and influence great men."

"I am sure that any woman your grandson chooses will be the right one."

Lady Goddard turned from the darkness of the window and continued to walk slowly back up the length of the room the black silk of her gown swishing across the floor like the hissing of a snake. "I have devoted my life to the cause of Archer's career. He has all the brains and ability needed to succeed, I have all the money."

Jane felt a little quiver of disgust. Surely service to your country was what was required in a politician. Why should money be a factor? But she was not so naive as to know that without backing, a gentleman stood no chance of succeeding in politics.

"It sounds like an ideal combination, Ma'am."

"That may well be the case, but I feel all his friends and acquaintance should know that I will only fund Archer's career if he marries wisely, if he marries a girl whom I think will help him advance in his chosen profession. If he chooses to marry someone else - " she cast a glance sideways at her companion's white, set face - "then I shall not give a penny piece to him from that day onwards."

Jane made no reply, indeed she could think of nothing to say that would not show her repugnance towards the elderly lady's attitude. She was, however, puzzled. Why was she being told this information? Could Lady Goddard possibly believe that Archer intended to marry her! How ridiculous. Everyone knew that Anne was his intended wife.

"I would like to think that anyone who considers themselves Archer's friend, would do all in their power to smooth his path. If, for example, you were a young lady who was totally unfit for the rigours of life as a politician's wife, then if you truly cared for my grandson you would give up all claim on him."

"And does Mr Maitland know of your decisions in this matter?"

"Indeed he does. I think I can safely say that Archer and I are in complete agreement regarding the situation. And now, here is my chair once more. Thank you for your arm, Miss Jane. Now, perhaps you would be kind enough to honour us with a few little tunes on the piano. I dismissed Purkiss for the afternoon and I think a little music before the afternoon comes to an end would be very agreeable."

She beckoned to Anne, who moved to her side and they began murmuring to each other, their voices too low for anyone else to hear.

Elizabeth Darcy glanced round the room, wishing heartily that she could just get up and leave. Bennetta's useful fit of coughing had saved her from saying something unforgivable to Lady Goddard. If Anne was to become Mrs Archer Maitland, then the two families would have to have at least an appearance of accord.

She sighed: she loved her eldest daughter dearly even though she irritated her a great deal. She saw all the faults that had been there in her husband's early character appearing once again and it seemed that however hard she tried, she could not eradicate them. And, what was worse, Elizabeth sometimes thought she could see a startling resemblance in Anne to her sister Lydia.

Not in looks or scandalous behaviour, of course. But the ruthlessness of putting yourself first, of obtaining what you wanted regardless of how it affected anyone else, allowed memories to surface of the young Lydia Bennet and all the shame she had nearly brought on her family.

Anne had decided to marry Archer but Elizabeth could not see that it would be a happy marriage. On the surface he seemed as hard-headed and ambitious as she was, but Elizabeth was not at all sure that was true. Her sharp eyes had caught sight of his face when he had entered the room with Jane earlier. His usually dark, saturnine face had been lit up, as if fired by some extreme emotion. But that expression had vanished when he spoke to Anne and his grandmother.

Surely he did not have feelings for Jane! She wondered, suddenly, what exactly had happened between them down in Dorset. Jane had said very little, but then she never did. If it had been Bennetta, then Elizabeth knew she would have had a word for word account of every conversation, but Jane had always kept her silence.

She relaxed a little as she glanced across to where the younger twin was standing beside the pianoforte as Archer entered the room once more and walked up to her and relaxed. There was no sign on Jane's face that she was delighted to be in his presence, that she liked him in any extraordinary way.

Then, once again, the past pushed its way into Elizabeth's mind and she was back at Longbourn, talking to her dear friend, Charlotte, now long departed this world, who felt that Jane Bennet should show Charles Bingley that she cared for him. Elizabeth had argued that it was not in her sister's character to do so and Charlotte had advised that the young man in question had no way of knowing that and might well feel that she was indifferent towards him.

She would have been glad of the opportunity to think more on the subject, but Celeste and Andrew Moore chose that moment to join her and conversation turned to what Greece would be like the spring and how Celeste longed for the sun once more.

Elizabeth smiled warmly at the couple: here at least was one relationship that was happy and straightforward.

⚜

ARCHER HAD WALKED THE LENGTH OF THE STREET AND BACK, GLAD OF THE cold night air on his face, fighting down his quick temper. With every fibre of his being he refused to believe that his feelings for Jane were not reciprocated, that she had been playing the dangerous game of jealousy between himself and Frobisher. He could recall, only too vividly, the kiss between them on the night of the fire. That had not been done to influence anyone. She had returned his embrace with all the passion he knew lay just beneath the cool calmness of her appearance.

No, until Jane told him in her own voice where her affections lay, he would not believe gossip or speculation.

Entering the drawing-room once more, aware of his grandmother, her gaze sharp, he crossed to where Jane was now standing, looking at sheet music lying on the pianoforte.

"Will you play for us, Jane?"

She looked up quickly and shook her head. "No, Sir. Not today. It is a fine instrument and I will not do it justice. Perhaps Anne will oblige you."

"She may well do so, if I ask, but I would prefer to hear from you."

There was another silence and he was aware that his grandmother was still watching them. He found himself saying in an abrupt fashion, "Anne has been telling me more of your attachment to Digby Frobisher, how he broke your heart earlier this year. I admit I had heard it mentioned by Celeste when we were all together in Dorset, but of course I did not enquire any further. I hope you are now fully recovered."

"Quite recovered, thank you."

"The gentleman in question is currently in town, I believe, perhaps anxious to renew his attentions. Is that the type of life that would suit you, Jane? Being married, living quietly in the country, much as you do at Pemberley, I imagine. Somehow you strike me as a young lady who needs more excitement than that."

His gaze caught and held her own and she reached down to grip the edge of the piano as the room spun around her. How easy it would be to tell him how she felt, that Digby had been a passing nonsense, that she had been flattered at coming before Anne in someone's affections, then realising that she would always be second. That half of her heartbreak had been because she had not fully believed her twin's explanation of her behaviour; consequently, she had felt betrayed by the two people she held most dear in life.

But that was impossible to say, just as she couldn't tell him that she could hardly bring Digby's face to mind, whilst Archer's, lived in her imagination every waking moment and came to her in her dreams as well.

Behind him, across the room, she could see Anne, smiling at something Lady Goddard had said. Her sister looked particularly elegant tonight in her new red dress. As Jane watched, she threw back her head and laughed. She was so happy. There was not a suspicion of doubt or worry in her manner. Throughout her entire life, Anne had always got what she wanted and her sister had no doubt that Archer must find her irresistible.

Why Lady Goddard felt that Jane could possibly be a threat to this happiness, she had no idea. Surely she hadn't shown by word or deed how she felt for

Archer? She had taken such care to control her face and her voice whenever she was in his company.

Pushing back the pain that threatened to overwhelm her, she realised that, if she could find the courage, this was her chance to make it clear to Archer that she had no feelings for him, except those of a would be sister.

"I find excitement greatly over-rated, Sir. If I am offered a quiet country life, I will accept it."

"I see." Archer's voice was harsh, his black brows drawn in a fierce line across his face. "I am surprised. You have given me the impression, especially of late, that you and I - despite our differences and arguments, that you might - "

Jane felt a flare of panic. She had given herself away that night by returning his embrace. This would not do. She took a deep breath. "I suppose you are referring to my behaviour the night of the fire. I think that is not the action of a gentleman, Sir. I was extremely tired and emotionally distraught, as well as being very scared. I had hoped that you had put it out of your mind."

Aware that Lady Goddard was still watching them, she sat down at the piano and pretended to arrange some music on the stand in front of her.

"It is a difficult thing to forget. "

Jane played a few soft chords. This was dreadful. "You must, Sir. Forget that it happened. I have."

Archer turned over a sheet of music, although she had played not a note shown. "Can you forget things so easily, Jane. I have no doubt that Frobisher is anxious to resume his friendship with you. Are you able to forget that he asked your sister to marry him only a few months ago?"

Jane played a gentle tune entirely from memory, the tears in her eyes blinding her from reading the score in front of her. The pieces of the puzzle were falling into place. It was now obvious to her that Archer was deeply jealous of Digby! And no wonder. He must think that Anne had led him on, given him reason to propose to her. And if he had seen the way she had flirted and danced with him at Pemberley, then he would have had all his suspicions confirmed.

Was it possible that gossip of such a nature had reached him in London? Mrs Caroline Tremaine had been at the ball and Jane had often heard her mother mention that she was the biggest gossip she had ever known.

Was this why he had not yet proposed to Anne? Was he seriously worried about her behaviour, that his wife had to be above reproach? Although it broke her heart to think of Archer marrying her sister, she realised she suddenly felt very sorry for her - something that had never happened before. Anne was so oblivious to Archer's concerns, so supremely confident in her appeal. She had Lady Goddard's approval and that, apparently, was all she felt she needed.

"I have no knowledge of Digby's forthcoming actions, Sir, and if you do not think me presumptuous, I would say that if you wish to marry a certain young lady, then you should propose to her, regardless of the circumstances surrounding her past actions." And before she could stop herself, her fingers came down hard on the keys and a loud, discordant note rang round the room.

She was aware of every head turning in their direction and felt tears burn her eyes. She cast a look of entreaty at her mother, who immediately rose from the sofa and crossed the room to her side as Archer muttered, "Thank you, Jane, for your advice. I shall do exactly as you wish."

"You look pale, Jane dear. I hope you have not over-exerted yourself." Elizabeth was all concern. "I think it is time we said our goodbyes. Lady Goddard has kindly offered us supper if we wish to stay for the evening. Anne and Celeste have accepted, but I have explained that your papa is expecting you and Bennetta at home and so the carriage has been called for."

Jane nodded, thankful for the chance to escape. She made her goodbyes to a frosty faced Lady Goddard and didn't once look back until they reached the door. Then she was unable to resist. But there was nothing to see to heal her pain - Celeste and Andrew were whispering together on the sofa and Archer was standing next to Anne, his face grave as he listened to her, seemingly intent on her beautiful, vivacious face.

Lady Goddard glanced her way, nodded her head, just the once and Jane was quite sure that she could see the gleam of triumph in her eyes.

CHAPTER 16

J ane was glad the following day for the simple pleasure of shopping with her mother and Bennetta for new dancing shoes. The temptation was strong to stay in her room, to be alone so she did not have to pretend to be happy, but she knew the rest of her family would begin to question her if she did so.

Anne and Celeste had surprisingly declined to accompany them.

"Celeste stayed at home in case Andrew called round," Bennetta said as the carriage finally drew up outside Matlock House. "And I imagine that Anne will have been anticipating Archer's appearance. Mama, can you not get Anne's engagement settled quickly. She's like an irritated cat all day long, waiting for him to propose. Why is it taking so long? We all know it is going to happen."

Elizabeth shook her head. "I have no idea. I can only imagine that he wishes to do so at the ball. Perhaps early on in the evening so he can then ask your papa for his blessing and then they can then make a splendid announcement."

Jane busied herself with collecting their various parcels, trying not to imagine how she was going to cope when that happened. She followed her mother and sister indoors where, to their surprise, they were greeted by the housekeeper, who asked for them to attend on Mr Darcy immediately in his study.

"My dear, whatever is the matter. Has something happened to Henry?" Elizabeth stood by the study door, all her fears for her youngest rushing through her as she saw her husband holding a letter. His face was dark with anger, though, she saw, not grief, which was a relief.

"No, everyone is quite well. Come in and sit down. You, too, Jane and Bennetta. I have sent for Anne but she has gone out to an appointment with her dressmaker. So I will tell her later."

"Tell her what, Papa?" Jane was growing more and more concerned. She had rarely seen her father angry. It was upsetting. Had there been some news regarding Archer, something that would stop her father giving his consent to the marriage?

"Read this, Elizabeth. Read it carefully and tell me that I am not mistaken in any fashion."

Mr Darcy handed his wife the letter and turned to gaze out of the window whilst she read it in silence. Finally Elizabeth raised her gaze from the page and sank down on a chair. "This can't be true! There must be a mistake."

"No mistake. Here are copies of all the documents sent in case we need to prove it."

"Prove what?" Bennetta wished her papa would get to the point.

Mr Darcy took a deep breath. "When I was informed about Celeste's arrival, I was very annoyed that her existence had been unknown to the Fitzwilliam family. It seemed to me that there had been a serious dereliction of duty in some lawyer's office. The Earl is not in good health, as you know. He did not feel well enough to meet the girl, so he asked me to enquire further. It has been worrying him because even though his father declared Rose no longer part of the family, claims for inheritance, the way wills have been written, there could be all types of confusion."

"Yes, it was obvious to all of us that there had been some dreadful lack of communication," Jane said quietly. "But letters do go astray and dealing with a foreign country in a different language must always cause problems."

"Rose Fitzwilliam, who was, of course, my aunt, did indeed run away to Sicily with a groom before I was born. She was just fifteen years of age."

He glanced across at his wife whose lips formed the word, 'Lydia!' and he nodded. Mrs Darcy's youngest sister had eloped at that age with George Wickham and that wicked man had, before that dreadful day, tried to marry Mr Darcy's little sister, Georgiana, when she was only fifteen!

"All that is true. Then news about her ceased completely. Of course it was not helped that my grandfather was so irate he cut her off and ordered his other children, including my mother, never to speak of Rose again. If he had been informed by some Italian lawyer or by Rose herself that she had had a child, the family was not told."

"But she must have had a baby because Celeste is her granddaughter!" Bennetta broke in impatiently.

"But this letter, from a respectable lawyer in Italy, states that she did not. Rose passed away in Rome, a year ago, at a great age. And she had no children. No children at all!"

Jane felt bewildered. "Then who is Celeste?"

"Exactly!"

"If you will allow, I will tell you." The voice from the doorway spun them round to find Celeste standing there, with Andrew at her side, holding her hand. Behind them Jane could see Archer, looking almost as confused as she felt herself.

"Dr Moore! Celeste - can I still call you by that name. Are you Celeste Fiorette?"

"Mr Darcy, Mrs Darcy, ladies - Celeste knows she owes you all an apology and an explanation." Andrew sounded very grave but Jane noticed he never once relinquished his hold on the Italian girl's hand.

"Why don't we all go into the drawing-room, where we can be comfortable." Elizabeth led the way, feeling the tension draining away once they were all seated. She knew that it was doubly hard to be confrontational when you were sitting down.

Jane was the last to leave the study - Archer was holding the door open for her. He seemed about to speak, then gravely stepped back to let her pass.

She entered the drawing-room to find her mother and Bennetta sitting on one sofa, facing Andrew and Celeste on the other. Mr Darcy was standing by the window and Jane quietly found a seat next to the chess table, gazing down to where the beautiful red and white marble pieces were still set out in the middle of a game. She remembered the set at Deerwood Park. The game must have finished because the King lay on his side, checkmated by a Queen and a pawn.

Jane was only too aware that Archer was standing behind her and felt a wave of pity for him. She knew how much he cared for his friend. This impossible situation must be hurting him deeply.

"Celeste - do you want to explain, my dear?" Andrew said quietly from his position next to her on the sofa. "And pray, may I make myself quite clear, Celeste confessed her wretched story to me this morning when I arrived at Matlock House. Let me make it plain - what she has told me makes no difference to my feelings for her. I have asked Celeste to be my wife and she has done me the great honour of accepting. We will marry immediately and travel out to Greece in the spring together."

"Andrew - my friend - listen - "

"No, Archer. I can guess what you will say. I repeat, nothing I have heard will make me change my mind. I love Celeste. And that is that."

His friend fell silent but Jane could see he was deeply affected by the words.

There was a silence, then Celeste shook back her long dark hair, raised her chin almost defiantly and said, "My name is, indeed, Celeste Fiorette. But I am not related to the Fitzwilliam family. I grew up in Rome, I lost my mother when I was very young and three years ago, my dear father died. He taught English at an Italian school, which is why I speak it so well. But he had no savings, no money to leave and I was penniless, facing an uncertain future of poverty for I had no relations to ask for help."

She hesitated, then went on, her voice never faltering. "I was lucky enough, through the church, to find a position as companion to a very elderly lady, Italian like myself, so I thought. But then I discovered she was not Italian but an English woman of aristocratic birth."

"Rose Fitzwilliam," Jane said softly.

"Yes. This lady told me many stories over the years I lived with her, stories of her family back in England. She had collected cuttings from the newspapers of weddings, deaths, births - so many that she knew exactly what was happening here. It seemed more important to her than her own life in Rome and Sicily where she had fled with her lover all those years ago.

"They had lived on a farm with his relations but times grew very hard in Sicily and the family, including her husband, decided to emigrate to America. But my mistress did not want to go and in anger her husband left her on her own and she moved to Rome. How she made a living she did not tell me, but I think she had many lovers in high positions in society."

"But she never had a child." Elizabeth was beginning to see how events had unfolded.

Celeste shook her head. "No. I became a substitute granddaughter and, wrongly, I hoped that when she, too, passed away, there would be a small legacy left to me."

"But there was no legacy," Archer added dryly.

Celeste shot him a sharp glance. "You are correct. All her money went to the local convent and I had a week to find myself a new home. As did Luisa, who was the old lady's maid." She shrugged, pouted and tears glistened in her eyes. "What should I have done? Begged on the streets? Taken in washing? Become a nun?"

"That would have been a great waste," Andrew said and, to her surprise, Jane thought she saw her papa's lips twitch into what was almost a smile.

"No, I decided to come to England as the old lady's granddaughter. Who was to say she had not produced a child? Italy is a long way from England. So I discussed it with Luisa and we agreed that I would introduce myself as the long lost cousin and she would be my maid. She has very little English, so I knew she would be in no danger of betraying our situation."

"But Celeste, what did you think would happen?"

Jane pushed some of the chess pieces around the board. She knew she should be thinking of how dreadful the girl's deception had been, but all that was in her mind was how poor Colonel Fitzwilliam would feel doubly betrayed. Not only had he been harbouring a deceitful woman in his home, but he had been prepared to give her his name!

Another shrug, another toss of the curly dark hair. "Who knows. It was just a game, useful because I had nowhere else to go. I live from day to day. I do not worry about the future. The Colonel is nice to me, kind, like an uncle. He buys me pretty things. It is nice house but lonely and oh, so boring! The Colonel he keeps wanting me to meet the old Earl, but I do not wish to do that. The game becomes serious and is spoilt.

"So, I plan to return to Italy, but first, because I am curious because of the scandal of their marriage that the old lady related to me many times, I want to meet the Darcys and see Pemberley. Then you arrive, Jane and I meet my dear Andrew and everything changes."

There was a silence following her last statement: even Bennetta seemed lost for words. Of everyone in the room, Celeste seemed the least worried by the situation and finally Andrew spoke.

"Mr Darcy, are you intending to take this matter any further? I appreciate that what Celeste has done is stupid and wicked but she meant no real harm. If we had not met and fallen in love, then she would have enjoyed her time in Dorset, then returned to Italy with the few guineas she had saved."

Without thinking, Jane turned in her chair, saw the expression on Archer's face and for a second they looked at each other in complete accord. Andrew was a dear, trusting man, too trusting if he genuinely believed that Celeste would have calmly gone back to life of servitude in Italy when she had tasted what it was like to be part of a rich and socially acceptable family. But love was blind and his feelings for her were only too clear.

Elizabeth crossed the room to her husband before he could reply and lay a hand on his arm.

"My dear, I know you are angry, and rightly so. I am, too. But no real damage has been done. I know you intended to formally introduce Celeste to our friends at the ball, but luckily that now need not happen. To all who enquire, she is just a friend of the family from Italy who is now engaged to be married to Dr Moore.

"We will write to the Earl and put his mind at rest, inform him that there was a misunderstanding, perhaps because of language difficulties. Celeste is not a Fitzwilliam, does not pretend to be one and he need have no more worries about the terms of the old family wills."

"My grandmother is extremely fond of Andrew," Archer said. "Indeed, she has always liked him more than me since we met as schoolboys! I think, once her initial annoyance has passed, that she will welcome Celeste to stay at her home until the wedding. Indeed, I have an idea that she will not be completely surprised at the news."

"Do you mean she has guessed that Celeste is an imposter?" Bennetta's eyes shone at the intrigue.

Archer ran his hand through his dark hair. "I would not go that far, but she has commented to me of her surprise that Celeste knows so little about Sicily, where she supposedly grew up."

Celeste nodded. "I have never been to Sicily! It was difficult when Lady Goddard and my dear Andrew asked me questions. But now, all is settled. I will pack and move to Mayfair. I will apologise most humbly to the good Lady Goddard. It will all be delightful."

She had no sooner finished speaking than a bell could be heard ringing and the housekeeper appeared - luncheon was now served.

Mr Darcy said he would have his in his study and Elizabeth did not try to persuade him otherwise. She knew he had been deeply distressed by the whole affair but hopefully with Celeste soon out of Matlock House she would be able to calm his anger. It had obviously slipped his mind that with Anne about to become engaged to Archer, this was not the time for a falling out between the two households.

The drawing-room emptied except for Jane who still sat, gazing at the chess board, wondering just who was going to tell Colonel Fitzwilliam what had happened. Her mind was racing; she could see no way of reporting the news without causing heartache and distress.

Archer turned in the doorway and saw that she had not moved and the anguish written on her face alarmed him. Surely Jane should now be delighted - the girl marrying Andrew was not a member of the Fitzwilliam family. Celeste's lowly background was surely no obstacle to their union. Andrew's family had no social standing to lose.

He walked across to the chess table and picked up one of the pieces, the white marble queen. "You do not seem over-joyed at the news, Jane. I thought you would be pleased to discover that Celeste is not a Fitzwilliam, that she is definitely poor enough in fortune for Andrew."

"Pleased? I confess I am at a loss, Sir, as to why you should think that."

"When we were in the Burlington Arcade, if you remember, you made it clear that you had the strongest feelings of repugnance against such a match."

Jane busied herself with putting the pieces back in their neat ranks. "No, Sir, you are wrong. There was a perfectly valid reason for my dislike of the marriage. That reason is still there and it has nothing to do with Andrew coming from a poor family!"

Archer wanted to smile. When Jane lost her temper, she was enchantingly pretty, her gentle eyes snapped and sparkled and a rosy pink flushed her cheeks. He wanted, badly, to kiss her.

"So as I have obviously misjudged you, I ask for forgiveness. Can you tell me the reason or is it a secret?"

She sighed; her vow to Celeste was obviously no longer needed and at least she could take one weight off her mind.

"Celeste told me that she and Colonel Fitzwilliam had an understanding. That they were to be married, but that it was a secret until he told his family. She said he had misgivings about the difference in their ages, but that did not worry her. So you see, I was sworn not to talk about it to anyone. I was very concerned that she would turn from Andrew as soon as my godfather appeared in London and that your friend would be bitterly hurt."

There was a short silence then, "I honour you for your strength of will in keeping such a promise. I do not know if I could have done the same, thinking I might lose your respect and affection."

Jane bent her head so he would not see the tears that were forming, willing herself not to cry. "Your respect is something I was saddened beyond belief to lose. I am grateful that you now know the truth of the matter and we can continue as we were before."

Archer tossed the queen from hand to hand. "And my affection, Jane. Were you sad to lose that, too?"

"Of course. Are we not to be family soon?"

"You mean Anne?"

A quick instinctive flick of her fingers and the chess pieces went rolling. "Of course I mean Anne! I had not imagined that you would be brave enough to take on Bennetta! I suppose your engagement will be announced at the ball? Everyone expects it, especially my sister."

Archer began to rearrange the board. "That distresses me. I have never said a word to her to give her that impression. Other people have done that. I am so tired of behaving exactly how everyone believes is right. Look, each of these pieces has a set path and the players know exactly what knight, pawn, bishop or queen can or can't do. I never cared for the game. I wish to make my own rules in life. I feel that I have always had to put other people's wishes first. Jane - look at me! Or don't you dare?"

Stung at the accusation, Jane flung back her head and found herself gazing into the dark eyes that haunted her dreams, eyes that sent a message she refused to read.

"I, too, have always followed the instructions given to me by loving friends and family. In that, I admit, we are alike. But we both know that we have very different paths in life to follow. They do not coincide. They cannot. You have a magnificent career ahead of you – why your grandmother believes you may end up as prime minister! I am but a mere pawn on the chessboard, you are a knight, at least, possibly a king."

"Even so, a pawn can capture a king, if it is brave enough."

"I have plenty of courage, Sir. But I am not foolhardy!"

Before she could say another word he pulled her into his arms and began to kiss her, stopping her from speaking, from breathing, from thinking. All she wanted was to wind her arms around him, bury her fingers in his hair and return his kisses with all the power of her being. When he finally let her go, she was shaking.

"Foolhardy? Yes, I suppose loving a fellow who would work long hours, often be away from home attending at the law courts might seem so to you, as would loving a man who no longer had the promise of money to fund his career. And you do love me, Jane, I know you do. Why do you deny it? You could not return my kisses if you did not."

"I think any girl would be proud to be your wife, Sir," she whispered, "And as you very well know, there is one Darcy who will be only too pleased to be given that honour, thus safe-guarding your career and income. It is foolish and unkind of you to play games with me when the moves on the board are already set in motion."

"And is that your final word? Well, at least I know where I stand and what I should do. Thank you, Miss Jane, for making things clear to me." And with a glancing blow, he scattered the chessmen onto the floor and left the room.

CHAPTER 17

The following morning found Elizabeth Darcy at her desk in the drawing-room, continuing a letter she was writing to her sister, Jane Bingley, who was living the quiet life of an invalid with her family up in Derbyshire. Jane had never fully recovered from the birth of her daughter Alethea who had arrived many years after her brother and sisters and Elizabeth worried about her constantly.

"....so my dearest, as you can imagine, the repercussions of the truth about Celeste are still ringing around my ears. Fitzwilliam is in a quiet fury that is aimed more at the Italian authorities than at the girl herself who swiftly packed and left Matlock House last night to stay with Lady Goddard.

"Celeste is a calculating little minx in my opinion, although like all men, Fitzwilliam just feels sorry for her! Poor Dr Moore - he is so in love with the wretched girl. But maybe she does care for him enough for the marriage to be a success and the formidable Lady Goddard will probably help them out if Celeste spends all of her husband's money. She is very fond of Andrew - far more, I fear, than her own grandson. Families are very odd.

"Speaking of families, mine will soon be altogether under one roof. Fitz and Henry will both be home for Christmas, which fills my heart with joy. It will be a happy relief to talk to two of my children and not have to deal with secrets and heartache."

She glanced across the room to where her sister's namesake was curled up on the window seat, a book in her lap. To Elizabeth's certain knowledge, Jane had not turned a page in the past fifteen minutes.

"I thought Jane had improved since her time in Dorset, but today she seems plunged back into gloom. She is pale and looks as if she did not sleep last night. I do hope all that nonsense regarding Digby Frobisher has not been awakened. I noticed that his name is on the list of invitations to the ball on Saturday.

I am very annoyed as Fitzwilliam and I have made our displeasure at his actions very clear and I have no idea why he was included. I am sure he was not on the list I approved and rather suspect Bennetta's fine hand in the matter. That child is a menace.

"Anne, on the other hand, is bursting with suppressed emotion, awaiting - as we all are - for Archer Maitland to make a formal proposal. Bennetta teases her unmercifully and I spend my time keeping the peace between them.

"I have no idea why the gentleman in question has not yet spoken - all I can imagine is that he is waiting for the ball. This is what Anne believes and I shall be so relieved when it is all out in the open. It will be fun to arrange their wedding. As you know, I enjoyed Cassandra and Catherine's but my own daughter's will be very special.

I am sure you feel the same way about your dear Beth. It is so hard to believe that the twins will be twenty at Christmas and Beth the same age a few days later! Where have the years gone?

"We are also awaiting the arrival today of Colonel Fitzwilliam and dear Susannah. It will be so good to see them both again. Poor Susannah has been away from home for far longer than she would have wished. Hopefully she will stay for the ball and then travel north. You will no doubt see her yourself and get all the latest news first hand..."

She paused and sat thinking. Would it be fun to arrange Anne's wedding? She had the uncomfortable feeling that she would not be allowed much involvement. Her eldest daughter was sure to have every detail already planned. Elizabeth sighed. That was the problem with Anne: she was an organiser with nothing in her life to organise. Marrying Archer would give that side of her nature full rein which could only be a good thing.

"Mama! Mama! Come quickly, they have delivered the most dreadful flowers for the ballroom." Bennetta ran into the room, her face a picture of despair. "They are all orange and brown, Mama! Orange and brown and I asked for white and yellow!"

With the sigh Elizabeth got up and accompanied the frantic girl out to the hallway to deal with the crisis. At Pemberley they had the redoubtable Miss Reynolds who would cope with all these problems, but the London housekeeper was very elderly and no doubt in as much of a frenzy as Bennetta!

Jane did not look up from her book - the book she was not reading. The words danced in front of her eyes and made no sense. All she could see and hear were Archer's harsh words as he left her yesterday.

"Oh this is where you are hiding!" Anne sailed into the room. "I wanted to know what you are wearing for the ball. It is so tedious when we are in the same colour, and people make all those stupid remarks about how alike we are."

Jane closed her book and gazed at her twin. With her brilliant golden hair, high colour and determined manner, she didn't think anyone would mistake them for each other anymore.

"I don't mind which dress I wear. But you have a new one, I believe."

Anne crossed to a mirror and inspected her reflection, delighted with what she saw. "I do indeed. It is gold with a fine silver embroidered overlay, cut in the very latest fashion. I need at least five petticoats under the skirt!"

Jane couldn't help smiling. "Well, sister, I don't think you need worry. I have nothing as wonderful as that. I think my cream silk or even the pink will be quite adequate. It is your night, after all."

"Well, I certainly hope so! I have been waiting long enough. His silence on the subject is very annoying. Everyone knows what must happen. I really think that if Archer does not advance our relationship tomorrow, then I will feel free to consider the approaches of other gentlemen."

"But how could you possibly do so if you love Archer?"

Anne laughed: sometimes her sister amused her greatly. "Love? I don't love Archer, you silly. It is a marriage that suits both of us. Lady Goddard's money is guaranteed for his career and I get a handsome, ambitious husband and a chance to get away from Pemberley and make a life for myself."

"But you love Pemberley!"

Anne's face hardened. "Of course I love it, but it will never be mine, will it? Or yours, or even if some disaster befell us both, Bennetta's. No, it will go to Fitz, and if he has no children, then to Henry. I love it more than any of you but if I can't have it, then I don't want to stay there."

Jane felt a wave of anguish, worry and pity sweep over her. It was bad enough losing Archer, but to a loveless marriage, to a girl who only saw him as a way of escaping from a life that didn't suit her - that was hard indeed.

"But what if you marry Archer and then fall in love with someone else? What if..."

she hesitated, then went on... "what if he finds someone he truly loves?"

"Oh Archer is far too honourable to cause me any embarrassment. I think he would just suffer in silence. But enough of me. Tell me, what is happening between you and the handsome Mr Frobisher? Have you made up your silly argument yet?"

"Digby? He means nothing to me. You encouraged him, to show me exactly what type of man he is. Well, you certainly succeeded."

"Oh Jane. I will say sorry if it makes you feel better. Perhaps I was wrong to act as I did. By pretending to like him, I pushed him into proposing to me, when I am sure he preferred you. But you gave him no sign of your feelings! The poor fellow had no idea you cared for him. Why don't you give him another chance? He is coming to the ball - although I have no idea how his name was added to the guest list - so you will have an opportunity to make everything pleasant once more. Now I must go and see what Bennetta and Mama are doing with the flowers. I've already planned out the decorations, but Benny will not listen!"

Jane wished with all her heart that she was back at Pemberley. Making an appearance at the ball had been hard enough to countenance; the thought that she would have to fend off Digby's insincere attentions gave her great cause for concern.

She crossed to the chess table. One of the servants had picked up all the pieces from where Archer had discarded them and placed them at random on the board. She reached out to pick up one of the little white pawns. So small and inoffensive, but if played correctly, it could make a huge difference to the game.

Was that what Archer had meant when he said that a pawn could capture a king? Her fingers tightened round the little marble figure, feeling the intricate carving digging into the palm of her hand. How could she possibly save him? And from what? Ahead of him lay a sparkling career and a position of great power which gave him the influence to do good in the world - all in return for a marriage that might be loveless but would be held together by mutual liking and ambition.

He seemed to be saying that it was within her power to change all that, but what woman who truly loved would destroy the recipient of her affections knowing it would ruin him?

The rest of the day dragged past. Jane hid herself in her room after lunch, tired of listening to Anne and Bennetta bickering about arrangements for flowers, food, champagne, musicians and who should open the dancing and with whom.

She knew she was being dull and annoying her sisters by her lack of interest and was determined to make more of an effort at dinner. It seemed strange not to see Celeste sitting at the table. Anne had shown only the slightest interest in the Italian girl's story, only wanting reassurance that she and Andrew would be attending on the following night.

"Oh they are sure to come," Bennetta said airily. "Lady Goddard will because she wants to be here when Archer proposes and in her eyes Andrew can do no wrong, so I am certain they will accompany her."

Anne looked content and Jane tried to stop herself from digging holes in the tablecloth with the prongs of her fork.

"Papa, you and Mama will lead the dancing, so please don't vanish into your study just when we need you," Bennetta said firmly. "And Jane, you need to be available as well, because there is sure to be some poor young man who will need a partner."

Mr Darcy raised an eyebrow at his wife. "I wonder if the esteemed Duke of Wellington could find a place for Bennetta on his staff? I fancy she would acquit herself well with her undoubted talent for giving orders."

Before another argument could break out, Elizabeth calmly turned the conversation by wondering when they would have the pleasure of seeing Colonel Fitzwilliam and Susannah, for surely they must have left Dorset by now and, unless something untoward had occurred to their carriage, they should have arrived in London.

"The Colonel has his own house in town, of course, but Susannah will have to come here until she goes back to Derbyshire. I have her room all prepared and obviously if she arrives soon, she will be in good time for the ball which will be a treat for her. I expect life has been very dull down in Dorset since you left, Jane.'"

Jane smiled. "I fear that the Colonel and dear Susannah's idea of excitement is sweeping up the leaves on the flower beds and deciding what should be planted next year. She will no doubt be glad to get back to her own garden."

"It must be very odd, to be a spinster, living with your younger brother and his wife. You must feel constantly in the way, an unwanted guest at their table. They would always be having to find her a partner for dinner or dances. I should hate it." Anne gave a dramatic shudder.

"I can't see the difference to us living with Mama and Papa," Bennetta said swiftly.

"If you are still living with us when you have reached the age of forty, I shall pay someone to take you away," Mr Darcy said absentmindedly as he tackled a particularly obstinate cutlet.

Bennetta laughed but, even as she did so, she felt that shiver of pain that she had experienced so many times whilst growing up. Papa was joking, of course he was. But she also knew that buried somewhere in that remark was the truth - he did not care for her nearly as much as he did his other four children.

The fire had been lit in the drawing-room and peace reigned as Elizabeth played a gentle tune on the piano whilst Mr Darcy turned the pages of her music. Jane sat listening, trying to put images of Archer out of her mind. Even Anne and Bennetta found common ground in discussing exactly who was coming to the dance on the following evening.

The peace was shattered when a peal at the front door bell heralded a footman announcing the arrival of Colonel Fitzwilliam who strode into the room with hardly a sign of a limp, looking fit and well. He was closely followed by Susannah Courtney and Jane just had time to notice she was wearing a very becoming winter coat and feathered hat in a shade of dark amber that suited her far more than her usual grey or dull brown.

Jane had been dreading this meeting, worrying about how the news of Celeste's betrayal would be received. She loved her godfather dearly and realised all over again just how angry she was at the girl for putting him in this invidious position. The only good thing she could think of was that the engagement had not been officially announced; no one except herself and probably her parents, knew about the liaison and so he would not be held to ridicule by society.

Mr Darcy welcomed him with a hearty hand-shake. "My good fellow! A pleasure to see you once more and to find you looking so well. We were all concerned by Jane's report on your health. And Susannah, welcome. Come and sit here by the fire."

"Darcy, Elizabeth, girls! Good evening to you all. I apologise for the lateness of our visit, but one of our horses lost a shoe outside of Guildford and we were somewhat delayed."

"You are welcome any time. I will ring for coffee, although I am sure a glass of brandy will be more to your taste." Elizabeth ushered them to seats closer to the fire. "It is a raw night for travelling."

"And where is the charming Celeste? I hope she has been enjoying her stay in London?"

Jane stepped forward and blurted out, "Such news, Godfather! I am sure you will delighted to learn that Celeste is shortly to be married to Dr Andrew Moore. She has moved to Lady Goddard's house in Mayfair, but I am sure she will be glad to see you once more."

No matter how unwelcome the information would be to him, how unhappy it would make him feel, she was convinced that the sooner he knew it the better, before he could make any announcement of his own intended marriage.

"That, of course, is not the most important part of the news," Anne added dryly. "It is typical of Jane to miss out the fact that Celeste Fiorette is an imposter. That she is not our cousin, not a member of the Fitzwilliam family. You have been sadly duped, I'm afraid, Colonel, by giving her shelter and introducing her to the world as such."

There was a silence, broken only by the spitting of the logs on the fire and the crackling of the flames. Then the Colonel sighed and said, "My wife had her suspicions many weeks ago, didn't you, my dear?"

"Your wife!" Bennetta's voice was hardly more than a squeak.

The Colonel stared round at his astounded audience, then held out his hand to Susannah, who removing her gloves to display a glittering gold and ruby ring, said with pride, "I know this will be a shock to you, Elizabeth and you Mr Darcy, but yes, the Colonel did me the honour of asking me to be his wife and I gladly accepted."

"We were married yesterday in Compton Forge." The Colonel was beaming as he shook hands once more with Mr Darcy and Susannah was hugged by everyone in a storm of chatter.

Jane was over-joyed and confused. The couple looked so happy; she could only imagine how Susannah felt, being elevated from spinster sister to the wife of a gentleman whose family stretched back for many generations.

"We have written to my brothers to tell them the news," Susannah said eventually, straightening her hat which had gone sadly astray from Bennetta's enthusiastic attentions.

"I know they will be very surprised, but I have no doubt that we will have their good wishes and I expect Richard and Cassandra will be happy to have their house to themselves."

"We intend to travel up to Derbyshire for Christmas," the Colonel was saying to Jane as his wife was surrounded by the other Darcy ladies all wanting details of the proposal, wedding day and wedding clothes. "Then back to Deerwood, which we hope you will always look on as your second home as usual, Jane dear."

She clasped his hand in hers. "I cannot express my feelings of pleasure and surprise. But Colonel, I do not fully understand. I was led to believe by Celeste that you and she had an understanding? When you spoke to me at breakfast on the day I left Dorset, you said you were going to propose when you could, that you felt the lady had feelings for you, but she was much younger!"

"Celeste! What a naughty child. Such stories, such an imagination. I am at a loss to know how to reply, my dear. I have not yet quite taken in that she is an imposter, or that Andrew intends to marry her regardless, although as I said earlier, Susannah had her suspicions. She was quite certain, for instance, that Celeste had never been to Sicily in her life.

"Why she should have made up such a story is outside my comprehension. But at least her silly tales have done no lasting harm. As for our conversation, I thought you had guessed as to the direction of my feelings, that I was already determined to make Susannah my wife. I had high hopes of her accepting although yes, she is over ten years younger than me."

Jane repeated her good wishes and managed to have a quiet word with Susannah as the Colonel was giving a highly amusing rendition of the travails that had beset them on their wedding morning when a flock of sheep blocked the road and the parson overslept.

"I can tell from your expression that you are truly pleased for me," Susannah said.

"Oh more than I can possibly say! But I must be blind. I never saw this happening, never saw a great regard between the two of you, although it was obvious that you liked the Colonel."

"We are both very quiet people who do not wear their hearts on their sleeves. I had never considered myself the type of woman who could fall in love so swiftly and completely, but I was wrong. I think I realised my feelings when we were arguing in the garden over the planting of lavender bushes! As for your godfather, I think he might never have spoken but for the advice of a certain young man we both know."

"You must mean Dr Moore."

"No, indeed. I mean Archer Maitland. I believe he saw the situation and dropped a very large hint to my now husband that he should speak his mind and his heart to me before I left Dorset for Derbyshire."

Jane gasped and felt hot colour flood into her cheeks. "That was good of him."

"Having fallen ill, I have never had the opportunity to thank him, but I believe we are to attend the ball here tomorrow night and, if I gather correctly from Bennetta's chatter and Anne's silence, we are to see a proposal from him to your sister. So hopefully I shall have a chance to thank him for orchestrating our happiness on an evening when his own will be at its peak."

Jane could only smile and agree and, after expressing her love and affection to the new Mrs Fitzwilliam once more, left her to Bennetta's excited declaration that the newlyweds should open the dancing at the ball tomorrow night and escaped to the quiet of her bedroom.

Her godfather believed that Celeste's mischievous words had done no harm and to him, they hadn't. But to Jane they certainly had. Archer had thought when they first met that she was a girl to whom snobbery was abhorrent. But because she had been unable tell him why she had been so against Celeste and Andrew marrying, he had thought the worst of her. And after all, there had been no need to keep her word, because he already guessed that the Colonel's affections were directed towards a very different woman.

It was easy to say now that he knew the truth, that her given word was important to her. But he had doubted her and that scar would take a long time to heal.

CHAPTER 18

Matlock House was *en fête* this late November evening. Every window was a brilliant yellow square of light and on either side of the front door, two flaming torches warmed the air, much to the relief of the footmen who stood on the steps, waiting to give help if needed. Straw had been heaped on the roadway to deaden the sound of the many carriages and hansom cabs that would bring those with a coveted invitation to the Darcy winter ball.

In the coach mews at the back of the house, stables had been prepared in case any gentlemen came on horseback and Elizabeth Darcy had made sure that there was a barrel of small ale, bread and cheese for any groom or postillion that needed to wait until the end of the evening.

As the guests arrived, they were ushered into the hall where garlands of white and yellow flowers hung from the chandeliers and decorated the huge gilt edged mirrors on either wall, throwing back their reflections in a kaleidoscope of colours as maids took capes, cloaks and overshoes.

In the ballroom, musicians were already playing and footmen were circling with glasses of champagne on silver trays. Bennetta and Anne, who were the official hostesses for the evening, welcomed their guests and felt great satisfaction as their dance cards were filled with the names of suitable young men.

Anne had kept the first three dances clear. She knew Archer would want them with her. Resplendent in gold silk, her waist pulled in to show off her full skirts and low cut bodice, she knew she was the most beautiful woman in the room.

Even Bennetta, whose dark ringlets were tonight kept under control with two brilliantly jewelled combs, could not outshine her. She watched as her sister moved around the room, tall, elegant, full of a suppressed excitement that made her eyes shine and her face glow with colour.

Celeste - whose red satin dress was so low-cut that Bennetta feared for her modesty when she danced - had arrived with Andrew and Lady Goddard. The Italian girl seemed not the slightest bit perturbed at the change in her role, and commented that she had never seen Anne so full of life.

"I take it that we will be receiving news of her engagement tonight," she murmured. "For some reason my dear Andrew has his doubts, but then he is a man and so cannot be trusted to understand these matters."

Bennetta nodded and watched as Anne received Lady Goddard - resplendent in purple lace and a high, feathered headdress - accompanied a few steps behind by Miss Purkiss, her companion, valiantly trying to carry two shawls, two reticules and in danger of dropping them both.

Her sister led the elderly ladies across the polished floor, already dusted with powder to stop feet from slipping, to seats next to Mrs Darcy, far away from the musicians but positioned so Lady Goddard could see and hear everything.

"Mrs Darcy! A pleasing room, not too many people, but enough for some interesting conversations. And I must compliment you on your eldest daughter." She patted Anne's hand, the diamonds on her fingers glittering in the candlelight. "A fine girl. You must be very proud."

Elizabeth nodded. "We are proud of all our children, Lady Goddard. Anne and Bennetta have worked particularly hard to make this evening a success."

The old lady turned her beady gaze on Elizabeth. "A success? Ah yes, well that is still to be seen. I am hoping that when my grandson arrives, he will have recovered from what seems to me nothing more than a temper tantrum - his mother was afflicted with the same trouble - and bring this long-drawn out dalliance with your daughter to a speedy conclusion."

Elizabeth nodded politely. She was uneasy about this much hinted about marriage: just hoping something would happen didn't mean that it would. Anne was not in love with Archer Maitland and, unless she was very much mistaken, Archer was not in love with her.

Was it wrong to want the bliss of overwhelming love to be experienced by your children? That was what she and Fitzwilliam Darcy had together and she thought it tragic that Anne was prepared to settle for anything less. She watched her talking to Lady Goddard, laughing, enjoying being the centre of attention, and felt concerned. It seemed to be the attention and influence she craved, rather than the man.

Anne's behaviour was also making Bennetta uneasy. Her elder sister was usually so elegant and refined in her behaviour - she would smile but not laugh, never raise her voice. Tonight she was different, as if she could not contain her excitement. For some odd reason Bennetta remembered a saying of her old nurse, Nanny Chilcot.

"You mark my words, there'll be tears before bedtime," had often been her dour comment when any of the Darcy children had become over-excited.

Celeste tapped her arm with her fan, attracting her attention. "And where is Jane? I do not see her anywhere."

Bennetta pulled a face. "Upstairs, no doubt. She is well known for disliking large parties and will no doubt slip into the room, unnoticed. Which is a pity, because that gentleman over there, in the plum coloured coat, is Digby Frobisher."

Celeste turned to stare. "Oh indeed. The man who broke poor Jane's heart. Well, he is certainly very handsome. What a splendid moustache!"

Bennetta privately thought he gave every appearance of being vain because he never missed an opportunity of checking his appearance in any mirror he passed. Earlier, on his arrival, she had watched with interest as he paid his compliments to her parents. Her father, in particular, did not look pleased to see him and made only the slightest gesture of welcome.

Digby obviously had no feelings of regret or shame for his actions that summer. Bennetta sighed: she had thought she was doing Jane a favour by asking him to the ball, but was beginning to think that perhaps she was wrong.

She peered towards the door, wishing Jane would hurry up and appear. And where was Archer? Anne was beginning to frown, obviously annoyed at his absence, especially as so many people at the ball would have been speculating and gossiping about what might happen.

Jane was, in fact, still upstairs in her room, sitting in front of her mirror, wondering just how long she could put off going downstairs. Tabitha, who had arrived back from Dorset with the Fitzwilliams had wanted to put up her hair into a very complicated style with many little braids woven into a coronet around her head, but Jane refused.

She had seen and admired Anne's gold silk dress and similar hairstyle and in no way did she wish to draw any attention to herself, to be accused of vying for popularity. So she had brushed her hair, then curled it into a thick bundle that sat at the nape of her neck and tied it with a silver ribbon.

Her mother had insisted that, like her sisters, she should have a new dress for the ball. It was still hanging in the wardrobe, a deep pink with a darker pink over skirt, adorned with many ruffles and bows. Jane hated it and much to Tabitha's disapproval, decided to wear the cream silk that she had worn when dancing with Archer down in Dorset.

At last she knew she could delay no longer, sighed heavily, and made her way down the sweeping, curved stairway. She could hear music and the swelling sound of many voices from the ballroom. Just as she reached the hall, the front door was swung open and a footman ushered in a familiar figure. Resplendent in a black coat, heavily embroidered with gold filigree, Archer Maitland cast an impressive figure.

"Jane!" He bowed. "Your servant."

"Archer." She curtsied, knowing she was blushing, but unable to hide her face.

"I hope I find you well?"

"Indeed, Sir."

"Are you looking forward to this evening?"

Jane had reached the final step on the stairs and realised her eyes were level with his. She forced herself not to drop her gaze, hoping that her love for him was not apparent. "It is always pleasant to find oneself amongst good company. One piece of news that may interest you, my godfather has recently married Miss Susannah Courtney. I take it that you will not be surprised and I thank you with all my heart if you helped the union along in some way."

Archer held out his hand as support as she stepped down onto the shining marble floor. He was smiling. "That is good news indeed. I doubt that anything I said or did would have changed the final outcome, but I did point out to

Colonel Fitzwilliam that the attraction seemed to be on both sides of the partnership, something he was having problems believing."

Jane released her hand from his; she found even the touch of his fingers on hers caused her exquisite pain and she forced herself to speak. "There is an old saying in our part of Derbyshire that everything goes in threes. Andrew and Celeste, the Colonel and Susannah - everyone is expecting a third announcement tonight."

"I am hoping for that as well," he replied smoothly and she fought down the cold shivers that swept over her. "Now, if you will excuse me, I must pay my compliments to your parents and my grandmother."

The door to the ballroom was opened in front of them and a wave of colour, heat and sound swept out, surrounding them, overwhelming Jane's senses. The air was thick with the smell of perfume, candle grease and the chalk that had been laid on the polished floor to avoid slipping had already been sent swirling up into the air by dancing feet.

Finding refuge on a small gilt chair on the far side of the ballroom, Jane watched as Archer approached her parents, making his bow, kissing Lady Goddard's cheek, listening gravely to something she said, then turning to speak to Anne and Bennetta, giving both, to Jane's surprise, equal attention. She could tell, even from a distance that her twin was not happy by this. She obviously wanted to be the only recipient of his regard.

"There you are, Jane! I have been looking for you." Susannah, regal in dark lavender, all diffidence gone from her manner, kissed her cheek and sat down next to her. "I was beginning to think you were unwell."

Jane shook her head and forced herself to smile. "Not at all. I am just tardy in my dressing. I am delighted to see you tonight. I had wondered if you might be too tired to attend after the long journey."

The new Mrs Fitzwilliam laughed. "Not at all. Happiness is a great reviver of weary limbs and nothing can dampen our spirits. Oh, Jane, I can hardly believe what has happened to me. To have found love at such a late time of life and for that love to be returned, why, it is nothing short of a miracle. Who would have thought our trip to Dorset could have ended in such a fashion."

Jane smiled and squeezed her hand. She wondered what Susannah would say if she knew that she was not the only person to have found love at Deerwood Park!

In a flash of gold, Anne crossed the room to sit next to them. Her eyes were sparkling with half-concealed excitement. "Goodness, Jane, you are so late coming downstairs and why are you hiding yourself away right over here, away from the rest of the family?"

"I am sure you do not need me."

"Need? No, but I want you here. I want all my friends and family around me."

Jane nodded. She had no doubt that the proposal was about to happen. Archer obviously intended to make it a very public affair. She wondered if a heart could actually break or if the pain she was feeling would ever lessen.

Just then the music started up again and she realised they were playing a waltz. By the time she had realised that it was the same piece of music she had danced to with Archer, the man who would always be her best beloved was walking across the floor towards them.

She felt, more than saw, Anne stiffen in her chair, then her fan moved swiftly and Jane knew she was gazing at Archer over the top of the feathers, her blue eyes sparkling with invitation.

"Miss Jane! How good to see you again. May I say how well you are looking? Surely I recall that dress. Why it was one you wore when we last danced together. Did you wear it tonight for that reason. Ha! Come, dance with me. I promise not to step on your toes as I did in the summer. Haha!"

To her horror, Digby had stepped out of the crowd, looming over her, his prominent blue eyes bright with what she could only suppose was feigned passion.

"Miss Jane, I believe this is our dance. The one we never finished." In two paces, Archer was standing next to Digby, ignoring him in an extremely arrogant fashion, gazing down at her, his dark eyes full of feeling as he held out his hand.

She was only just aware of a muffled exclamation from Digby and a stifled gasp from her twin and out of the corner of her eye she saw Susannah's hand shoot out to grasp Anne's arm, to stop her from rising from her chair.

Then nothing else mattered but the warmth of Archer's fingers clasping hers, his hand on her back, the closeness of his body and the way they moved to the music as if they had been born to dance together.

"This is madness," Jane whispered as they circled the room, aware that people with expectations of seeing a different couple, were viewing them in puzzlement.

"I agree."

"We must stop! You must ask Anne to dance. You must - "

"I am dancing with the woman I love, the woman I believe loves me in return."

She gasped. "Archer!"

"Be a coward and tell me you do not love me, Jane!"

The music faded away and all she could hear was the thumping of her heart as she realised that with those few words he had thrown open the doors to the cage that had both protected and imprisoned her entire life. He was giving up wealth and a life of power and influence for love. And he was asking her to join him.

"Sir, I am not very brave... no, you may not laugh... I know I am not. But, Archer Maitland, I love you with all my heart and soul and will do so until the day I die."

"Jane, my dearest, sweetest Jane. God, I want to kiss you so much, but I fear that would scandalize our fellow dancers even more. Marry me, Jane! We will not be rich, but I will do everything in my power to make you happy. I have repeated tonight to my grandmother my decision that I will not choose a wife at her command. My mother married a poor lawyer and she was happy. I am asking you to do the same, although I fear your family, especially your sister will not be over-joyed at our union."

Jane glanced over his shoulder: Anne and Lady Goddard were no longer in the ballroom, Bennetta, Celeste and Andrew were sitting watching them, their faces pictures of astonishment. Then as Archer spun her round once more, she saw her parents standing, side by side, and they were smiling at her with a warmth and affection that told her they guessed what had happened and gave their blessing.

She glanced up at her beloved's face, his usual stern expression wiped away by joy, and before she could think twice, she stepped out of her prison, stopped dancing, stood on tip-toe and with her hands on either side of his face, kissed him, the gasps of the onlookers ringing in her ears.

"I will marry you, no matter what lies ahead for us. I love you, Archer and always will."

And, oblivious to the audience, he pulled her tighter into his arms and kissed her with all the passion in his soul.

ॐ

MATLOCK HOUSE, LONDON, NOVEMBER 1834
.....And so, my dear Catherine, that is all the news I have to share. Not, perhaps as exciting as yours and Sir Robert's - I do so hope the baby is boy, I know that will be your dearest wish. But as long as it is healthy, another girl would find no disfavour with me and will grow up with Cassandra's little Victoria as a new generation of Pemberley cousins! I wonder what their world will be like in 1854, twenty years from now. Good Lord, I shall be thirty-eight, old and wrinkled, no doubt. Probably still living at home, unmarried, unloved!

I am delighted for Jane, she is a changed girl, laughing where once she would have smiled, all diffidence and shyness quite vanished. I rather miss my gentle sister, but Mama assures me she is still there, that when you are so very happy, it overwhelms you and you cannot help but show it. She insists the quiet sister I now miss will return.

As I am not shy and retiring, as you know, I dread to think how unbearable I shall become if I ever fall in love. Which, I fear is unlikely! Finding the right man to spend the rest of your life with seems very difficult. Finding someone you can trust with your heart seems impossible.

The happy couple are to live in London, which is probably a good thing. It will give time for the scandal of Archer proposing to "the wrong sister" and the two of them embracing so passionately in front of all our guests, time to die away. I have not spoken to Anne and have no idea how she feels. She laughs a lot and spent the rest of the ball dancing with Digby Frobisher.

I long to see you again and will hope to travel to Courtney Castle once the baby has arrived. Don't forget, I am now quite proficient at taking care of infants. I have had plenty of practice with little Vicky!

Give my very best love to dear Robert and Matilda and my sincere regards to his Great-Aunt, Lady Honoria.

Your devoted cousin, Bennetta

P.S. Cousin Miriam has sent Henry a parrot from Africa. It arrived this morning, makes a deal of mess and squawks very loudly. Papa is not impressed!

P.P.S. Miriam writes she will send bolts of silk when they reach the East and the welcome news that she is now Mrs Nicholas Sullivan!

❧

MATLOCK HOUSE, LONDON

....And so, my dearest Jane, that is my news. I so wish you could see how happy your namesake is today. You would hardly recognise her. She glows with love and joy and Fitzwilliam and I are so very glad that she and Archer are to share the same type of marriage that you and Charles and ourselves have had these past twenty or more years. If they are as content with each other as we have been, then I can only be delighted.

I trust the gossip will soon die down; it has surely been dampened by Anne's impeccable behaviour since the engagement was announced so publicly in the middle of the ballroom!

I have always loved my eldest child, as you know, but these past few days I have come to admire her immensely. I know she did not love Archer, but he was still at the centre of her hopes and dreams, all of which have now been shattered. But she makes no fuss, cries no tears, pretends that this was her wish the whole time, that Jane should find someone who appreciates her finer qualities.

Sometimes I worry that she is being too sensible, too off-hand, but time will tell.

Lady Goddard left the ball in high dudgeon, hardly able to pay me her compliments, white with anger. I fear that although our two families will be linked by marriage, she will not easily forgive Jane for ruining her plans for Archer's future.

Now, you must gather all your strength for the wedding which will be in January. I suggested they wait until the Spring, but they do not wish to and from the way they kissed in front of everyone, I think that is probably a good idea!

A new year looms -1835, can you possibly believe it? I am looking forward to undertaking all the arrangements, although heaven help us, it means having Lydia, Kitty and Mama all under the same roof at the same time! I am only glad Pemberley is big enough.... and chiding myself for hoping for thick snow so they will not be able to travel.

News from Mary! I expect you will have received a letter as well, telling that Miriam and Captain Sullivan are now married and, even as I write, are on the high seas on their way to the Far East.

And what of Colonel Fitzwilliam marrying Susannah? I have never seen my dear husband so lost for words before. And, of course, as he has now made clear to me, when the old Earl dies, should his young heir break his neck out hunting, then the Colonel will inherit the title and Susannah will become a Countess. Hopefully, Lydia would then have to stop treating her like a superior servant!

I will close now as I must gather in the lovebirds for dinner. They are sitting on the sofa, gazing at each other with such solemn expressions. He is a very earnest, rather stern faced gentleman but it is obvious he loves her so I am sure all will be well. Watching them brings back such happy memories - do you remember those first conversations with Charles when you both admitted your feelings for each other? I recall mine with Fitzwilliam only too well!

Your loving and devoted sister, Lizzy.

⚜

THE FIRE CRACKLED AND FLARED, THE WARMTH IT SENT OUT INTO THE ROOM not quite responsible for all the high colour in Jane's cheeks. That was due to the heavy weight of Archer's hand on hers as it lay between them, the way his thumb was caressing the soft skin on the inside of her wrist in a way that sent hot flushes across her body.

She glanced up at him and smiled. "So, Mr Maitland, Sir, when did you actually fall in love with me? I have a distinct memory of your disapproval when we first met."

Archer stretched out his long legs towards the blaze. "I have given the matter some thought, sweetheart, and although I cannot give you the date when I suspected, I knew for certain when I felt the first wave of jealousy."

"For what?" Jane was alarmed.

"You were sitting in the garden at Deerwood Park, a young gardener gave you a pretty ripe apple and you smiled up at him. I knew from that moment that I never wanted you to smile at another man, ever again! Just me."

Jane bit back a giggle. "So, I am to be solemn and dour of face to Papa, my brothers, even dear Colonel Fitzwilliam, for the rest of my life?"

Archer squeezed her fingers and turned to her. "No, I love to see you smile. But now I know that special look in your eyes is for me alone and that gladdens my extremely stupid heart."

He wrapped his arm around her shoulders and pulled her close, not caring what Mrs Darcy thought from her seat at the writing desk. "Sometimes I don't feel good enough to be this happy. You're like a beautiful bird that has escaped its cage. Have I trapped you again by proposing? I never want you to feel anything but free."

Wickedly, Jane slid her hand under the edge of his coat and felt his heart thumping through the silk of his shirt. She rested her head on his shoulder.

"We have both broken from our former lives," she murmured. "We have given each other the freedom to make a new life together and I give thanks for it."

And they sat in silence, gazing into a future that dazzled them with its wonder, until Elizabeth Darcy gently called them for dinner.

ends.

COMING SOON:

BOOK 5: MERRYN

When a young woman is to become the recipient of a great fortune, her life can be stressful. Lady Merryn Bowyer has many problems - including dealing with relatives who hate her and men who wish to marry her! Can she learn to trust, find a way to survive, to love? Luckily Merryn has two advantages - strength of character, inherited from her formidable grandmother, Lady Catherine de Bourgh, and a reckless, dare-devil cousin, Bennetta Darcy.

Printed in Great Britain
by Amazon

17304294R00115